GONE
TOO FAR

Also by Angela Winters

View Park

Never Enough

No More Good

A Price to Pay

Published by Kensington Publishing Corporation

GONE
TOO FAR

ANGELA WINTERS

KENSINGTON PUBLISHING CORP.
www.kensingtonbooks.com

DAFINA BOOKS are published by

Kensington Publishing Corp.
119 West 40th Street
New York, NY 10018

All Kensington titles, imprints, and distributed lines are available at special quantity discounts for bulk purchases for sales promotion, premiums, fund-raising, educational, or institutional use.

Special book excerpts or customized printings can also be created to fit specific needs. For details, write or phone the office of the Kensington Special Sales Manager: Kensington Publishing Corp., 119 West 40th Street, New York, NY 10018, Attn. Special Sales Department. Phone: 1-800-221-2647.

Dafina and the Dafina logo Reg. U.S. Pat. & TM Off.

ISBN-13: 978-0-7582-2957-1
ISBN-10: 0-7582-2957-7

First Printing: June 2010
10 9 8 7 6 5 4 3 2 1

Printed in the United States of America

This book is dedicated to all the fans who came to love and hate all these characters just as much as I did.
Thank you all for your words of encouragement.

1

When the elevator opened up on the penthouse floor of the exclusive downtown L.A. high-rise, Avery Harper heard a sigh. She stepped out, expecting to see an elderly woman, because that was what the sound reminded her of. But it wasn't an old woman. No one else was there. It was her thirty-year-old body sighing. She was beyond tired and couldn't remember a day in the last six months when she wasn't. She looked at her reflection in the hall mirror. Her large, doelike eyes were red with dark circles underneath. Her medium-brown skin looked a couple of shades paler.

Six months ago, Avery's husband, thirty-seven-year-old college professor Anthony Harper, was paralyzed from the waist down in a car accident. He hadn't been drinking or sleeping, but he had been frantic. Frantic because Avery had just told him that she was leaving him after less than one year of marriage, leaving him for Carter Chase, the man she loved and the father of her fifteen-month-old daughter, Connor. Avery had never felt such guilt in her life, and that was saying a lot considering how guilty she already felt for going against her own values and entering into an extramarital affair with Carter last year.

She had tried so desperately to be a faithful wife. Anthony had been there for her when she ran away from her then-fiancé Carter, after finding out that he had lied about being behind the heart-breaking end of her engagement to another man in order to have her for himself only a year before.

In retrospect, she realized that she shouldn't have run away, but she didn't have much choice. After all, Carter was a Chase, and no one went against America's richest, most powerful black family and won. They always lost—and lost big. Carter had made it clear to her that he wouldn't let her go. Finding out she was pregnant on top of that was all she needed to know that she had to get as far away as possible from a family that believed anyone with Chase blood running through their veins was their property.

Anthony comforted her and loved her. He made her believe that she could be happy without Carter. Even when family emergencies forced them to return to View Park, the black, upper-middle-class suburb of Los Angeles, he supported her. He was devoted to her and treated Connor like she was his own. But she wasn't, and once Carter had found out that Connor was his daughter, Anthony's life began to spiral down the drain, much like the lives of anyone else who became inconvenient to the Chase clan. They had billions from the Chase Beauty empire, which Carter's father, Steven, had built from scratch. Anthony had done all he could, but it wasn't enough; it couldn't have ever been.

Avery had never stopped loving Carter. How could she? The thirty-two-year-old alpha male was perfect in every way. He was handsome, successful, driven, ambitious, frustrating, confident, sexy, arrogant, and rich. He challenged her, made her laugh, and when he touched her, he made her feel more like a woman than she knew she could. They'd had an explosive chemistry from the start. Just being in the same room with him could light Avery up. She had tried to stop loving him, wanting him. She'd thought she could do this—be co-parents without being to-gether, especially when Carter seemed to accept her resolve to stay with Anthony and stopped trying to get her back. But it wasn't enough; it couldn't have ever been.

When Carter was in a plane accident a year ago, Avery had thought he had died. When she realized he was still alive, her suppressed feelings for him surged to the surface, and she couldn't control herself anymore. Despite Anthony, and despite Carter's girlfriend, Julia Hall, the two of them gave in to their desire for each other. Every time they were together, Avery's mind went away and her body caught on fire. They had never stopped loving each other, and the quenched thirst was too much to deny. It was that love and their mutual love for the daughter they made together that made both of them believe nothing could keep them apart any longer.

Anthony took it very hard, and after Avery left him, he lost it. That was when the accident happened and lives were ruined. Anthony begged her to stay, to help him, but he hadn't needed to. Avery knew she couldn't leave him now. This was her fault. She had committed adultery and left a man who had no one else but her. There was always a price to pay for such selfishness, but it was Anthony, the innocent party, who paid the price. She couldn't make it worse by leaving him alone when he couldn't even walk.

Carter refused to accept that they couldn't be together. He had waited too long to get her back, and she had promised this time. He warned her that this was her last chance, and even though it killed her, she knew she had to stay with Anthony.

That was six months ago, and Carter had been busy making her suffer for what he saw as a choice. It began with a very sudden announcement of his engagement to Julia. He knew Avery still loved him and that it would hurt her. It did hurt her, but she couldn't be angry. She had chosen to stay with Anthony and had hoped that all Carter would do was try to find some happiness for himself. But she knew better, and that wasn't all he was doing. The engagement was just the first step in Carter's plan to cause Avery pain at every turn.

Avery expected him to be cold to her, but she wasn't prepared for the cruel and callous nature of his behavior. He immediately began demanding more time with Connor beyond what had been agreed to, and he wanted to change the custody and child-support agreement. He was giving her $10,000 a month for child support while still paying for everything that Connor needed. He knew that Anthony could no longer work, and she had to stop working at her mother's art gallery to take care of him. He knew that Anthony's care was very expensive and made no effort to hide his desire to make their lives financially difficult. As one of the best lawyers in L.A., he knew exactly what to do.

Avery had tried so many times to talk to him, to make him understand and to quell his anger, but he wasn't having it. She still loved Carter, but he hated her and refused to talk to her about anything but Connor; even then, he was short and mean. Every now and then, Avery would let it get to her and they would fight. But mostly she just took it. She took it because she felt guilty for breaking his heart again, but most of all, she took it because she was just too tired to do anything else.

The fact was, Avery knew she had to be delicate. Carter's disdain for her broke her heart every time she interacted with him, but he was a Chase, and he never passed up an opportunity to exert his power and influence. He didn't need a reason to start a war with her, even though he had reasons. In particular, he would remind her of how she and Anthony had initially tried to make him believe that Connor wasn't his. They'd even gone so far as to fudge medical records. He was trying to scare her so she would take his verbal abuse, and Avery knew that a legal battle with a Chase was one she couldn't win.

She was about to ring the doorbell a second time when it slowly opened. Standing in the doorway was Carter's fiancée, Julia. She was a very elegant-looking woman, not flashy. Her brown skin was smooth and glowing, and her features were perfectly sculpted. She had long, shiny, wavy hair and was very tall. Julia was the kind of woman Carter was supposed to marry. While Avery was a middle-class girl, the daughter of a cop and a hippie artist, Julia was from one of the finest black families in all of Texas. Like the Chase family, from Carter's mother's side, Julia's family had been one of the finest for generations, dating back to the late 1800s. She was a bona fide member of the black blue blood, Ivy League, exclusive society. She was born for Carter's world, and from the smug look on Julia's face, Avery knew she was enjoying every second of being in it.

"Avery." Julia looked her up and down and sighed as if she felt sorry for her. "You look ill. Are you ill?"

Avery knew she wasn't a beauty queen like Julia. She was a pretty girl-next-door, not at all glamorous. She cleaned up very well but mostly showed a natural, cute face and casual style that Carter had always told her he loved. Her rosebud nose was always his favorite. Lately, though, Avery was so tired from looking after her husband and her daughter that she neglected herself a bit. She was never more aware of this than in the presence of Julia.

"I'm fine, Julia." Avery spoke tersely, knowing that the worst thing she could do was appease this woman.

Julia hated Avery because she knew that Carter still loved Avery despite Julia trying to do everything to make him fall in love with her. She found out about their affair and wanted desperately to keep him. Julia cared more about being a Chase than she did about having a faithful man. Avery assumed Julia hadn't been prepared when Carter told her that he was leaving her to be with the mother of his child. But the devastation was only temporary, because Carter soon came back with a marriage proposal. Julia had gotten what she wanted—a key to the inner circle of America's black version of the Kennedys.

Of course, Avery was jealous. She hated the idea of Carter being with anyone, and every time she ran into Julia, which she tried to avoid at all costs, Julia found a way to mention her impending wedding to Carter to make it worse.

"I just came to get Connor." Avery looked over Julia's shoulder. "Carter was supposed to drop her off two hours ago, and he's not answering his cell."

"So?" Julia asked, placing a haughty hand on her slim hip.

"He can't keep doing this," Avery said, but regretted it as soon as she did. She had to remember the less she said to Julia, the less she would have to listen to Julia talk back.

"Actually, he can." Julia offered a flat smirk as she tilted her head. "She's his daughter too."

"I know that," Avery answered. "But . . . Look, Julia, just let me in so I can get her."

Avery took a step forward, but Julia didn't move. "She isn't here."

"Where is she?" Avery was starting to get worried. Carter often failed to stick to the terms of their custody agreement, but usually she could find him here or . . . "Is she at Chase Mansion?"

Chase Mansion was the family home in View Park, and it was famous all over the country because of who lived inside of it. Despite its modest size, considering the family's wealth, the elegantly designed 15,000-square-foot redbrick and white-columned masterpiece had graced the cover of several home, design, society, and celebrity magazines and Web sites. Its seven bedrooms; nine baths; exercise, game and media rooms; library; and more intrigued everyone. Avery had experienced an endless amount of awkward, uncomfortable moments in that home and wasn't looking forward to going over there.

"I don't have to tell you," Julia said.

Avery's hands clenched into fists at her sides. She tried to be civil, but Connor was where she drew the line. "Fine, then I'll go there myself."

"You shouldn't," Julia said just as Avery turned away. She waited for her to turn back. "You're not welcome there. He'll bring her to you when he's done."

"Done with what?" Avery asked.

Julia shrugged. "With whatever. Really, Avery, I have a big wedding in five months. I'm very busy, so I can't keep track of him all the time."

That wasn't subtle and was successful at reminding Avery that she had been only six months from marrying Carter when she left him, and in her heart, she was only seconds from marrying him just six months ago. Now he was marrying Julia, and that was that.

Avery didn't bother to say good-bye. She just turned and walked away. She heard the door slam behind her but never took her eyes off the elevator door in front of her. Julia wasn't her problem; Carter was, and he was getting worse.

Kimberly Chase was lounging her long, model-figure body in the soft chair on the patio near the pool of her house. It was dark out, so the lights from inside the large pool surrounded by expensive Gavea, a rare Brazilian stone, reflected the ripples in the water around the back area of the Tuscan-inspired Hollywood Hills home. She felt at peace, which was a rare thing, a gift that she never thought she could ever get again.

Just as she lifted the raspberry martini to her lips, the cell phone on the table next to her began to vibrate. She contemplated whether or not she wanted to interrupt her peace, but when she saw who it was, she decided to answer it. It was her money man.

"It's kind of late for a business call, Glenn." She placed the drink down.

"Mrs. Chase," he answered with his middle-class British accent. "My clients pay me a lot of money to forget nine-to-five. I thought you might want to hear this."

"It's Ms. Chase," she corrected, "and as long as it isn't bad news, I'll listen."

"I've rearranged the money from your divorce settlement as you asked. I'm glad you decided to get back into the riskier market. I really do believe the stock market is safe again. You stand to make millions."

"I just don't want to lose the millions I have," Kimberly said.

Her millions were precious to her, because Kimberly didn't think she'd actually get them. Being Mrs. Michael Chase wasn't a dream come true for her, because a girl with her past didn't dream of anything but surviving. Leaving an abusive home in Detroit at fifteen, she worked the streets for two years before using one of her johns to hitch a free ride to New York, where she cashed in on her exceptional beauty and became a model. She hadn't known she'd hit the jackpot when she met and had a one-night stand with the youngest son of the Chase dynasty. All she knew was that there was a fire about Michael that drew her to him.

It was love at first sight for both of them, but Kimberly thought she had ruined her chance when she found out she was pregnant. But unlike most men in her life, Michael didn't leave. Not only did he stay, but he also wanted to marry her. He went to the ends of the earth to hide her past before introducing her to his parents. It didn't matter. Even though they never knew about the seedier sides of her past, Kimberly would never be good enough. A prince is supposed to marry a princess.

Her mother-in-law, Janet Chase, made her life hell. While she wanted the marriage to happen to avoid having a child with the Chase name born out of wedlock, afterward Janet wanted Kimberly out so she could be replaced with a suitable woman to bear the Chase name. Their battles reached levels neither had expected. Things got so out of control, it began to harm the marriage that Kimberly had to pinch herself every morning to believe she had. An unbelievably sexy, handsome, smart, successful, and rich guy loved her, adored her, and she had the two most perfect twin boys in the world. She was living the highlife every day, except for the fact that she was never allowed to forget that she didn't belong.

She'd made mistakes and her marriage began to show cracks. She had assumed that Michael loved her more than anything but found out he loved his father's approval more. Steven Chase was a man among men, and he never let his boys forget it. While the eldest son, Carter, had found a way to get out from under Steven's shadow, Michael hadn't, and Kimberly's desire not to be the cause of more strife between Michael and Steven made her make bad decisions. The worst decision was not telling Michael that her pimp, David, had come to Los Angeles to extort money from her, threatening to expose her past and embarrass a family that was always under the microscope. David proved more than she could handle. His demands continued to escalate, and even though she had slept with him to make him leave, he wouldn't. When he threatened to release a tape of them having sex, Kimberly could no longer bear it. There was a struggle and David died.

She was a Chase, so it was all covered up. This family was expert at keeping scandals from the public and overcoming those that seeped through their hands. There was never a moment when they weren't actively trying to keep up their appearance of perfection. A lot had been done that was wrong, but murder, even though it happened in self-defense, was the last straw.

Her dream man had become her nightmare. He hated her because she had slept with her ex-pimp and, mostly, because she had Steven threatening to cut Michael off from his chance at the CEO seat of Chase Beauty—the dream he had above all others. She hated him because he used their children to hurt her. He threw his affairs in her face and practically kept her prisoner in their home. She had tried to leave with her boys, not caring that she wouldn't get a penny, but she learned quickly that she would never be able to.

Things reached the brink when Michael finally broke down. In his own sick way, he still loved Kimberly too much to let her go, and he hated her for it. But it was interfering with every aspect of his life, and it was starting to wear on the family name and image. Kimberly played the last hand she had left and, surprisingly, won. He had threatened to never let her go with more than the clothes on her back and to never let her see her kids again, but when she appeared to be willing to do that, he caved to keep her near.

In the divorce settlement, she was given their $5 million home, $10 million in cash, $75,000 a year in alimony, and $300,000 a year in child support. Certainly better than the clothes on her back, but most importantly, she had her boys. And that was all that mattered; it was all that ever mattered, but the other stuff was nice too. Of course, it wasn't nearly half of what Michael had. He kept their home in Maui and had at least a $300 million investment in Chase Beauty. There was also the matter of his trust fund, which was worth millions, and he never relinquished his control of the trust funds of their two boys, Daniel and Evan, which was at least $10 million each and growing.

The money was a headache at times. She had spent the almost eight years of her marriage spending money and nothing else. She had no idea how to manage it, so she hired one of the best to manage it for her. It had taken him almost six months, but Glenn had finally convinced her to make riskier investment decisions. She had been willing to live without the money if she could keep her boys, but now that she had them, she didn't want to lose the money either.

"Not only will you not lose the millions you have," Glenn answered, "but you also stand to make millions more. You just have to trust me."

"I won't trust you," Kimberly answered. Since Bernie Madoff, no one trusted their money managers. "But I will give you a closely monitored chance."

"That's all I ask. I'll let you get back to your family."

Kimberly said good-bye and hung up. She placed the phone lightly on the table and looked around. Her family. What had become of that? It seemed insane, but there were times when she missed Michael. Even after the hell he put her through, she hadn't forgotten how happy they had been once. She hadn't forgotten how he loved her despite knowing about her past and how hard he had worked, although ultimately unsuccessfully, to protect her past from his family. What they had shared at one time, she had been certain was stronger than any problems they could ever have. She was wrong. During the bad times, Kimberly had feared so much, but now all she feared was the belief that she would never feel that kind of love again.

The phone rang again, and she was hoping it was Michael, telling her he was bringing the boys home from dinner at Chase Mansion with their family. It wasn't. She noticed the caller ID, and the grind in the pit of her stomach brought her peaceful evening to an end. She wasn't going to take that call. She wasn't in the mood to talk about the revenge she was planning for Steven and Janet Chase for trying to buy her children away from her six months ago.

Carter leaned back on the large, plush, regal sofa in the great room of Chase Mansion, the home that was famous around the world not just for who lived in it, but also for the fact that it was nestled in a decidedly upper-middle-class black suburb rather than in Bel Air or Beverly Hills. He was tired after spending the morning at Chase Law, the law firm that he started several years ago, and spending the rest of the day with his little angel, Connor. He was still getting used to the energy it took to be a dad.

It was all worth it, he thought as his little princess rolled onto her side and fell on his lap. She looked up at him, rubbing her tiny little nose with her chunky fingers, and yawned. He picked her up and brought her to him, kissing her on her fat cheeks before laying her against his chest.

Carter had never known he could love like this. After more than thirty years of a father who seemed to have only enough emotion to offer his wife, Carter wasn't familiar with an affectionate type of fatherly love. Of course, he knew he would love his child, but what he imagined was nothing like what he actually felt. Connor was the sun and the moon to him. He would give his life for her. There was a time when he'd do the same for her mother, but now it was only Connor. She was the only good, pure thing in his life, and he loved her beyond words.

Carter's twenty-nine-year-old sister, Leigh, sat down on the sofa next to him with a glass cup of strawberry ice cream in her hand. She looked down at Connor. "She's tired. You don't usually keep her up this late, do you?"

Carter kissed Connor's head. She now had a full head of soft, curly hair that smelled like lavender. "She's fine."

"Avery's going to be mad," Leigh said, "but you don't care about that, do you?"

Carter shot Leigh a look. His very pretty sister, the doctor, looked like an angel with her unassuming beauty; soft, tender features; and short curls. But she could, on occasion, be passive-aggressive when telling you how she felt, especially when she didn't approve.

"Is that what you came over here for?" Carter asked. "To get on me about Avery?"

"That's none of my business." Leigh looked at the ice cream and wondered if there was whipped cream in the fridge. "I was just stating a fact."

"I decide how late my daughter stays up," Carter said defiantly. "It's been a peaceful family evening, Leigh. Everyone is getting along. Let's let this rare occasion last."

Leigh laughed. He was right. She was well aware that, in the dictionary, the word *Chase* could be defined as "dysfunctional family." Why would they need to discuss battles they had with others when there were more than enough battles just between them? The most constant battle was between Carter and their father. Steven and Carter got along only sporadically, something that existed their whole life but escalated when, after Harvard Law, Carter decided to start his own law firm instead of joining Chase Beauty. Steven, a man who relied on his influence over his children to get them to do his bidding, had never fully recovered from the rejection. They were closer now, ever since Carter and Michael had been in the Chase jet that crashed in Denver last year. They had tried their best to put aside their differences—

differences that hit a height when Steven found out that Carter had known all along that Kimberly had been a teenaged hooker and kept it from the family.

"You forget Michael and Daddy," Leigh said. "You should know better than to mistake not fighting with getting along. You're an expert at it."

Carter looked over at the bar, where his father was fixing a drink. You could never not notice Steven Chase. He was a powerful, tall, dark man who commanded attention. While his distinguished white temples hinted that he was well into his fifties, he was still in remarkable shape. He carried himself with a unique mastery very few men had.

And he was married to a woman, standing next to him, of a very rare caliber. Janet was Steven's introduction to the world of black blue blood. She was an exceptionally beautiful woman who had always looked ten years younger than she was. She was always impeccable, even when she was a mess inside, which was more often than she'd ever admit.

Carter turned his attention to the floor, where his little brother by one year, Michael, was playing chess with his eight-year-old son Daniel, while Daniel's twin, Evan, looked on with a discontented look on his face. Six months ago, everyone thought Michael would implode. His life had gotten so out of control that it threatened to destroy the whole family. No one knew what to do. Even Carter was on the verge of hopelessness, despite the fact that he and Michael had been best friends their whole lives and usually helped each other out of their biggest messes.

Everyone was shocked beyond belief when Michael, whose one and only dream in life was to take over Chase Beauty, resigned from his position on the Chase Beauty board of directors and took an indefinite leave of absence from his position as CFO. This was in response to his parents' attempt to force him to divorce Kimberly and run her out of L.A. with $20 million and nothing else. He eventually came back within a month, but you could still feel a chill in any room in which Steven and Michael were together. Things had changed forever.

"If anything good came from Michael and Dad's drama,"

Carter whispered to his sister, "it's that Michael isn't under Dad's finger anymore. His entire existence rose and fell on Dad's approval, something I warned him could never fully be achieved."

"I'm still worried about him," Leigh said. She always worried about Michael and Carter and their little sister, Haley, who . . . "Hey, where did Haley go? She was here like five minutes ago."

"She probably went back to her new house," Carter answered as the doorbell rang.

"You mean the guest house?" Leigh was speaking of the 2,500-square-foot house behind the main house and the pool but in front of the basketball court.

"Mom's latest attempt to keep her close," Carter said. "You know the kid can only stand peaceful family moments for so long. Dysfunction is her energy source."

"Hello, everyone."

While everyone expected to see whoever had rung the doorbell, they turned their attention in the other direction as Peter Hargrove entered the room from the back with that always-too-cheerful smile on his face and those constantly ruffled dark brown curls.

"Well," Michael said out aloud, "if it isn't Haley's first of what's certain to be a minimum of five husbands. Nice of you to join us, Pete."

"It's Peter," the young man corrected with an annoyed glance at his brother-in-law. "Is Haley around?"

"You mean your wife?" Michael asked. "Why is it that I know more about your wife's whereabouts than you do?"

"Michael." Janet spoke sternly as she nodded to her son. "That's enough."

Janet took a deep breath and forced a kind smile as she turned to Peter. "Haley is in the game room downstairs. Peter, have you had dinner?"

"I ate out," he answered with his strong Australian accent. He ran his fingers over his unruly hair as he stood looking pleased with himself. He knew he was handsome in the rebellious rich boy sort of way, and his dark skin and half-Australian, half-Aboriginal features made him stand out.

"Where the hell have you been?" Steven asked, not trying to conceal his disdain for this boy who had forced himself into his family.

"Out and about, mate." Peter, dressed in faded black shorts and a Manchester United T-shirt, seemed unaware or unconcerned of his father-in-law's disdain for him.

"You wouldn't have possibly been looking for a job?" Michael asked sarcastically.

"Don't need a job," Peter said with an above-it-all grin as he strode through the middle of the room. "I'm rich, remember?"

Steven let out a low groan, and Janet placed her hand firmly on his arm to get him to calm down. She waited until Peter was gone before letting go.

"I'm not going to warn you again," she scolded. "You must try to be nicer to him."

"This is as good as it's going to get," Steven answered, taking a quick sip of his drink. "I can't stand that kid."

"Carter." Maya, the Chase Mansion maid for almost twenty years, stood in the archway to the great room, and with her strong Caribbean accent said, "It's Avery."

Carter took a second before nodding to Maya, who quickly left. *Here we go,* he thought as he lifted himself off the sofa with his baby in his arms. He ignored the insolent glances thrown his way as he left the room. This was none of their business.

"No one is happy about this situation," Janet said, "but I—"

"He's happy," Steven said. "He's happy and so is Haley. And we're all supposed to just put up with it."

What Steven was having a hard time putting up with was Haley's surprise husband and his presence in their home. Six months ago, they were embroiled in Haley's latest mishap, which was getting herself involved in a murder scandal through her current lover, Garrett Collins. It seemed to be solved just before a young man from Australia showed up at the house claiming to be Haley's husband. It wasn't until then that Haley told her parents that nine months prior, while spending the summer in Sydney, she had gotten married.

This was a shock for everyone, even for Haley, who had established herself as the hell-raiser and chief scandal-maker within the Chase family. A significant part of Steven's and Janet's lives, and money, was spent repairing the damage caused by their youngest child, now twenty-six years old. Sadly, her involvement in last year's murder mystery wasn't the first of that kind, but a hidden marriage had the family floored.

After regaining their composure, Steven and Janet listened to Haley explain that she had met Peter, an heir to oil billions in Melbourne, while spending a summer prancing around Sydney on her parents' dollar. Peter's eighty-five-year-old grandfather had recently died, but Peter's access to his share of the inheritance, $300 million, hit a snag. Peter was always a wild child and an outcast because of his father's choice to marry an Aboriginal woman, and Peter's grandfather thought he could calm Peter down by demanding he be married for at least two years before he could collect his inheritance. They were on month fifteen.

As Haley explained, Peter, who wasn't the least bit interested in settling down for real, needed a wife quick and he needed money. Haley had grown tired of Steven holding her trust fund— estimated to be between $12 and $15 million after the most recent stock market crash—over her head and using it to control her. Her disdain for her father, which she made no attempt to hide, led her to the idea that she needed a different source of income. In her own words, she explained, "At least until you both die and I can get more."

Once Peter got the $300 million, she would get $30 million for all her help in the ruse, and they would get a divorce. He would have his money, and she would be able to live her life as she pleased without regard for her father's orders. Steven hadn't asked if she had gotten a prenup, because he knew she hadn't bothered.

"The best way to keep control of the situation," Janet said, "is to keep her close and keep an eye on him. You don't want to push him away, because she'll go with him."

"She doesn't even like him," Michael said.

"She likes him," Leigh added. "They get along at least."

"I don't want to talk about this anymore!" Steven turned and headed for the back patio.

*   *   *

When Carter saw Avery standing in the marble-floored, well-appointed foyer, he could tell right away that she was angry, but when he got up closer, he could see that she was also very tired. Despite it all, damn her, she still looked beautiful to him. The simplicity and careless elegance of her natural beauty still got to him despite the way he felt about her.

And what he felt was hate. Avery had broken his heart too many times for him to forgive her ever again. He had tried and tried, but she ripped his insides to shreds and still expected him to hold no grudge. Well, he held a grudge, and he was determined to make her pay for it. He hadn't wished Anthony's accident or physical condition, but it was no excuse. He had offered to pay for all of Anthony's medical needs, including a full-time, top-quality nurse. But Avery didn't care. Once again, she decided to give in to morals that had no basis in what was right or what was real. His heart paid the price, and his anger had not yet subsided. He didn't know if it ever would. Avery was his enemy now, because if she was anything else, he would fall for her again. He would redefine their relationship on his own terms before she could ever get a chance to destroy him again.

"What are you doing here?" he asked harshly, keeping his almost asleep baby close to his chest.

"I came to get my baby," Avery said. She could see that all-too-familiar look of anger on his handsome face, those hostile light eyes of his. He never offered her anything else, but she was too tired to care tonight.

To Carter's dismay, the sound of her mother's voice brought Connor to attention. Her head shot up from his shoulder, and she swung around in his arms. Once she saw Avery, she reached her arms out, squealing, "Mommy!"

"Your baby?" Carter asked. "What the hell does that mean?"

"That is generally what you call someone you gave birth to." Avery held her arms up. "Just give her to me, please."

Carter didn't want to oblige, but Connor was not going to cooperate. When Avery was around, no one else would do. "I was going to bring her back soon."

"Soon?" Avery wanted to tell him that with the agreement, she was supposed to get Connor back more than two hours ago, but he didn't care and she didn't want to fight with him. She had what she came for.

"Don't start with me," Carter said. "I could've not brought her back at all."

"Are you threatening me again?" Avery asked. "Because I'm not impressed. You're not her custodial parent, Carter. I am."

"Well maybe you shouldn't be." Carter felt a sick sense of satisfaction as the expression on her face changed. She was paying attention to him now. "You're too busy taking care of that husband of yours. Maybe you don't have time to take care of a baby anymore."

"You've been saying that for six months." Avery tried desperately to control her temper. She knew these were just threats, but just the thought made her want to explode. "And despite what you hoped for, I'm making it work."

"That's a matter of opinion," Carter shouted just as she turned and headed out the door.

It made him angry that she could walk away. She had stopped trying to calm him, trying to make peace. She didn't care that he hated her anymore, and that bothered him. The one thing Carter knew was that, even though she had torn his heart to shreds by choosing Anthony over him yet again, she had still wanted him. He could see it in her eyes and in the jealous looks she shot in Julia's direction. But he didn't see that anymore. If she didn't care that he hated her, then he'd have nothing.

"Very foul."

Carter swung around to see Michael standing right behind him with a disappointed expression on his dark, intense face. He'd been so focused on his anger for Avery that he hadn't even heard him approach.

"What are you doing? Sneaking up on me?"

"How long do you plan on being the apex asshole?" Michael relished the opportunity to be the less dysfunctional brother for a change—at least for now. "You thought things were going to end up one way and they ended up another. You're the most logical person I know. Logic would suggest you make the best of it. An emotion-driven person, which you are not, would choose . . . well, what you're doing. Acting like a vindictive, bitter bitch."

"*You're* giving *me* advice on how to deal with women?"

"Yes, I am," he answered. "You know why?"

"Because you are uniquely unqualified?"

"The opposite." Michael let the aside go by. "I am uniquely qualified because I was you."

Carter's laugh was laced with sarcasm. "Is that what you think?"

"Filled with animosity and hate for a woman who I, at the same time, loved." Michael grinned as Carter's expression turned to resentment, because he was right. "You think the meaner you are to her, the more you can prove to yourself that you don't love her. It doesn't work. Riding that thin line between love and hate will eat you from the inside out."

Carter ignored his brother and walked away. That thin line was his obsession, and he wasn't ready or willing to let it go.

2

When Haley Chase entered the kitchen, she had hoped to find Maya, because she was hungry. But the only person she found was Leigh, who looked up at her with a smile that Haley did not return.

"Where is Maya?" Haley rushed over to the large double-door stainless-steel refrigerator, her long wavy auburn hair flying behind her. She was a natural seductress with a smoldering sex appeal that drove men crazy. She was heartless and bold and wicked to the core. Despite seeing the danger in her eyes, men still chased her because they wanted to tame her. She found it amusing that they thought they could.

Opening the refrigerator, she spotted and grabbed a large plate of cut fruit. She placed the plate on the large, dark, granite-topped pinewood kitchen island. "What's the point of having a maid if you have to do stuff for yourself?"

"Well," Leigh replied, "to begin with—"

"Rhetorical," Haley shouted back. "For an Ivy League doctor, you're not that bright."

Leigh shrugged off her baby sister's insults. After all this time, she had gotten so used to them that she knew they didn't mean anything and they didn't matter. In her own psychotic way, Haley loved Leigh and knowing that was enough. She would show love only to their mother. Everyone else was out of luck.

Leigh put down the croissant she was eating and swung around in her chair. "Why does Mom have the idea that you're planning on staying married to Peter beyond your—*arrangement?*"

Haley crinkled her small nose. "I can't really tell her more than I have."

Haley hadn't wanted to tell her family anything. Peter was supposed to stay in Australia and not bother her until the two years had passed, and then he was to let her know she could get her money. After trying for the last five years to rip her trust fund out of her father's grip, Haley had given up. She hated the man, and he used every chance he got to control her or place her aside. She wasn't going to let him banish her to Europe for a third time just because she dusted up a little trouble.

The trust funds in the Chase family were not very complicated. All of them had been set up with $10 million and were managed by the best private wealth trust firm in the world. Steven's orders to the trustees were clear. After eighteen, all of the children would receive a modest salary from the fund of $150,000 a year. It was meant to supplement whatever income they would make from the career they were expected to have. After twenty-five, that salary would go up to $250,000. After they reached thirty, the trustee was to hand the fund over to the manager of their choice and give them full, unlimited access to their millions.

Haley's lifestyle had passed $250,000 by the time she reached fifteen. Steven had thought that he could manipulate his children and force them to work, but Haley had found a way around it. She lived rent-free at home and charged as much of her life as possible on her parents' credit cards and Chase Beauty business accounts at the various high-end hotels and restaurants. When she traveled, she flew on her parents' jet and stayed at her parents' several homes around the world, but Steven was cutting her off more and more. She went to graduate school like they asked, but now they wanted her to work, and Haley wasn't going to be treated like this. Peter was her way out from under that awful man's thumb.

"It's not a big deal," Haley said after tossing a chunk of pineapple in her mouth. "It's marriage in bank account only."

"But he sleeps in your room."

"He's my husband, Leigh. Where do you expect him to sleep?"

"Does he know you were sleeping with other men after you came back from Sydney?"

Haley wasn't sure what had happened to her sister's supposedly superior brain. "One man, and Peter is my husband, but he's not my husband-husband."

"But you seem to like him," Leigh said. "At least as much as you're able to like anyone."

Haley smirked at that last comment. She made no secret that she didn't have much respect for men. They were worth what she could get from them—access, money, sex, or just to piss her parents off. She never intended to keep any of them around long.

"Why is my marriage the topic of every conversation in this house? This is why I wanted to move out."

"Mom doesn't want you to do that," Leigh said. "There is no reason you two can't stay in the guest house."

"Except for the fact that it is the size of a closet," Haley said. "They only want us there so Dad can keep his eye on Peter. He's not fooling anyone."

"He's not trying to."

Haley shrugged as she bit into a gigantic strawberry. "Whatevs. I just don't see how it's such a big deal. I'm going to meet Peter for lunch at Equator later today. Wanna come?"

Leigh knew the invitation wasn't genuine, so she didn't respond.

"Oh, yeah, that's right," Haley added with a laugh. "You're busy tending to whores and drug addicts. The same thing you do every day."

Haley was referring to Hope Clinic, the free clinic Leigh started more than two years ago to give the poor access to some form of adequate health care. She specialized in HIV/AIDS patients but offered other services, since the need was so great. It was upsetting to her parents. Although they had always reminded the children of their privilege and responsibility toward charitable behavior, they expected the Duke Medical School grad to join a top-notch private practice. Like Carter, she chose another path.

Leigh had two clinics now, and they were her pride and joy. She had seven doctors and four nurses working for her and had become almost as good as her society maven mother at fund-raising. Of course, the Chase Foundation, the multimillion-dollar family charity run by Janet Chase, was Hope Clinic's biggest donor.

"For your information," Leigh countered, "I'm not going to the clinic today. I'm going into the city to lobby for the new state health care program."

Haley held up her hand. "Please kill me before you start explaining what that is."

"I won't bore you."

In addition to her fund-raising skills, Leigh had been honing her lobbying skills. She was constantly lobbying for funding and legislation that supported getting decent health care to the poor and uninsured. She had worked hard to get a new health care bill all the way to the governor's office in Sacramento, but she needed help.

Haley suddenly remembered something. "Wait a minute! Are you talking about Senator Cody?"

Leigh smiled sarcastically. "So you do actually listen to me when I talk about important things. I thought you were allergic to them."

"I usually never remember anything you say," Haley said. "But I do recall you mentioning Senator Cody—or as I like to call him, Senator Hottie—to Mother."

"Yes, I am." Leigh sighed. "I'm not looking forward to it, but he has the ear of the governor, so I need his help. He's on district break, so he'll be here a while."

"He's a hard audience to get," Haley said as she walked over to her sister. She surveyed Leigh, who was wearing a black suit with a stark-white button-down shirt. "Can you please, please, please wear something that doesn't make you look like you're allergic to sex."

"I'm wearing a suit," Leigh responded. "This is a professional meeting."

Haley rolled her eyes. "You're never gonna get any ever again, are you?"

Leigh didn't respond, but the question wasn't as crazy as it may have sounded. Leigh had horrible luck with men. As a young woman, she had been obsessed with pleasing her mother, so she dated the "right" type of boys but felt nothing for them. The first time she fell in love, it was with Richard, a doctor who helped her open her first clinic. She was prepared to deal with her parents' disappointment, since Richard wasn't "one of us," but before she got the chance, he was killed by a "right" type of boy who just happened to be a psycho, obsessed with Leigh. Leo, after shooting Richard dead, immediately shot and killed himself right in front of Leigh.

Leigh was devastated and it took a long time for her to get back in the game. She had not planned on becoming interested in famous action-movie star Lyndon Prior, and their relationship was more than enough to upset her parents, who had no respect for wealth obtained by the talent side of sports and entertainment. However, his being white seemed to bother them even more.

It was Lyndon's friend Nick who had given Leigh a bad vibe from the get-go. While alone in Lyndon's mansion, Nick attacked Leigh, trying to force himself on her. While Lyndon came to her aid, he was more concerned with his career than Leigh's desire to get justice for what had happened. In the end, Steven and Janet Chase did what they always did to anyone who tried to hurt their children. Nick was put in jail after he was found with an enormous amount of drugs, and Lyndon's career as a heart-throb action star was ruined, because someone had convinced Nick to say that he and Lyndon were lovers.

Leigh never asked her parents what had been done. She didn't want to know. She had been too angry about what Nick had done to her that she didn't care that his life was ruined. That had been over a year ago, and Leigh was in no rush to get back into the dating game. The clinic was her lover for now, and she was satisfied with it.

* * *

Kimberly stood in the archway to her living room, trying to figure out how to deal with her ex-husband as he helped himself to the sofa and reached for a magazine from the glass coffee table. When her maid, Marisol, informed her that he was here—again—Kimberly's first inclination was to be angry. Despite his promises to leave her alone, except for matters regarding the children, Michael always found an excuse to come over at least once every couple of weeks. But she wasn't going to get angry. After all, compared to what things had been like before the divorce, this was nothing.

"Hello, Michael." Kimberly walked confidently into the room as Michael turned around to look at her.

"Kimberly." Michael tried not to be obvious as he took her in. She was exceptionally beautiful, and although over the years he had gotten used to her perfect curves and glowing skin, he was seeing it a lot less frequently these days, bringing back a newfound appreciation.

"You don't have a visitation today," she reminded him.

"I know," he answered, "but I want to get some stuff I have in storage in the basement."

"I thought you cleared everything out." She sat on the tall chair across from him, trying to appear not at all emotional. Her voice was calm and cool as she reminded herself that he could not hurt her anymore. She had what she wanted, so there was no need to rock the boat. At some point soon, his unrelated-to-the-children visits would stop. The truth was, it bothered her to see him, because it reminded her of how much she once loved him and hated him at the same time.

He looked much better than he had in a long time. Toward the end of their marriage, Michael had slept with anything he could get his hands on, justifying it by Kimberly's refusal to let him touch her. He was drinking too much and not taking great care of himself. He was obsessed with getting his father to forgive him for forcing his hand in covering up David's death and was constantly afraid of his power position at Chase Beauty. He was angry, suspicious, vindictive, and obsessive, and he was making her life and the lives of their children a living hell.

In the last six months, he had come to accept the fact that he couldn't control Kimberly anymore, and his life had spiraled out of control. The anger was still there to an extent, and, like all the Chase men, he hated losing. That was what these visits were about, Kimberly suspected. They made him feel as if she was still his.

"You mean everything you didn't burn?" Michael didn't like the apathetic look on her face. He was okay with her loving him or hating him, but he couldn't stand her being indifferent. She had ruined his life. She should at least offer him some regretful emotion. "I heard you're selling this house, so I wanted to make sure you didn't sell anything that was mine."

"Nothing here is yours anymore, Michael." Kimberly leaned forward. "This house became one hundred percent mine in our divorce. I could ask how you found out about my choice to sell, since I haven't told anyone but my money manager, but why bother? You seem to make a practice of knowing every little thing I do."

"Is there something in particular you have a problem with?"

"No," she answered. "I have a problem with all of it. Including having a man investigated just because I had lunch with him."

Michael was willing to let Kimberly go, but he was not yet willing to let any other man near her. That, he was not ready for. "I just came here to—"

"Daddy?" Evan walked into the living room in his one-piece sky-blue pajamas with Star Trek characters on them. He seemed unhappy to see his father. "What are you doing here?"

"Why are you in your jammies?" Michael asked.

"I can't come over today," he said. "I'm not feeling well. I'm sick."

"Sick?" Michael's brows furrowed in doubt. "Like you were sick when your intestines were broken?"

Evan nodded in agreement. "They broke again today. I can't come with you."

"Daddy isn't here to take you," Kimberly said. "He's here to talk to Mommy."

"Oh." Evan seemed relieved. "Well, I don't feel good."

"*Well*," Michael corrected. "I don't feel well."

"Go back to bed, sweetie." Kimberly pointed back to the hallway. "I'll be up there in a bit."

After Evan left, Michael asked, "Are you going to tell Dr. Bryant about this?"

Dr. Bryant was the boys' psychiatrist. The animosity between Michael and Kimberly had affected the boys in a very bad way. They had stopped respecting Kimberly, because Michael had treated her with such disrespect, and they hated Michael because he had grown so cruel and cold. Dr. Bryant was one of the best child psychiatrists in L.A. and was helping them recover.

In the past month, though, Evan had gotten in the practice of claiming to be sick whenever Michael had visitation time. He made all kinds of excuses, but his physician, Dr. Brown, found nothing wrong with him. Dr. Bryant, his psychiatrist, suggested Evan was acting out on his remaining anger by finding excuses not to spend time with his father.

Michael couldn't help but be hurt by this. He loved his boys. They were the only people he felt he could love completely and without precaution. Trying to help them was the main reason he decided to get his life back together. He accepted that it would take time for the boys to forgive him, but that didn't mean it wasn't very painful.

"He did have a bit of a fever," Kimberly said. "That's why he's in bed. Dr. Brown didn't find anything the last time. Maybe Leigh can look at him."

"No," Michael said. "The less my family knows about the boys' psychiatric counseling the better."

"Fine." Kimberly stood up. "You know where the basement is. Please make it quick."

She didn't look back as she walked out of the living room and toward the stairs. This bothered Michael and she knew it, but he had to learn. Like she told him, nothing here, except the boys, was his anymore.

"All right, all right, you little monster." Avery placed a kicking and struggling Connor onto the floor as soon as they entered the Baldwin Hills home they recently moved to because they could no longer afford to live in View Park.

Her daughter began waddling into the living room, running as fast as lightning.

"Let's go to the kitchen, sweetie." Avery smiled as Connor immediately headed to the left, toward the kitchen. Avery's mother, Nikki, told her she was training her like a little dog, but Avery was doing what she had to. It was hard to look after a rambunctious baby and a—

"Where in the hell have you been?"

Avery stopped in the dining room, just before crossing into the kitchen. She turned to see Anthony Harper, her husband, sitting in his wheelchair near the window, where he could look out at the front of the house. He looked his usual surly and suspicious self. Avery was sick and tired of going through this. For the last six months, any time she was more than ten minutes later than she said she would be, Anthony gave her the third degree.

"Nice to see you too," she responded, but it only seemed to make him angrier.

"Can you answer my question?" Anthony asked shortly.

She didn't feel like it, but as Avery looked at her husband, sitting in the chair, twenty pounds lighter and with dark circles under his eyes, she knew she had to. She had to because it was all her fault. She had cheated, and that cheating had ruined so much of Anthony's life. It was fair that he was suspicious of her.

Avery lifted the bag of groceries in her right arm. "Where I said I would be. I picked Connor up from Mom's and ran by the store."

"I called your Mom. She said you left more than an hour ago."

Avery ignored him and headed into the kitchen, where Connor was sitting on her butt, talking gibberish to her fingers. She could hear Anthony's automatic wheelchair purring behind her.

"It takes more than an hour to buy one bag's worth of groceries?"

Avery responded while taking the groceries out of the bag. "With a one-year old, an hour is good damn time."

"You think this is funny?"

She turned to him. "Did I laugh? You asked where I was and I told you."

"Then why didn't you answer your cell?"

"Anthony," Avery said as more of a sigh than anything else. "I don't know. The battery must be dead. Just, please."

"Please what?" Anthony asked, his voice holding an injured tone. "Or maybe you just turned it off."

Avery slammed the can of soup on the counter. "Where do you think I was? What do you think I was doing? Why not stop wasting our time with these same questions and just tell me where you think I was."

"I wasn't going to say you were with Carter." Anthony's expression darkened as it always did when he said the name of the man he believed had ruined his life. "I know you aren't sleeping with him, but I know the only reason you're not is because he doesn't want you."

Avery was taken aback by the sting of his words. "You're an evil asshole."

"You made me that way," he retorted. "Let's face it, Avery. If he wanted you, you'd be fucking him, wouldn't you?"

"Leave me alone, Anthony." Avery went to place the soup in the cabinet, but something shiny caught her eye. She looked down at the sink and saw a silver-label bottle of whiskey.

She grabbed the bottle and noticed that it was almost empty. "I see you've been doing some shopping yourself."

"That's none of your business," Anthony said. He rolled toward her, holding his hand out. "Give it to me."

Once Anthony had been through a couple of months of physical therapy, the doctor approved the addition of a disabled hoist and braking system in his car. It was an expensive transition, but it allowed Anthony the ability to drive. He took lessons, and within the last month, he was driving it regularly—that was, when he wasn't feeling phantom pain from his injuries. He was in pain often and had decided to use the new freedom the car provided him to go and buy liquor. That and driving by the art gallery where Avery worked to make sure she was there.

"Dammit!" Anthony yelled as, instead of giving him the bottle, Avery turned it over and let the rest go down the drain of the sink. "You are such a bitch!"

Avery was ready to come back at him, but Connor began to cry. As she hurried to her baby, Avery felt horrible. She had practically forgotten that Connor was there.

"It's okay, baby." She picked Connor up and tried to soothe

her. "We're making too much noise? It's okay. Sorry, sweetie. Don't cry."

Avery thought of what had happened between Kimberly and Michael as their marriage fell apart and how angry it made her over what it was doing to the kids. She couldn't let that happen to Connor. It was bad enough that she no longer got along with Carter. If Connor had to witness the strife between her and Anthony, too, it was bound to harm her psychologically.

"I'm sorry," Anthony finally said, although he was already turning and wheeling out of the kitchen when he said it.

Avery wanted to cry. He looked so pitiful, and she was too tired to try and do more for him. Fortunately, his upper body was intact, so he was able to take care of his most personal needs, but besides that, Avery was doing everything for him. Because of his mobility issues, and because they were financially strapped, they sold the View Park town house they lived in and moved into a much smaller ranch-style home in a less pricier suburb.

Avery had tried to help him by staying positive and holding on to hope that he could regain the use of his legs. The doctor said it wasn't an impossibility, because Anthony's injury was just below the point on his spine where damage was always permanent. But Anthony had fallen behind on his physical therapy, and ever since he had been able to drive himself, he told Avery he didn't want her coming with him to his doctor's appointments because it was humiliating.

As Connor's cries subsided to sniffles, Avery sat down in a chair at the kitchen table and lowered her head to pray. She prayed for the same things she prayed for every day. She prayed for herself to be a better wife and mother. She prayed for Anthony's recovery. She prayed for Carter's anger to subside. Most importantly, she prayed that she would never lose her baby.

When Michael walked into his father's office, he was a little taken aback by the reception. Usually Steven was at his oversized mahogany desk that Janet had won at a Sotheby's auction a year ago, looking down at his laptop or papers, talking to someone on the phone, waving him in without a look, or doing something else. Michael was used to it, but today it was different. He hadn't knocked, because Steven's administrative Fort Knox had ushered him in. When Michael entered, Steven wasn't sitting at his desk. He was sitting in one of the leather chairs on the opposite side. He was half turned around and met Michael with a smile on his face.

"Come in, son." Steven gestured for Michael to sit in the other chair right next to his.

Son? Steven always called him Michael when they were at Chase Beauty or doing business elsewhere. When he was mad, he would call him *boy*, but never *son*. What was going on?

"What's the matter?" Steven asked, noticing the look of apprehension on his son's face.

"Nothing." Michael sat down. "I was told you summoned me."

Steven sighed. "Is it that painful to be alone with me?"

Steven knew that his son still held animosity toward him. They had been so close that everyone referred to Michael as the favorite. He was a clone of his father in many ways and was the exact opposite in others, but while Carter seemed determined to make his name without Chase Beauty, Michael ate, slept, and breathed the company.

Their relationship had been a series of dysfunctional ups and downs. Steven was a harsh father, and he knew it. He loved his children and would give his life for them, but he wasn't an affectionate man, and he believed strongly that you had to be firm with boys to make them tough and prepared for manhood. Still, Steven had always been confident in Michael's succession to his empire.

That was, until Michael's wife, Kimberly, killed David and the truth about her past was revealed. To say it was a shock that his son had married an ex-runaway hooker and, with Carter's help, had gone to such lengths to hide her past from his parents would be an understatement. To find out who he had paid off, what records he had stolen, and especially that he had framed David and had him locked in a Mexican prison was completely unexpected.

None of that compared to the nightmare that the murder, which Kimberly claimed was an accident, had been for Steven and Janet. They had to call in all their favors and do things that even they, with all they had done to protect their family, had a hard time living with. It had worked, but Steven couldn't even talk to Michael. He was so angry that every time Michael tried to appeal to him, he shut him down. Janet had been more understanding toward Michael, but the fact that he had chosen to stay married to Kimberly made things worse. Her presence in the family put them under a constant threat of disaster.

But things changed last year when Carter and Michael were on the Chase jet returning from New York to L.A. It malfunctioned and crashed. The pilot was killed, but Michael and Carter survived with minor injuries that healed within months. The thought that he had almost lost his sons, neither of whom he was barely talking to, floored Steven to a point where he didn't know who he even was. It put him in a spot so vulnerable that he didn't know how to deal with it. What he did know was that he loved his sons more than anything and would never treat them the way he had in the past. Never again.

The problem with this was that Michael's life had fallen apart and was threatening to put him over the brink. He was embarrassing the family in public and, worse, was making decisions that could put Chase Beauty at risk. Most of all, he looked as if he was turning an emotional and psychological corner that Steven and Janet feared he couldn't return from. It was all stemming from the breakdown of his marriage to Kimberly, and it was damaging their grandchildren, so Janet and Steven made the choice to force Michael to give Kimberly a divorce and offered Kimberly $20 million to leave L.A. without the children and never come back.

While fear that Kimberly would accept this offer urged Michael to give her a divorce, but on his terms, he hated Steven and Janet for what they had done. He took a leave from Chase Beauty and refused to speak to either parent. He kept them out of the divorce and custody proceedings and didn't involve them in putting his life together. He had stopped drinking and was seeing a psychiatrist but was still keeping Janet and Steven at arm's length.

Steven suspected it was all to impress Kimberly, but he was happy nonetheless and tried to convince Michael to come back to Chase Beauty. Everyone in the family urged him to return, and eventually, with an exceedingly generous compensation package and increased authority, Michael came back.

It had been four months since he'd been back, and while he was working at the same top-notch level the Columbia MBA grad always had, Steven knew there was still deep-seated anger. Steven listened to his wife tell him he had to be patient and wait for Michael to come around, but patience had never been one of Steven's strong points. It just wasn't in his blood.

Michael looked down at his watch. "Dad, I'm very busy. Do you need to talk to me or not?"

"Yes, I do." Steven stood up and walked around his desk to his chair. "But first I wanted to know if you would like to come home for dinner tonight."

Michael shook his head. "I'm looking at a condo after work today."

"It will be nice to get out of that hotel room after all this time." Steven thought he might try again. "You know your mother and I would love to have you stay at the house until you find a place."

Michael nodded an acknowledgment of the offer. "Dad, what is this about? Is it the Mexico contracts? Because legal has them right now and dealing with—"

"It's not about work," Steven interrupted. "It's about Jerry Gregoire."

Michael shook his head with a sarcastic smirk. "Since when did you start looking at my expense reports?"

"Since someone brought to my attention that you are using Chase Beauty funds to pay for a private investigator to follow your ex-wife."

"I'll pay you back."

"Michael," Steven said impatiently. "That isn't the point. You have to stop following Kimberly around."

Michael shot up from his chair. "Stay out of it."

"I'm not done talking to you," Steven said as Michael turned to leave.

Michael turned back around. "Unless you have business to discuss, I'm done talking to you."

"It's not healthy," Steven said. "You know this."

Michael nodded in agreement. "Yes, I know. But I'm not ready to . . . I'm just not ready."

"I want to help you."

"I don't need your help," Michael responded. "I don't want it."

Steven let Michael go, knowing that to push the point would be useless. While Carter stood toe-to-toe with Steven when they argued, Michael simply shut down and gave nothing. He said he didn't need his help, and Steven believed him. He told himself that this was a good thing, that he had held on to Michael for too long. But he wanted his son back. He wanted Michael to need him again.

"Would you like to see another pair?" asked Natalie, the personal attendant that always dealt with Chase family members when they shopped at Neiman Marcus. While Michael's divorce gave Janet Chase the excuse to cut Kimberly off from most perks the Chase family had access to—and there were countless perks—her personal shopper was one Kimberly was not willing to give up. Natalie knew what she liked and always had a great selection ready for her.

Today, Kimberly had come for shoes, and the selection was, as always, top-notch. Of all the choices, she had picked two. A $1,200 pair of Christian Louboutin black floral lace over pink satin platforms and a $1,000 pair of silver double-platform sandals.

"No, these will be fine," Kimberly said, feeling extremely pleased with herself. Shoes had that kind of effect on her. "Just have them wrapped up and delivered to the house by the end of the day."

Before Natalie could respond, Kimberly's phone rang, and she reached into her oversized Bottega Veneta purse. She felt a pang in her belly when she saw the caller ID but knew she couldn't avoid him much longer. He'd just keep calling. She dismissed Natalie before answering.

"Hello, Keenan." She spoke with the polite, unemotional voice that she had learned from Janet. The bitch was perfect at polite coldness.

"Why haven't you called me?" Keenan Chase, Steven's younger

brother by a few years, had a low, raspy voice that made him seem like he was always on the verge of being angry.

"I have other things in my life to do besides check in with you," she responded. "We're supposed to be partners, remember? I don't work for you."

"You aren't working at all," Keenan said. "I need progress."

Keenan was asking for information on Steven and Janet Chase that he could use against them with the ultimate goal of destroying them. Last year, while trying to find out more about Michael's latest mistress, Elisha, Kimberly stumbled upon Elisha's real reason for being in Michael's life. While he believed Elisha was helping him purchase an upscale publishing company to add to Chase Beauty's portfolio, she was actually trying to help Keenan, her real secret lover, attach Chase Beauty to a corrupt company so Steven could be held responsible and made bankrupt through fines and consumer lawsuits.

Keenan had been using Elisha, and Elisha had been using Michael, but she ended up developing real feelings for Michael, and she slipped up when Kimberly challenged her by threatening to expose the plan. The business deal was dead before Steven could even realize his brother, head of the White-Collar Crime division of the FBI, was behind it.

Kimberly thought nothing of Keenan's foiled plan until Janet and Steven offered her $20 million to divorce Michael, leave L.A., and never see her kids again. She had always hated Janet for the way Janet had treated her. The first second Kimberly had been alone with her future mother-in-law, Janet told her that she wasn't good enough for Michael. She intended to get rid of Kimberly as soon as possible after the children were born, but Kimberly fought her every second. She had taken Janet down at different times, but she always got back up, and Kimberly ended up the worse for wear.

The offer, which Steven and Janet told her was not really a choice, was the last straw. Now Kimberly hated Steven just as much as she hated Janet, and she wanted their perfect image and all its glory to turn to dirt. She wanted them to hurt for thinking they could buy her babies from her, and the only thing that could really hurt them was destroying Chase Beauty, their legacy to the world.

This was why, after she was assured of her divorce and custody rights, Kimberly contacted Keenan herself. He was skeptical at first, but as they shared their stories, they both came to believe that they could help each other.

"What have you done?" Kimberly asked.

"I'm in Washington, D.C.," Keenan answered. "You're right there."

"We've been through this before," Kimberly said. "I'm not in 'there' anymore, and Janet has pretty much made it so I can't get in there at all. I'm shut off. What can I do?"

"Use your husband." Keenan's tone gave away his desperation.

It worried Kimberly. While her lust for revenge had softened somewhat as she settled into her new, free life, she realized that Keenan's hatred for Steven was more of an obsession than she'd originally thought. A childhood of comparisons had left Keenan feeling bitter and unloved. Steven had everything, including Janet, who Keenan says was interested in him before she met Steven. Steven got all the breaks, and Keenan had failed at almost everything. Although he had made it up the government law enforcement ladder, his brother's success through life and marriage only made Keenan hate him more. *It should have been my life,* he'd told Kimberly more than once.

"If everything you tell me is right," Keenan continued, "then he'll want you back in his life. Use him to get access to the family. There has to be something."

"It isn't time yet," Kimberly said. "I worked so hard to get away from him. They will all be suspicious if I try to get closer to him so soon."

"Kimberly." Keenan sighed and paused for a few seconds. "You're my only hope. If I can't . . . If something doesn't happen . . . I can't stand to see his success anymore. I just can't . . ."

"Calm down," Kimberly said. "I'll do what I have to, but I think after the . . . Things have happened to make Steven hold everything even closer to his chest than before."

Kimberly had told Keenan of all her pain and suffering at the hands of Janet and Steven Chase, but she left out the details of her past and David's murder. She sensed that Keenan knew she was keeping something from him, but her hatred was pure enough for him not to care.

"You have to be patient," she said.

After a few seconds, Keenan responded with, "I don't think I can anymore."

After he hung up, Kimberly once again wondered what she had gotten herself into. At the time she had agreed to partner with Keenan, she had been consumed with despair and anger. But now her life was under her control again, and although she still wanted Steven and Janet to suffer for what they'd done, she didn't have the passion to spend every waking hour trying to figure out how to get that done.

3

The second Leigh entered the L.A. office of the Republican Party's only black senator, Max Cody, located on the ninth floor of a Santa Monica Boulevard office building, she could see the pace was hectic. It was a relatively small office, but there had to be at least ten people running around, carrying stacks of paper, or talking on at least one phone at a time.

The middle-aged Hispanic woman who sat at the front desk was wearing an early '90s-style flower dress and talking very fast on a landline while at the same time holding a cell phone in her other hand. Leigh waited patiently, as no one seemed to have even noticed she was there. After the woman hung up both phones, she went straight to an appointment book on her desk, never looking up until Leigh cleared her throat.

"Oh, hello. Do you have an appointment?" she asked curtly, although she seemed to admire Leigh's suit.

"Yes, I am supposed to see Senator Cody at one." Leigh spoke loudly to be heard above all the noise. "I'm Leigh Chase."

The woman's green eyes widened. "Oh, Ms. Chase. I'm sorry, I mean Dr. Chase. Yes, the senator is expecting you. I think he's on the phone, but I'll let him know you're here. He wouldn't want to keep a Chase waiting."

When she said this, a young staffer walked by and looked at Leigh suspiciously. It always made Leigh uncomfortable when people treated her differently because of her last name, because it gave the impression to others that this was what she wanted. Expressions of indifference immediately turned to disdain and envy.

The woman, who never gave her name, was up and away in a second. Leigh looked around for an empty chair to sit in but couldn't find one.

"You can move anything," said a woman who approached her with a clipboard hugged close to her chest. She was white and looked to be the same age as Leigh. She was pretty, with Nordic blond hair that was almost white. She wore a hunter-green sharp skirt suit that Leigh assumed cost a lot more than she expected a legislative aide could afford.

"I don't want to mess up your papers."

"Here." The woman reached down into the closest chair and picked up a stack of the *L.A. Times*, dumping them on a nearby coffee table. "Good?"

Leigh didn't like the woman's attitude. She was acting as if Leigh was demanding she do this for her and being difficult about it. She thought she might try to clear the air. "My name is—"

"I know who you are," the woman said, looking Leigh up and down. "I'm Senator Cody's chief of staff, Kelly Smith. I know everyone he meets with."

Leigh could feel the freeze from the woman who stood only two feet away. "Is it common for a chief of staff to leave D.C.?"

"I go wherever the senator goes," she responded coldly.

I'll bet you do, is what Leigh wanted to say. From the possessive tone of Kelly's voice, Leigh assumed that she was probably sleeping with the senator or at least wanted to. Max Cody was married at a young age, but his wife was killed in a car accident seven years ago. He had no children, and rumors of his dating were few and far between. Maybe, Leigh thought, it was because he was dating someone he'd wanted to keep secret.

Just as Leigh was about to sit down, the woman from before called her name and waved her over to the main office behind a dark wooden door.

Once inside, Leigh noticed that the senator was not as ready as she'd hoped. He was talking on the phone, and just as Leigh was about to close the door behind her, Kelly squeezed through and rushed past her to his desk.

Leigh stood unnoticed as Max switched between the phone and Kelly's questions about a charity dinner in Sacramento later this week. Leigh considered herself a patient person, but she was getting angry. It didn't help that when he finally acknowledged her, Max gestured for her to sit down across from him as if he was a father directing his child.

Leigh ignored the gesture and gave it a few seconds before she loudly cleared her throat. When he looked at her, she gave him a look she had learned from her mother—one that, without words, made it clear that there was about to be trouble. He seemed to understand, because he quickly hung up the phone and gestured for Kelly to leave. Kelly tossed Leigh a contemptuous look before turning and leaving.

"What was I thinking?" he asked in a deep voice. "I shouldn't have expected a Chase to share time with anything else."

Leigh rolled her eyes. "Is that what you think that was about?"

Max stood up and reached across his desk. "It's nice to finally meet you, Dr. Chase."

Leigh shook his hand before finally sitting down. She had to remind herself that she needed his help, so she had to suck it up. "I can see that you're busy. I appreciate the time."

"I always have time for the people I represent." He leaned back in his chair with a charming smile.

Leigh admitted he was very attractive. He was a few inches over six feet but was much more than the traditional tall, dark, and handsome. He had dark, penetrating eyes, a broad nose, and a hard jawline. He was young and very fit at thirty-seven, but he still was able to look distinguished, like he belonged where he was even though most men and women in his position were ten or more years older than him.

Everyone knew he came from a middle-class family in Freemont and found his way to Yale before receiving his MD at Johns Hopkins University. He married one of his med-school classmates and practiced for eight years before running for Congress. He was elected twice to the House of Representatives for his home-town district. He took two years away from politics after his wife was killed in a car accident, but then returned to run for the Senate. He won in a landslide. He was a political winner who at-tracted young people and minorities, and the Republican Party hoped he would be their Barack Obama.

"Especially," he continued, "one from such an important family."

"I'm not here on behalf of my family," Leigh responded. "I'm here—"

"That's good," Max said. "Because despite my requests, your family did not see fit to support my campaign for the House or the Senate despite being Republicans."

Leigh realized she wasn't going to get around this. It hap-pened all the time. She wished she could be anonymous at times but knew that if she was, she probably wouldn't get anywhere.

"Do you know why that is?" Max asked. "Why the richest, most prominent black family in the country would not support a black candidate for office in their state who belonged to their party?"

"My parents don't clear their political motives with me, but I imagine they will return to the Republican Party when the party returns to them."

Max blinked in response to her unexpected retort. "Interest-ing. You're one to believe that the neocons have taken over the party. You'd like the moderates to regain control."

"I don't care either way," Leigh said. "I'm a Democrat."

"I imagined as much considering your advocacy for such a big spending bill."

She ignored the connotation. "So you actually read the infor-mation I sent you on the health care program?"

"No," he answered, pulling closer to his desk. He flipped through some folders as if looking for something. "I'm sure some-one on my staff has. But I know what bill you're here to talk to me about, and I have to tell you, if you can't figure out how to pay for it without raising taxes, you're not going to have much luck."

"I believe when you are passionate about something, you find a way."

"Having billionaires for parents doesn't hurt."

Leigh's eyes turned to slits. This asshole was intent on making her squirm. What a politician. "I thought you had passion as well, Senator. Being a former physician, you can understand how important health care is."

"No one argues that point," he answered. "But this . . . soda tax . . . is not fair to taxpayers, and I can't tell the governor that this is a good idea despite the worthiness of its purpose."

"The amount is so insignificant." Leigh opened the portfolio she had brought with her. She pulled out an article by the *L.A. Times* and placed it on his desk. "That report says that it would cost only five cents extra for ten ounces of soda."

"Only?" he asked, not bothering to look at the article. "Tell that to a family of four who has to—"

"This is a sin tax, Senator. Just like cigarettes and alcohol. No one is being forced to buy soda. And for those who do choose to, they can regulate based on what they can afford."

Max's expression made it clear he wasn't used to being interrupted. "Do you know how much movies cost these days?"

"Is this about to be another dig at my last name?"

"No, it's a question," he said. "It costs twelve bucks a person now. A hot dog costs five bucks. Popcorn costs about five bucks and soda about four bucks. Now you want to add more money to that? What about all those Californians for whom the movies are the only form of entertainment they can even barely afford?"

"That's your concern?" Leigh asked, unable to conceal her anger. "So regarding the pregnant woman in Long Beach who doesn't have any health insurance but needs a sonogram because she hasn't felt her baby move in a week, your concern is that someone might have to pay an extra fifteen cents for their six-pack of Diet Coke?"

Leigh could tell she had gotten under his skin, and that was what she wanted. He was a jerk, so she wasn't going to further appeal to his sense of decency. All she had left was to appeal to his sense of self-preservation. Any politician puts their image ahead of anything else.

"Is that what you stand for?" she asked, realizing he hadn't intended to respond.

"I underestimated you," Max finally said. After a short pause, he continued. "I certainly won't do that again."

When Carter entered his bedroom, he wasn't expecting what he saw, but he was very pleased.

Lying in their bed, Julia Hall had her arms spread across the pillows, her perfect body on display for the man she loved. Her brown skin was glowing, and she was wearing a firebrand-red satin slip dress that was see-through sheer in the middle and shaped like a burst of flames. It accentuated her very fit and trim figure and stopped just at her hips, revealing her lack of underwear. Her long hair was flowing over her shoulders and over her left breast as she tilted her head with a welcoming smile.

"What are you doing home so early?" Carter asked, beginning to undo his tie. Julia was a public-relations executive for a large L.A. firm.

"I thought I would surprise you." Julia sat up with a seductive grin on her face. "Just because we're getting married doesn't mean the excitement has to go."

Carter joined her on the bed. Julia was a very attractive woman, and although her exterior was generally cold and aloof, she could be very experimental sexually. She was more needy than Carter would prefer, but her background made her a good match in so many ways.

"Last night," Julia said as she scooted over to him, helping him with his jacket, "I wanted to make love, but I fell asleep before you came to bed. You spend too much time in that office down the hall."

"Trust me," Carter said, "if you had come into that office last night with this on, I would have stopped working."

He took hold of her and suddenly pulled her to him. He brought his mouth down to hers and kissed her firmly. Her lips were soft, and as she moved her body against his, he could feel his body begin to heat up. He wanted her.

As Carter lay her back on the bed, he could feel her unbuttoning his shirt. His mouth went to her neck, and as he positioned himself on top of her, he reached down to unzip his pants.

"I love you," Julia whispered as her hands slid his shirt off his shoulders and down his arm. "I love you, Carter."

As her hands gripped his bare arms, Carter returned to her lips and reached his hand down between her legs. He rubbed the soft, hairless skin around her center and kissed her deeper, doing everything he could to not think of anyone but her.

"I love you," she repeated into his ear before bringing her soft lips against his again.

Carter was trying to unzip his pants with his free hand when he felt Julia pull away. When he looked up at her, he could see the look of hurt on her face. He hadn't any idea what had happened, but was sure it was his fault.

"What?" he asked.

"How many times do I have to tell you I love you before you say it back?" Julia scooted away from him, looking ready to cry.

"This again?" Carter felt his growing arousal skid to a halt as the familiar complaint lowered his temperature by a hundred degrees. "It's not something I—"

"You're going to say it isn't something you like to say, but the truth is," Julia said, "it isn't something you like to feel."

"Julia, you know how much I care about you." Carter sat back on the bed, not as bothered by the pain in her eyes as he knew he should be. "We're getting married for Pete's sake."

Carter wanted to love Julia, but he didn't. When they'd met, Carter was in a bad place. Avery had made it clear she was going to stay with Anthony, and he was trying to forget her by sleeping with any woman he met. As always, there were more volunteers than he could ever want. Julia was different from the other women in the sense that her background didn't make her a prospect for a one-night stand. Her family, rich doctors from Dallas, were not at the level of the Chases in terms of power and influence, but they were their sort of equivalent in the Southwest.

His father had warned Carter not to toy with a Hall, but as Carter decided that getting Avery back was his priority, Julia soon became very useful. He had devised that the best way to get back into Avery's heart was to get her to let her guard down about his intentions. Pretending to care about Julia was part of that.

Julia was not a stupid woman. She knew that Carter didn't love her, but she wanted to be a Chase, and the opportunities that could open for her through Carter were more than enough to overcome the inconvenience of the affair he and Avery began last year. Carter had ended it with Julia once he thought that he and Avery were going to be together again, but then Anthony's accident changed everything.

In a fit of rage, Carter thought of a way to hurt Avery the most. He proposed to Julia as part of an overall plan that was supposed to end with him taking Connor away from Avery. He hadn't been able to bring himself to that yet, because, despite trying desperately, he still felt something for Avery that prevented him from hurting her to that degree.

"I have tried," Julia said, shaking her head. "I have tried to make you love me, make you forget about Avery, but you won't."

"Avery is the mother of my daughter," Carter said. "But I'm marrying you."

"But you love her." Julia's voice sounded as if she was on the verge of tears.

Carter was not in the mood for another self-pity session. "I don't want to talk about her!"

"Do you think I do?" Julia asked desperately. "How can I ignore her when I see you look right through me whenever she is around?"

"You're getting what you want," Carter shouted as he shot up from the bed. He zipped his pants back up, looking down at her. "Let's not fool each other, Julia. You want me more for what I can give you access to than my heart."

Julia's expression flattened. "I want it all, Carter. Is that so wrong?"

Carter turned his back to her, headed for his balcony. "No one gets it all, Julia."

Carter welcomed the fresh air as he stepped out onto his balcony. He wondered how he was going to manage this. He didn't love Julia, but love had ripped him to shreds. He wasn't going to let it do that again. He had always assumed that he would find someone to share a life with, because he wanted what his parents had. Whatever their faults, Janet and Steven had shown their children, through example, what a loving marriage was. But after Avery, Carter had just come to accept that this kind of love was very rare, and it wasn't going to happen for him.

It hurt just to think of how foolish he was to believe that he and Avery could stay as happy forever as they were for that short time. He was filled with regret and was sick to his stomach playing over and over in his mind whether or not every step he made was right or wrong and what could have been if he'd chosen differently. He had admitted to all his missteps, his lies and deceptions. None of it mattered. She still left him, and he doubted that she ever really loved him.

That morning, Avery was just closing a deal with a customer for a Nubian princess sculpture created by a seventeen-year-old artist from Compton when Carter walked in. He had that all-too-familiar look of contempt on his face as he darted right for her. She quickly thanked the customer and promised to have the piece delivered in two days. Carter had done this before, stormed into Hue, the art gallery owned by Avery's mother, Nikki, and interrupted Avery with some gripe or another. He never cared that there were customers around.

"What are you doing here?" he asked as soon as he reached the counter.

Avery noted the $5,000 gray suit he was wearing. "You came all the way down here from L.A. to ask me why I'm here? I work here, Carter."

"Not on Tuesdays," he said. "I've been calling your cell phone for two hours."

Avery reached into the back pocket of her jeans, expecting to find her cell phone, but it wasn't there. "I must have left it in my purse in the back room. What's wrong? Is it Connor?"

"How in the hell would I know?" Carter asked loudly. "I'm frantic wondering what is going on with my daughter, and—"

"Our daughter," she corrected. "And she's with my mother."

"I found that out," Carter said, "after I called her. Dammit, Avery. You don't work on Tuesdays. You're supposed to be taking care of OUR daughter."

"For your information," she replied, "I am always taking care of our daughter. I told you two weeks ago that with the ethnic art festival in L.A. this week, we were going to get extra traffic and I would have to work extra hours."

"And I told you no."

Avery's eyes closed to almost slits. "I wasn't asking for your permission. I was telling you so you would know."

"Your mother can't take care of Connor the way she needs," Carter said.

Avery laughed. "You're ridiculous. My mother raised three children perfectly fine."

"Yes, but she's taking care of your father. She can't watch a baby and a sick husband at the same time."

"You're really reaching now," Avery said. "My father is just fine now. He doesn't need any extra care at all."

Avery's father, Charlie Jackson, was the police chief of View Park. One evening, while out for dinner with Avery's brother, Sean, they came across a group of kids trying to steal a car. Charlie was shot twice in the stomach and almost died. It was this emergency that made Avery come out of hiding in Miami, where she had gone to keep her pregnancy a secret from Carter, and return to View Park with Anthony, thus letting her secret out. Although he was not fit enough to return to the force, he had recovered nicely and was doing fine.

"I'm stretching?" Carter asked, fuming. "The only thing that I'm stretching is how long I'm going to let you keep our daughter if you keep handing her off to other people."

Avery rushed around the counter to come face-to-face with him. "Don't you dare threaten me! I don't pawn her off on anyone. Nikki is her grandmother!"

"Well, she may be Connor's grandmother, but she's acting like a better mother to her than you!"

Carter didn't have a second to think before he felt Avery's hand slap against his cheek like a cold whip. He blinked at the burn before locking his bright hazel eyes with Avery's large and raging ones. His entire body lit on fire, and without thinking, he grabbed her by her upper arms and pulled her to him.

When his mouth came down on hers, Avery was shocked. She was so filled with rage that to have it mixed so unexpectedly with desire was a jolt to her system. But only for a second because as soon as she felt his strong lips against hers, Avery experienced a ferocious pull in her gut that set her body on fire. His kiss was hard and demanding, and her body melted into his as she received it, feeling the longing inside her awaken at rapid speed. The intensity of so much anger and passion sparked an all-consuming craving.

The taste of her lips was so good to Carter that it was painful. It had been so long since he tasted them, but it had not been long since he'd dreamed of tasting them. There was something about her mouth that made him want more and more. He aggressively drew her even closer to him and drank up her sweet taste that sent electric waves through his body.

"No," Carter said in a tortured whisper as he pushed her away. He was so angry with himself for being so damn weak when it came to this woman. How could he hate her so much but within seconds want nothing more than to touch her, kiss her, and be inside her? What was she doing to him? What was this power she had?

"This isn't going to work," he said, trying to catch his out-of-control breath.

Avery was too stunned to even think or focus. Her entire body was like a volcano, and all she could think was that she wanted him, needed him, more. "What isn't . . . What . . . What won't work?"

"You're not going to seduce me," Carter said, finally able to look her in the face. How is it that a man who had spent his life controlling his feelings for women easily could have absolutely no control over himself when this woman was near?

"I wasn't trying to seduce you!" Avery's anger at his audacity brought her senses back. "You arrogant jerk! You kissed me."

"You knew that was going to happen," Carter accused. "Every time you slap me, we end up kissing or making love. You know the effect you—"

"What?" Avery asked. "The effect I have on you? That's my fault? And what effect would that be, Carter? To make you want me and then hate me?"

"How is that different from how you feel about me?" Carter

took a step back, because while his mind was in control, his body still wanted her.

"I don't hate you, Carter." Avery sighed, looking him in the eyes. "I love you. I'm sorry that we couldn't—"

"Don't show me your pity," he exclaimed. "Don't tell me how sorry you are that you couldn't love me enough."

"I can't do this again," she said. "I can't keep explaining to you that my choice wasn't about how much I love you."

"Don't waste your time," Carter said, feeling the resentment boiling inside of him. "Quote your scriptures to yourself. If you really loved me, you would have chosen me."

Avery tried to control her emotions, feeling tears begin to creep into her eyes. She had cried so many nights over this, but she couldn't let him see her do it. Not anymore. "I did love you, Carter. I still do, but I—"

"Bullshit," he responded, and was gratified with the angry expression that took over Avery in response to his dismissal of her feelings. He wasn't going to be her fool again. "It's not going to work anymore. If you insist on neglecting MY daughter in favor of everything else, I'll see to it that you don't have that choice anymore."

As he stormed out of the gallery, Avery let herself go and tears began streaming down her face. She ran behind the counter to grab a Kleenex and push the bell that rang in the back room, asking for help at the counter. Her coworker was on break, but Avery had to get some air. She knew what Carter meant by taking away "that" choice. He meant taking away her custody, and there was nothing that Avery feared more in this world.

"You're doing a great job, Darryl." Leigh was warmed by the proud smile of the twelve-year-old boy sitting on the patient's table in room 5 of Hope Clinic in South Central Los Angeles.

"I feel good." Darryl's dark brown face lit up, showing his bright white teeth. "I was outside playing for like five hours yesterday."

Leigh looked at Aliyah, Darryl's thirty-year-old mother, sitting in a chair a few feet away. Aliyah shook her head with a laugh.

"It was only two hours," she said. "And not more than that."

"I'm sure it felt like five hours," Leigh said as she turned back to Darryl.

Four months ago, the diabetic preteen showed up at Hope Clinic very weak. The normally active boy broke into an exhaustive sweat after only twenty minutes of activity. After years of struggling, Aliyah had finally gotten off of welfare and was working as a part-time receptionist at a veterinary clinic. Unfortunately, the new job didn't include health insurance, so she came to the clinic.

Leigh diagnosed him easily. A drug he had been taking to manage his diabetes had turned on his kidneys and was damaging them. They were degrading fast, and if he hadn't come to her when he had, they would have likely failed. There was no way Aliyah would have ever been able to afford dialysis, which is what he would have needed to stay alive.

However, switching his medications, Leigh was able to stop the damage, and his kidney filtration rate was back to normal. It was the minimum of normal, but he was on his way. It was such a small change but meant the difference between life and death, and this was what Leigh lived for.

"Two hours sounds good," Leigh said, "but you want to take it slow. Your mom will tell me if you don't."

"I will." Darryl had a light in his youthful eyes that had recently returned after months of having the dimming eyes of an old man.

Leigh looked around the makeshift medical room, separated from the other rooms by partitions. The closed rooms were reserved for patients with much more personal health issues, such as HIV or pregnancy.

"I don't see my prescription pad anywhere." She placed her hand gently on Darryl's knee. "You get your shirt back on and I'll go find the pad so I can write you a new prescription. I'll be back in five minutes."

Leigh winked at Aliyah as she walked by her and was satisfied with the appreciative smile. Aliyah was like many girls in her neighborhood who had gotten pregnant too young, but unlike so many of the young girls in her neighborhood, she wasn't satisfied with the life she was living. She wanted more for herself and for her son and had struggled to get it. She was a great mom in a world that made it real hard to be one. Mothers like her needed this health insurance bill Leigh was fighting for.

Leigh quickly made her way to the front lobby of the clinic, where she was confronted with a roomful of waiting patients. This always reminded her that she had to open up that third clinic quickly. Both Hope Clinics were always full to the brim, and Leigh and the doctors and nurses on her payroll had only so much time.

"I'll be ready in a second," Leigh said to Lauren, the receptionist. "Do you have an extra prescription pad?"

"They're locked up," Lauren said as she reached into the top drawer of her desk for her keys. "You've been here since five in the morning, and you're going to act like you don't see this?"

"What?" Leigh, who had been surveying the patients' sign-in sheet on the desk, looked up. The second she did, she realized what Lauren was talking about.

It was an enormous bouquet of flowers that Leigh recognized as very expensive lilies of the valley and Casablancas. Casablanca lilies were her favorite.

"There is no—" Before Leigh could finish her sentence, Lauren handed her a small, pink-colored, petal-shaped envelope. "Did you read it as well?"

"Since when did you start dating Senator Cody?" Lauren didn't bother to whisper, which caught the attention of several in the waiting room.

"I'm not dating him," Leigh responded loudly. "I barely even know him."

She opened the envelope and read the message.

> *You made me think more of the issue than I have*
> *since learning of it. You're an amazing advocate.*
> *—Max*

Leigh felt a reluctant smile form at her lips. They were kind words, considering that when she left his office yesterday, she felt he was throwing daggers at her from his piercing eyes. She had met his opposition as best she could, but her time had run out when Kelly interrupted to tell him he had to catch a flight to Sacramento.

"Well?" Lauren said impatiently.

"Well nothing." Leigh stuffed the card back in the envelope and placed it on the desk. "He's a politician, Lauren. He's just schmoozing to try and make up for being a . . . well, a politician. I'm trying to get his support for the health insurance bill, and he's giving me the regular Republican line."

"Line or not," Lauren said, "you're due for a little lovin', and you could do much, much worse than a future president of the United States."

"President?" Leigh asked. "Do you know something I don't?"

"Everyone knows that he's being groomed for the White House. He's too perfect not to be. The only thing missing is a family, and who better than an American princess?"

Leigh rolled her eyes. "I'm not a princess. I'm a doctor, and I have patients to tend to."

Leigh accepted the prescription pad and made her way back to the rooms. She didn't doubt that a man like Max could be president. He had all the superficial qualities that voters seem to like no matter how much they consistently prove to be insufficient in the long run. He certainly wouldn't have her vote.

4

Leigh knew something was up when her mother walked into the state-of-the-art gym located in the basement of Chase Mansion. It was a little after one in the afternoon, and Leigh had just gotten home from her shift and hoped to get some exercise in.

As Janet approached her, Leigh jumped up on the sides of the treadmill so she could stop moving without having to pause the machine. She removed only one of her iPod earphones.

"I thought you were going to be secluded in your office planning the charity breast cancer ball," Leigh said.

"I just happened to be walking past the foyer when Maya was receiving a messenger." Janet's voice was tinged with genteel excitement. "It was a lovely invitation in a very classical black and ecru envelope. The lining and design are just choice. Very elegant."

Leigh was amused at her mother's stir. A lady of the best breeding, Janet was given an Emily Post etiquette book at age eight. She was the epitome of self-restraint and appearances, but every now and then, she let herself go and could have a good time. She seemed ready to burst right now.

"Sounds intriguing," Leigh said. "Stop teasing and tell me. Is it an elaborate invitation to some high-society wedding? What?"

"It's funny you should say wedding," Janet said, holding up the opened envelope in her left hand. "Because that is exactly what I was thinking of when I read it. It's for you by the way."

"What is it with people?" Leigh jumped off the treadmill and snatched the envelope away from her mother. "Everyone feels free to open any card with my name on it?"

"You've been holding back on me." Janet watched eagerly as Leigh opened the card.

When Leigh realized who the card was from, it all made sense. She turned to her excited mother with a look of dread on her face. "Sorry, Mom. This isn't what you think."

"I can read," Janet said. "Senator Max Cody has invited you to dinner. At Bastide no less."

"I know what's going on in that mind of yours." Leigh stuffed the paper back into the envelope. "You're always trying to marry me off to some upper-class well-to-do society guy. You know, Max comes from the middle class. You've never been too keen on those types."

Janet waved a dismissive hand. "He's like your father. It's just a mistake of the stars that he wasn't born in high society. He's of superior quality. High society is where he's always belonged."

Although she shouldn't be after all this time, Leigh was astonished. Not because of what her mother was saying, but because she knew she meant it. "Well, I hate to burst your bubble, but I am not dating this man, and I never would."

"Then why the invitation?" Janet asked.

She was treading lightly. Janet knew that her involvement in Leigh's personal life usually led to disaster, but she wanted so desperately for her angel to be happy. She had had such bad luck with men. Leigh had always been the jewel of the family, and Janet expected greater things for her than even herself in life. Max Cody could offer that.

"I was trying to get his support to lobby the governor for the health insurance bill." Leigh handed the envelope back to her mother. "But he isn't on board. He just likes to be lobbied. I think the attention turns him on."

"This man is likely going to be president someday," Janet said. "His time is very valuable and in demand by some of the most powerful political and business leaders in the world. For him to ask you to dinner—"

"Makes him a man," Leigh interrupted. "He just wants his ego stroked. Besides, I'm pretty sure he's sleeping with his chief of staff."

"Future presidents don't marry staff," Janet said. "They marry women like you."

"Marry?" Leigh found this amusing. It was a bit much, even for her mother. "You're insane. I'm not going. He's not serious about this bill, and I'm not going to let him use it to amuse himself."

"Fine." Janet raised her arms in acquiescence. "I will stay out of it."

"When have I heard that before?" Leigh asked.

"But," Janet added.

"Here we go," Leigh said.

"You have been passionate about this bill for a very long time," Janet said. "If charming a man who is arguably the most powerful in the state can get this bill on the governor's desk, why would you let anything stop you?"

"It's called integrity," Leigh said.

"I think you're just afraid." Janet noticed a defiant expression on Leigh's face. As darling as she was, Leigh enjoyed proving people wrong about her. "I hope you can tell all those people you were fighting for something better than 'it's called integrity.'"

As her mother left, Leigh knew she had been tricked, but she was used to it. Janet always found a way to get Leigh to do what she wanted her to. She was right. If a little charm could help save the health and lives of thousands of Californians, who was she to stand in the way? If he wanted dinner, he could have it, but she intended to let him know that it would never be more than that before he even poured the first glass of wine.

Besides, a dinner at the ultraexpensive Bastide in Melrose wasn't a bad place to get a free meal.

"Avery!"

Avery blinked, coming back from her trance as she relived in her mind the kiss she and Carter shared yesterday. She had been unable to think of much else. She wasn't sure how long Kimberly had been calling her name, but from the look on her face, it had been more than once.

"I'm sorry," Avery said. "What?"

"What is your . . ." Kimberly paused as the country club waiter brought their grape, Asiago cheese, and toasted pine nut salads to their table. She waited until he was out of earshot. "What is your problem?"

"Nothing," Avery said. "You were saying something."

"Are you not hungry?" Kimberly asked. "I know this isn't your favorite place, but I feel like every time I come here, I'm sticking it to Janet. She tried to get me kicked out of this place after the divorce, but Michael stopped her."

"So I'm party to your ongoing revenge?" Avery asked, picking at her plate.

"Shit." Kimberly leaned back in her chair. "Not just you. Since the bill still goes to the Steven and Janet Chase account, I'm bringing every bitch I know here."

Avery let out a weak laugh, appreciating Kimberly's attempt to lift her mood. "You're crazy."

"She made me crazy," Kimberly said. "That whole family did, and I'm assuming your far-off, distant zone-out is due to a member of that psychotic clan too."

"It's Carter." Avery looked at her sleeping daughter in the baby seat next to her. "He threatened me again yesterday."

"Stop it," Kimberly said. "He is not going to take Connor away from you."

Avery was shaking her head. "I'll never let him take her, but I'm just afraid of the fight. I don't have the energy to deal with this hate. I've tried to make peace with him."

"Just be patient," Kimberly said. "He's Carter Chase. He's had women at his feet his entire life. He's never lost a woman. He never loses anything, and he certainly never expected to lose the one thing he wanted most in the world."

"I didn't have a choice," Avery said.

Kimberly tilted her head to the side with a faint smile. "You know how I feel about that, but your choice is your choice. I just think Carter always assumed you would come back to him. We all did. Once he gets some joy in his life, his anger will subside."

"I thought Julia was going to be that," Avery said. She could tell what Kimberly was thinking from the expression on her face. "Before you say anything, no, I'm not happy that he's with her or anyone else, but I want him to be happy and I thought—"

"No, you didn't," Kimberly said. "You know he never loved her. Everyone knows. Hell, she knows. Julia is all about hurting you and making him feel better. Carter isn't going to find happiness until he makes it for himself, genuinely. A loveless marriage is only going to spread the pain."

Avery didn't know what to think. Sometimes she found herself so insanely jealous over the idea of Julia becoming Mrs. Carter Chase. Other times, she just wanted Carter to be happy with Julia so he would stop being so mad at her. The kiss they shared yesterday made her angry and left her excited in ways that Anthony, even when they were having sex, never could. The kiss made her remember what it felt like to want to be devoured.

"This is just such a mess," Avery said just as a young woman with short red hair approached their table with a disagreeable-looking Evan in tow.

"What did he do, Rachel?" Kimberly asked as soon as the club day care assistant approached.

"Sorry to interrupt you, Mrs. Chase."

"Ms. Chase," she corrected.

"Sorry." Rachel kept her saccharine, Disneyland smile without fail. "Ms. Chase, Evan is saying that he isn't feeling well."

"Again?" Kimberly asked, looking at her son, who kept his face looking downward at his shifting feet. "Come here."

He stepped over to her, and Kimberly reached her palm to his forehead. Expecting to feel nothing, she was surprised to feel a little heat but wasn't sure if that wasn't from running around. She cupped his chin with her hand and lifted his face to hers.

"You sick for real, baby?"

Evan nodded slowly.

"Okay, love." Kimberly sighed as she pulled him to her and hugged him before looking up at Rachel. "Can you please get his brother?"

"Right away," Rachel answered, and shot off.

Avery could see that Kimberly was concerned. "Do you think it's serious?"

Kimberly shrugged. "I'm sure it's just a regular fever, but I'm going to take him home and make an appointment with Dr. Brown as soon as possible. I hope you don't mind if I cut this short."

"Of course not." Avery looked down at Connor, who was squirming around but still fast asleep. She knew what it meant to be a mother with a sick little one. Nothing could be more upsetting.

"Follow me *s'il vous plait*," said the French host as he led Leigh through Bastide's dining room.

Leigh hated how much she cared about the way she looked. After telling Max's office that she would meet him for dinner, Leigh spent the rest of her time wondering what she would wear. She didn't want to give him the impression she was trying to impress or look sexy for him, but it was one of the most expensive restaurants in L.A. and had a dress code, and if she went out of her way to not look nice, he would know that she was doing it on purpose. She didn't want to give him the satisfaction of the truth.

She had settled on a fitted bodice gray twist dress with a sheath silhouette and neck twist. She accented it with a black belt. It was soft and slid against her skin with ease without hugging any curves too tight.

She took her mind off of what she looked like for the first time when she realized the host was leading her past all of the patrons, and they were heading for another room.

"Are there more tables back there?" Leigh asked.

"Private dining is back here, mademoiselle." He opened the door and stepped aside so she could walk in.

When Leigh stepped in the doorway, she was a little confused. There was nothing private about this back area. There were people walking all over the place.

"Dr. Chase." Max seemed to come out of nowhere as he made his way to her with a glass of wine in his hand.

Leigh tried to smile kindly, but not too kindly, as he approached.

"I'm glad you could make it," he said. "You look beautiful."

Leigh brushed aside the bit of pleasure his compliment brought her. "So glad I could make it? Your office told you I agreed to meet you for dinner, right?"

"No." He gestured for a passing waiter to come over and retrieved a glass of wine. "I guess they never got to me. Wine?"

Confused, Leigh took the glass without thinking. "Then what are you doing here?"

It wasn't until then that she realized he was wearing a suit—but it was an office suit. She looked around the room and noticed that everyone in the room was wearing suits. When it hit her how wrong she'd been, she immediately became horrified at the prospect that Max could figure out her mistake. She only hoped that he wouldn't notice, but she was too late.

"Dr. Chase." Max spoke through laughter. "Did you think this was a private dinner invitation?"

"I . . ." Leigh was too caught off guard to come back with a safe response. "I just . . ."

"Well, you certainly fancy yourself, don't you?" he asked.

Her face was taut and strained as she looked at him. "It was an easy mistake."

"If you say so." Max shrugged. "You're more entertaining than I thought."

"Entertaining?" Leigh asked. "Am I here for your entertainment?"

"Don't be mad at me," Max said. "You're the one who read the message wrong. I sent that same invite to everyone here. No one else thought so highly of themselves to assume it was a date."

"I didn't assume it was a date," she lied. "I just didn't know other people would be here."

"Don't get so upset," he said. "I'm flattered."

"Don't be," she quickly shot back. "I wasn't coming because I wanted a date. I was coming despite thinking you wanted one. I'm very serious about this bill, and I was only coming for that."

Max quickly looked her up and down, not lingering in any one spot long enough to be offensive. "This is what you usually wear to lobbying events? I can't imagine anyone saying no to you in that."

Leigh wanted to slap him now. "Are you finished having jokes at my expense?"

His eyes grew openly amused. "I think I have a few more in me."

"Well I hope you enjoy telling them to yourself." Leigh turned to leave.

"Dr. Chase, please." Max reached out and placed his hand on her shoulder. "Don't leave."

Leigh jerked her shoulder away from his touch, but she did turn around. "You may not have meant for this to be a private dinner, but you clearly don't mean for it to be a serious one, so there is no need for me to be here."

"Even if you could talk to Alan Bud?"

Leigh looked at Max to see if he was serious, then looked around the room. "The governor's chief of staff is here?"

Max nodded. "I was just talking to him five seconds ago. Him and Ned Artus."

Leigh immediately recognized the name of the head of pediatrics at Cedars-Sinai Medical Center. "Where?"

Max pointed to the right corner of the room. "He's over there talking to Anna Wagner, CEO of Pacifica Health Insurance. She's the one who implemented the free flu shot initiative at schools across the West Coast, right?"

Leigh couldn't hide her enthusiasm. "I have to talk to her."

"There are a lot of health care power brokers here, Leigh. That's why I invited you." He took a sip of his wine.

All was forgiven as Leigh realized the treasure trove of health care professionals before her. She turned to Max with a smile as apologetic as she could muster and still have some pride.

"I'm very happy you invited me," she said.

"So you're going?"

Leigh wasn't sure how long Kelly had been standing behind her, but when she turned around, the woman was barely a foot away. "Excuse me?"

"You said you're happy he invited you." Kelly's expression was flat. "So you're coming to Africa."

Leigh turned back to Max, who had a look of disappointment on his face. "Kelly, can you give me and Dr. Chase a moment?"

Kelly huffed before walking away.

"Africa?" Leigh asked.

"I was going to wait until you had happily talked to a lot of people and maybe had a glass of wine or two before asking," Max said. "But, yes, I am going to Nairobi to review and assess our health care–related programs in caring for the thousands of Somali refugees living there now. I'm doing it on behalf of the president, not California."

"Doing what, exactly?" Leigh asked.

"Assessing their success, worth, and value, among other things."

"Worth and value?" Leigh asked. "Isn't that just another way of saying you're looking for reasons to explain cutting the funding?"

Max pointed his finger at her. "You are a very suspicious one, Doctor."

"You're going to go and get publicity shots to add to your political portfolio and come back recommending the government slash aid to needy Africans in half."

"If you haven't noticed, Leigh, money to take care of Americans is sparse. You can't expect us to cut that before we cut money spent abroad."

"It's Dr. Chase," she corrected. "And, no, I wouldn't expect you to, but I imagine this president is going to have a higher standard than you."

"Ouch." His brows drew together in an agonized expression. "Despite what you think, Dr. Chase, I'm a human being, and I actually want to do an honest assessment. That is why I wanted to invite you. You've been to Kenya, and you have a unique perspective. You can help me do what's right."

Leigh couldn't help but be tempted. It was a great opportunity to prove him wrong and protect much-needed international programs. This was what she wanted. She would have to check to make sure this trip was on the up-and-up, but how could she refuse an opportunity to have such a direct effect on a report going straight to the president?

"I'll need some time," Leigh said. "I'll have to—"

"You don't have time," Max said. "We're leaving tomorrow."

* * *

When Avery heard a banging sound, she rushed from the kitchen into the living room. Connor was safely in her playpen, so Avery was worried that Anthony had fallen. It hadn't happened in a while, but it was always a danger.

But when she rushed into the room, she saw Anthony sitting in the La-Z-Boy situated across from the television. His wheelchair was right next to him.

"Are you okay?" Avery asked.

"I'm fine," he answered, reaching for the remote on the coffee table next to him.

Avery noticed he sounded out of breath, but she also remembered something. The second after she entered the room, something had caught her eye; she let it pass out of concern for Anthony, but his quick breathing brought it back.

The sofa had decompressed. While being firm, it was made to conform to the shape of whatever pressed against it. Once you got up, the sofa had an indentation of your shape. It slowly decompressed and came back to its natural form. It happened so often that Avery almost didn't notice it, but something about Anthony's voice bothered her.

Why was he out of breath? The only time Anthony was breathless was when he was doing his upper-body exercises, but he hadn't been doing those. Had he? Wondering about this was what brought the decompression of the sofa back to mind. It was no longer indented, but Avery thought it had been the shape of something small, like a hand, and it was three feet away from where Anthony was sitting.

"What was that noise?" she asked.

"A book fell off the end table," Anthony said, gesturing toward the other end of the sofa.

Avery walked over to the book and placed it back on the table. She threw her ridiculous thoughts aside and went over to her baby. She got on her knees outside the playpen and held her arms out, but Connor was too preoccupied with a set of mini-soccer balls to notice.

"Come on, sweetie," she said. "You should have been to bed an hour ago."

"I thought I asked for some dessert an hour ago," Anthony said.

Avery kept her back to him. "I'm tired, Anthony. Just get some ice cream from the refrigerator."

"So you would like me to spend the next half hour trying to get a pint of ice cream from the kitchen when you could do it in a couple of minutes?"

"Come to Mama," she cooed.

Connor dropped the ball in her hand and let out a loud yawn. She leaned over and reached for her favorite toy, her black Baby Stella doll. She wouldn't go anywhere without that. . . .

As Avery reached for the doll in order to lure her daughter to her, it suddenly struck her that only an hour ago, she had taken Baby Stella away from Connor as punishment for a tantrum. Connor wanted her pacifier, but Avery was weaning her off of them and wouldn't give it to her. Connor threw Baby Stella at Avery in a fit. Immediately after, she grunted her demand for Baby Stella, and as punishment, Avery took the doll and placed it on the third shelf of the walled bookcase.

So how did it get back in the playpen? She looked over at the bookcase and gauged its height. It was possible for Anthony to reach it if he tried very hard. Wasn't it?

"Avery?" Anthony's tone was impatient. "I'm still waiting."

Avery picked up Connor, with Baby Stella in hand. She had to be crazy to think what she was thinking. No, she wasn't crazy; she was just tired. Her mind was playing tricks on her. She had to have given Connor her Baby Stella back at some time but just forgot about it. Anything else would just be impossible.

"I'll get your ice cream," she said, heading toward the kitchen.

"It's okay, sweetie," Kimberly said as she kissed her son on his cheek.

Evan was cringing as the nurse drew his blood. He hated needles, and it killed Kimberly to see him in pain. She cradled his face to her chest with one hand and gently rubbed his head with the other.

"That's all," the nurse said in a sweet voice as she pressed against his arm with a cotton ball. She quickly covered the cotton with a Batman Band-Aid. "That wasn't so bad."

Evan responded with a grunt as he leaned into his mother.

Just as the nurse was leaving, Dr. Brown entered the room. He was one of the best pediatricians on the entire West Coast, and he had cared for Daniel and Evan since they were born. They had both become attached to him, and Kimberly found him, a black man who had lifted himself from the L.A. projects to the Ivy League and graduated at the top of his medical school class, an inspiration. It was hard to get an appointment with him earlier than a week ahead, even for his richest clients, but the Chase name, not to mention his involvement with the Chase Foundation and his friendship with Leigh, could get her in within a day or two.

But she wasn't so happy with him right now. "Are you going to tell me it's nothing again?"

"I've never told you it was nothing," Dr. Brown said. He was almost fifty but looked much younger, with a shaven bald head and a fit figure. He was a very dark raisin brown with light brown eyes. "I told you it was nothing serious. It was just a little bug."

"What do you say now?"

Dr. Brown placed his hand on Evan's chin, gently lifting his head. "Well, I need the blood results and the urine test back before I can say exactly, but it looks like a flu."

"Swine flu?" Kimberly asked, feeling her chest tighten.

He shook his head. "I've seen several of those cases in the past year, and this isn't that."

"He has a fever, and he says he's very tired." Kimberly kissed the top of his head. "His neck hurts, he won't eat, and on the way over here he said he wanted to throw up."

"That could be several things," Dr. Brown said. "Maybe a flu just hitting him hard. You need to take him home and get him in bed. His temperature is one hundred and one, so keep him cool, give him a fever reducer, and keep him hydrated."

"For how long?" Kimberly knew she would be up all night. She could never sleep when her babies were sick.

"I've given the test a rush," he said. "I should be able to call you tomorrow afternoon with the results. We'll go from there, okay?"

"I just . . ."

Kimberly stopped talking and looked down at Evan, who seemed to be struggling to get away from her.

"Nurse!" Dr. Brown screamed out as he reached for Evan.

"What?" Kimberly asked, panicked. It took her a second to realize what the doctor had realized immediately. Evan wasn't struggling—he was convulsing.

As the doctor snatched him away from Kimberly and laid him on the table, he was shaking all over.

Kimberly was screaming, running to the other side of the bed as the nurse came in. "What's happening?" she asked frantically. "What's happening?"

The doctor ignored her as he barked orders to the nurse. Kimberly reached for her son, but the doctor pushed her hands out of the way. She tried to stop screaming, but the sight of the whites of her baby's eyes and his trembling body filled her with shattering fear.

5

"Thank you so, so much," Leigh said to the flight attendant who met her at the door to her flight. "I know I'm so late. I really appreciate you waiting for me."

"Thank Senator Cody." The woman smiled as if just saying his name was exciting. "We were going to take off without you, but he convinced the pilot to wait a few minutes longer."

"I'll be certain to thank him." Leigh stepped aside as the male flight attendant, not interested in being nice, reached for the door.

"Please take your seat," he said.

"You're in Three-B." The woman gestured toward the first-class section. "I'll take your bag and put it in the overhead."

Leigh handed her the bag and rushed down the aisle.

"How nice of you to join us," Max said as she approached.

Leigh looked up and realized that he was in 9A. "Did you do this?"

"Do what?"

"Never mind." She sat down quickly, shoving her purse underneath the chair in front of her.

"You're welcome," he said.

"I know you got the plane to wait." Leigh fastened her seat belt. "But I'm not thanking you, because it's your fault I'm late."

"Can I get you something to drink?" The stewardess was asking Leigh but was looking and smiling at Max.

"No, thank you," Leigh said, annoyed by the woman already.

"How do you figure I'm at fault?" Max asked.

She turned to look at him and was immediately struck by how much he looked like a model out of a Lands' End catalog. He was wearing a dark camel, thin British sport coat over a white T-shirt and jeans. This was the first time she had seen him in his more "rugged" attire, and it definitely suited him.

"At seven o'clock last night, you tell me we're leaving tomorrow. I had to do a million things to make this happen."

"You're a Chase," he said. "Don't you have people to do that for you?"

"No, I don't," Leigh answered sharply. "I'm not you. I have to plan my own life. I had to make sure I could get a substitute doctor to work at the clinics."

"And?"

"That was not easy," Leigh said. Now that she was saying it, it seemed like a small thing. "Packing for Africa can be complicated. It's not like a weekend in the Bahamas."

Leigh left out the opposition her father had to her going back to Africa. Neither of her parents wanted her to go there the first time years ago after she finished her first year of residency. Africa was dangerous and far away, but Leigh was passionate about the Peace Corps program and went despite her parents.

When she told them of her plans to go back there on a noon flight later today, her father attempted to forbid her. Her mother hadn't wanted her to go but seemed to calm down a bit when she told her she would be with Senator Cody. After agreeing to allow her father to hire his own private security in Kenya, Leigh focused on packing and getting to the airport.

"Well," Max said, reaching into the pocket of the chair in front of him. He pulled out a copy of the *L.A. Times*. "At least you're in first class. All the way to our layover in London."

"What is that supposed to mean?" she asked defensively. "I

can't afford first class. I make nothing at the clinic. I'll have you know that I used miles to pay for this flight."

"Whose miles?" Max asked. "You never go anywhere, Leigh. From what I hear, you go to your clinics and back to View Park."

"From what you hear?" Leigh rolled her eyes. "You don't know what you're talking about. My father has hundreds of thousands of miles with this airline from business traveling."

Max smiled. "You're certainly sensitive today."

"What about you?" she asked. "Are the taxpayers footing this bill?"

"Please." Max flipped open his paper just as the plane started taking off. "Traveling from D.C. to L.A. and all over California, I probably have more miles than your daddy."

Leigh bristled at his use of "daddy," indicating that he considered her spoiled. "How nice for you to have so many miles that only you can fly in first class. What about your security or staff? Shouldn't Kelly be sitting where I am?"

Max paused for a moment, his expression suggesting he was analyzing Leigh's tone and expression as much as her words. "Kelly isn't coming, Dr. Chase. Can I ask why that matters to you?"

"It doesn't," she responded.

"You're lying," he said matter-of-factly. "But if you're wondering, there is nothing going on between Kelly and me. She's my staff. It would be highly inappropriate, and she's not my type."

"She's very pretty," Leigh added.

Max nodded and said, "But my life is focused on the governor's race next year. I'm not seeing anyone right now."

Why did she care? Leigh asked herself. She had already made such a fool of herself in front of this man with her assumption last night.

"The governor's race?" she asked, even though she probably should have stopped talking. "Isn't that a done deal? I hear that an actual election is a formality. Why be so concerned?"

Max smiled a winning smile as he placed his paper on his lap. "So you can believe what you hear, but I can't? Interesting."

Leigh laughed her way out of awkwardness, but her mouth

pulled her back into it. "This country doesn't often elect unmarried governors."

"You offering something?" he asked.

Leigh's brows set in a straight line. "Now it's you who flatters yourself. I'm just trying to make conversation. If we're going to be sitting here for an endless amount of hours, we might as well be civil."

"I thought I was," he said. "Nevertheless, dating is extremely complicated. The only serious girlfriend I had since my wife passed . . . Well, politics can be unkind at times."

"Your Republican backers weren't that excited about you dating a white woman," Leigh said. She could tell she was getting a little too personal for his taste and enjoyed having the upper hand in this conversation for once. "That was what was rumored, of course."

"There is some truth to that," he answered, "but I would have never let that end a relationship if I really loved her."

"If that's what you want," Leigh said, "you're better off being with her and hoping people see your courage as a positive thing rather than wanting her but tossing her aside for a more politically safe woman."

"Is that what you think I would consider a black woman? Politically safe?"

"I don't know," Leigh said. "Your wife was white. The only woman you've been serious with since was white. I'm not dogging you, Senator. I—"

"You couldn't possibly be," he said ardently. "Since you've swirled yourself. Recently, I believe it was an actor?"

Leigh didn't want to talk about Lyndon. She would rather forget that ever happened. "I'm not running for office."

"Your assumptions about my . . . preferences are wrong," he said. "I married my wife because I fell in love with her, and I dated . . . Well, I guess I didn't love my girlfriend as much as I thought. If I had, I wouldn't have let anything keep us apart."

"You guess?" Leigh asked. "You don't know if you were in love?"

"It's hard to tell," he said. "After my wife . . ."

Leigh watched his entire face soften, and his eyes seemed to look somewhere that was far away. "I'm sorry. I shouldn't have gotten so personal."

"Don't worry about it," he said. "I'm sure you understand how difficult dating can be when you or the person you're with is famous."

That was the understatement of the year.

As CFO of Chase Beauty, monthly division finance reports didn't reach Michael's desk until they had been scoured over by several levels of finance. Still, he demanded to see the details, because he could always find a mistake. He thought he'd just spotted an error in the expense reports for the marketing division when his assistant buzzed his phone.

"I told you not to disturb me until I'm done reading the reports."

"It's your wife," she answered quickly, sounding very upset. "She's been trying to reach you on your cell. You have to take this."

Michael had thought to remind her several times that Kimberly was his ex-wife. "What is it?"

"It's an emergency. It's your son."

Michael dropped the pen and grabbed the phone. "What is it? What's wrong?"

He could barely understand her. She was panicked, screaming and crying at the same time as she tried to tell him what was happening. He felt a sense of terror rise within him that he couldn't control.

"Where are you?" he asked, shooting up from his chair.

"UCLA," Kimberly cried. "Hurry!"

Michael threw the phone down and was out the door in two seconds. He rushed past his staff, yelling out for anyone who could hear to call his father.

"Where is my son?" Michael's voice boomed down the hallway of the Emergency Medicine Center at Ronald Reagan UCLA Medical Center, considered the best hospital in L.A. "Where is he?"

Everyone was rushing around, and it wasn't clear who could

help him. He was feeling frantic. It had taken him fifteen minutes to get over here, and he kept getting disconnected from
Kimberly on the phone.

"Michael!"

Michael turned and walked back to the hallway he just passed.
Standing there was Kimberly, looking unhinged. The look of
dread on her face made him think the worst, and he barely had
the strength in his legs to make it to her. She started running for
him, and he opened his arms for her. There was no thought in
this, no thought of the fractured state of their relationship. They
had done this so many times, finding comfort in each other's
arms at times of pain or fear. And although it had been a long
time since they'd last done that, right now it was the only thing
they could do.

"Please." His voice cracked as he held her away. "He's not . . ."

Kimberly's red eyes were full of panic. "No, but . . . Michael,
he's in a coma."

"What?" Michael looked up. "Where? Where is he?"

"We can't go in yet." She grabbed him by his suit jacket as he
started down the hall. "The doctor said that we can't go in for
another half hour or so."

"What are they doing?"

"I don't know." Kimberly started crying again. "It was so awful,
Michael. He just started shaking all over and . . ."

Michael wrapped his arms around her again, squeezing her
tight. He was trying to think, trying to figure out what to do,
while at the same time he felt like he was losing his mind. This
was his son. "Where is Dr. Brown?"

"He's in there," she said, pointing to the area they were holding him. "He said he'll be out in a few—"

Before she could finish, Dr. Brown came out of the room.

"What in the hell has happened?" Michael demanded. "You
said he was fine."

"Mr. Chase, I need you to calm down."

"Calm down? What the fuck?" Michael stood only inches from
the doctor. "You said my son was fine, and now he's in a coma.
You better tell me right now what is going on, or I swear I will
bring hell down on you."

The doctor seemed to be a little afraid. The problem with dealing with the rich was, although there were a lot of perks, if you pissed them off, they could destroy you. Dr. Brown looked as if he was aware of that.

"Michael." Kimberly placed her hand on Michael's shoulder to try and calm him. "Doctor, just tell us."

"I believe Evan has—"

"You believe?" Michael asked. "You still don't know?"

"Mr. Chase," he said sternly. "Let me talk."

After a pause, the doctor began again. "I believe that Evan has acute disseminated encephalomyelitis."

"That sounds like encephalitis," Michael said.

"It isn't that," Dr. Brown said. "That is good news. ADEM has some of the same symptoms as encephalitis, but that isn't what he has. This is very hard to detect and is completely unpredictable. It is a very rare condition."

Feeling her knees about to fall out from under her, Kimberly had to sit down as Dr. Brown explained to her that ADEM is a neurological disorder characterized by inflammation of the brain and spinal cord that attacks mostly children after having caught the flu, measles, or other viral infection. Its symptoms were like the flu but could come on even faster. A coma was one of the symptoms of the disorder, but Dr. Brown told them that he believed Evan's coma was going to help him.

"How can a coma help?" Kimberly asked, frantic.

Dr. Brown motioned for a nurse standing nearby to come over.

"What is this?" Michael asked as the nurse gave Kimberly a stack of brochures.

"This is information on the disorder," Brown said.

"What now?" Michael asked. "Who are the experts in this? I want them here now. I will send the Chase jet to get them if they are in this area."

"Now," Dr. Brown said, "we will transfer him to the Children's Critical Unit, and we'll monitor him to make sure his immune system doesn't deteriorate. I know the coma is very upsetting, but it can be a good thing. The body is shutting down all its other functions so it can focus on fixing this problem. He is otherwise very healthy, which means—"

"Do children die from this?" Kimberly asked, feeling a sharp pain through her heart just at the question she had no choice but to ask.

Dr. Brown seemed hesitant to answer but finally said, "Yes, they can."

"Oh, my God." Kimberly felt her heart leaping out of her chest, and she couldn't breathe.

"But you need to know that death is very rare," the doctor added. "This is an acute condition. It isn't chronic, so he should recover. It has about a five percent mortality rate."

She starting pacing in a circle before Michael grabbed her. "Kimberly, look at me," Michael told her. "That's not going to happen."

She looked at him through her tear-filled eyes. "You don't know that."

"He's gonna have the best doctors. He'll be fine." Michael turned to the doctor. "Who are the experts?"

"We're looking into this now." The doctor stopped for a moment as a nurse whispered in his ear. "There was a similar case earlier this year in San Francisco. I'm on my way to contact the doctor now."

"What happened then?" Michael asked. Based on the expression on the doctor's face, he knew the answer wasn't good. "The kid died?"

Dr. Brown nodded slowly. "But that was a rare case. It's possible there were underlying factors, and as I've said, Evan is healthy. It is more likely that he will recover with minor residual disability and that he'll make a full recovery."

"Oh, my God," Michael said just above a whisper. "When can we see him?"

"As soon as the team has set him up and made sure everything is okay, you and Kimberly can go in and see him for a short while, but they have rules and you'll have to follow them."

"Michael!"

Michael turned to see his parents rushing down the hallway toward him.

Janet Chase felt every bit of pain her children experienced, and Michael had had more than his fair share in the last year.

Much of it was his own fault, but he was her baby, and it didn't matter. Pain is pain and to a mother, it was unbearable. When Steven called her and told her something was wrong, she headed out immediately.

"What's wrong with Evan?" she asked, reaching out to him.

Michael let Kimberly go and hugged his mother. He looked up at his father and saw something so odd.

Steven Chase was scared. The sight took Michael aback a bit, and if the situation had been any other, it would have stood out more.

"What's going on?" Steven asked. "Where is he?"

"He's . . ." Michael pointed toward the room.

"Let's go," Janet said.

"No." Michael held on to his mother. "You can't yet."

"Why not?" Janet asked. All she could think of was Evan, and it made her sick to her stomach.

"He's in a coma," Michael said.

Both Janet and Steven gasped at the same time.

"What in the hell happened?" Steven asked. "Where is the doctor?"

Michael hadn't noticed that Dr. Brown had left, but he told his parents everything they knew so far. While they both took it in, Michael turned to look for Kimberly. She had made her way to a bench several feet away. She was sitting, looking so alone and so afraid as she stared at her shaky hands on her lap and rocked back and forth.

Michael started for her before his mother took hold of him, turning him back.

"Son," she said. "He's going to be okay. We'll take care of this."

"This isn't a problem money can solve." Michael didn't think he'd ever have to say that, especially after he had seen money cover up a murder.

Janet wrapped her arms around him, unable to think of what to do. This was Steven's specialty. When disaster hit, he was the calm and collected one. Her job was to comfort her children, and right now she had to focus on getting Michael to see Evan as soon as possible.

* * *

When the plane finally dropped down in Nairobi, Leigh found herself lost in the melee. She was sort of disappointed. After the initial awkward moment, her conversations with Max took a good turn as he told her about his days in medicine and travels throughout Latin America. He had been a part of Doctors Without Borders and had done many things that she admired. After being judged so quickly by so many because of her last name, Leigh thought she should know not to do the same.

Once the plane landed, she and Max separated. She was taken away by security to meet her bodyguard, a very large man who looked miraculously cool for such a hot climate. Twenty minutes off the plane and Leigh was already sweating. His name was Bem, and he spoke almost perfect English as he explained the details of his coverage to Leigh. She was barely listening, trying to keep her eyes on the group until Bem told her what hotel she'd be staying in.

"What?" she asked. "No, we're all staying at the Nairobi Hilton downtown."

"Your father has changed that on my advice," Bem said. "You will be staying at the Serena Hotel. It is—"

"No," Leigh interrupted. "I'm with a group. I can't be separated from them. It's the Hilton. It's a nice hotel, not a hostel."

"Dr. Chase," he said mindfully. "We must provide you with the utmost security while in Kenya. The Serena Hotel is where the most powerful people in the world stay. It is more secure."

"I don't care," Leigh said. She kept looking back as she saw that some of Max's group were heading out to the bus they were told would be taking them to the hotel. Then she finally spotted Max and an unexpected smile came across her face as she noticed he was looking for someone, and she was certain it was her.

"It is the nicest hotel in all of Nairobi," Bem added. "Your reservation at the Hilton has been canceled. Your bags have been removed from the group. We should go."

Leigh had already started walking toward the group when she heard Bem call her name. Max had indeed been looking for her, because when he saw her, he smiled and stopped looking.

"Where did you go?" he asked, shooing away staffers who wanted to prep him for the press outside.

"My father." Leigh sighed. "I'm sorry. He's moved me to the Serena Hotel."

"Nice." Max seemed a little disappointed but was laughing it off. "Upgrade most definitely."

"I want to be with everyone else," Leigh said. "I don't want to—"

"Dr. Chase!" Bem caught up with her, and the expression on his face was very serious. "You cannot run away from me like this. I cannot protect you if—"

"Stop," she said. "I wasn't running. I thought you were with me. Can I at least talk to the senator?"

Bem nodded, looking Max up and down before taking a couple of steps back.

"You have your own security?" Max asked.

She could see the sarcastic smirk on his face, and it made her angry. "It isn't my choice. It's the only way my parents would allow me to come."

"Allow you?" His brows centered in confusion. "Aren't you almost thirty?"

"You don't know my father."

"You're right," he answered. "I never got the chance, considering he never supported my camp—"

"This isn't about you," Leigh said. "Look, I just want to know what the schedule is so I don't miss anything."

"We're taking it easy tonight. We're all meeting for dinner at Traveller's." He looked at Bem. "That is in the hotel. She can make it, right? We have a private dining room."

Bem nodded.

"I haven't introduced myself," Max said as he stretched his hand out to Bem. "I'm Senator Max Cody."

"I know who you are, sir," Bem said. "Mr. Chase told me to keep a particular eye on his daughter when she is with you."

Max turned to Leigh before they both busted out laughing.

Avery was filled with joy the second the double doors of Chase Mansion opened, and Connor, in Maya's arms, screamed with excitement at the sight of her mommy. Avery held her arms out, and Connor practically leaped into them.

"Someone is certainly happy to see you," Maya said with a warm smile.

"That just made my day," Avery said, and couldn't have meant it more. She hugged her baby tight, tighter than usual considering the situation.

"Where is Carter?" Avery asked.

She hated to admit it, but she wanted to see him. After news of Evan's coma, Avery first thought of Kimberly. Then she thought of Carter, who she knew loved those boys very much. And because Carter and Michael were so incredibly close, Carter had to be feeling pain for his brother as well.

"He's upstairs." Maya stepped aside so Avery could enter. "I'm not sure why he didn't just drop her off at your place instead of here."

"He probably doesn't want to see me," Avery said. There was no point in keeping secrets from Maya. She knew more of everything that went on in this house and with this family than anyone else.

"They're in the process of transferring Evan to Children's Hospital Los Angeles."

"Transfer?" Avery asked. "I thought UCLA had the best children's wing."

Maya shrugged. "They said this is the best for children with his condition. Carter dropped her off here for you to come pick up, and he was heading over to the new hospital. I think he just wanted to rest a bit."

Avery looked up the stairs, unable to come to terms with her own emotions when thinking of Carter exhausted and worried.

"Here," Maya said, opening her arms. "Give her to me and go talk to him. We'll go back out by the pool, and you can come get her when you're ready to leave."

Avery hesitated for a moment but knew she was going to do it, so she handed a very disappointed Connor over to Maya and headed upstairs.

Carter's back was to the door as he looked out the window of the baby room his parents put together for Connor. He had watched as Avery drove up the large, black, half-circle driveway to the front of the house, where some of the family's other cars were parked.

He had hoped to avoid this, which was why he brought Connor here instead of to Avery's. He expected to be gone before she got here. After kissing Avery the other day, Carter was livid with himself. He had built up such a wall against this woman, convincing himself that he detested her, but all of that was blown apart when he kissed her. Yes, he recovered as best he could, but there was no ignoring that he still wanted her, wanted her badly.

He could feel her now. She wasn't in the room yet but was just standing at the doorway. There was an energy between them that aroused him whenever she was in the same room, and he hated it.

"I didn't expect you to come up," he said, keeping his back to her. His head was so messed up right now; he didn't even trust himself to look at her.

Avery took small, cautious steps into the room. "Did you think I would ignore you?"

"I was hoping you would."

"I don't care what you say to me, Carter. I'm just here to say that I'm sorry that Evan is sick, and I'm praying for him."

"You know I don't believe in that," Carter said. He took a deep breath before adding, "But thank you."

"I've had a hard time reaching Kimberly," she said.

"They don't let you use cell phones where she is." Carter finally found the courage to turn around and face her, knowing that she was only a few feet from him now.

Avery's breath caught at the look on his face. His light eyes were red, and he had dark circles around them with large bags. He looked tired and sad. She hated this and she hated that it affected her so much.

"Carter, I'm so sorry." Avery had a hard time fighting the urge to walk closer to him. "What can I do? I'll do anything."

Carter kept still despite the emotion her plea evoked within him. "For who? Kimberly?"

"For you," she answered.

"Why?" Carter asked. "After everything I've—"

"I love you," Avery said, feeling the tears well in her throat. "I know you hate me, but I love you and I love Evan."

Carter didn't have the strength to control his reaction to those words, and he didn't want to. Too many times he had returned her words of affection with hateful words of his own. He had done it not because he didn't want to believe she loved him, but because when she said it, it made him feel so weak and vulnerable.

Carter lowered his head, feeling so ashamed of his inability to respond the way he knew he wanted to. There was just so much pain that surfaced when he tried to face his real feelings for Avery, and right now he just didn't have the desire to worry about that.

"I thought of . . . I thought of Connor," he said.

Avery felt the tears stream down her cheeks as she watched his shoulders slump and his body lean back against the wall. She placed her purse down on the sofa as she rushed over to him. She wanted to touch him but didn't.

"I know," she whispered. "I thought of her too. Everything changes when you have a baby, and . . . you feel so helpless."

"I look at her and . . ." Carter looked up and his eyes caught Avery's. Her tears touched him and choked him up inside. "What is the point of having all you have if you can't save the one thing you love most in the world?"

"Carter." The skip in his throat as he spoke grasped hold of Avery's emotions, and she forgot all those times she had reached out to him and was burned. His pain over Connor was her pain, and it compelled her to reach out to him.

When her hand came gently to his chest, Carter felt tormented by conflicting emotions. He was reminded of the tenderness in her eyes and how comforting her touch was. He was reminded of how far-reaching her compassion could be. He was reminded of how much he loved her once.

"He'll be okay," she said. "We have to have faith."

"I don't have your God, Avery. I need more than faith."

"No, you don't," she answered. "And you do have Him whether you believe in Him or not. He loves you and He loves Evan."

For several seconds, they stared into each other's eyes, and the one thing that connected them no matter what the world did to them, no matter what they did to each other, was what they thought of: Connor. They didn't grab each other in a desperate, sexually charged embrace that characterized so much of their encounters. They both simply leaned forward until their lips connected.

Unlike the hard, punishing kiss from days ago, this kiss was so tender and warm that it made Avery's knees go weak. She pressed her lips against his, feeling a rage of fire sweep down her throat, into her chest, and through her entire body.

The salty taste of her tears mixed with the sweetness of her soft, full lips made Carter immediately want more. All of his senses exploded to life as his body began to pulse with need.

When their lips separated, Avery leaned away with a gasp. She wasn't sure what had just happened, but she had to get out of there, so she started for the door.

"Avery," Carter called after her. He didn't care about anything but touching her again.

"I have to leave," Avery said, but just as she reached the door, Carter stepped in front of her and closed the door behind him. Avery looked up at him, her mind not clear enough to decipher what he could be thinking.

"Move, please."

"You say you have to leave," Carter said, his eyes compelling and magnetic, "but do you want to leave?"

"How can you ask me that?" Avery knew he was aware of the answer to that question.

"Answer me!" he demanded angrily.

"Yes!" Avery pushed him aside. "I want to leave. Get out of my way."

"Fine," Carter said as he moved aside.

She wouldn't leave. This was what happened between them. Once they got started, they couldn't stop, and as much as his head told him that he was a fool to make love to this woman he claimed to hate so much, his body had taken over the second she placed her hand to his chest. Avery had that effect on him, and maybe it was his large ego, but Carter was certain he had the same effect on her.

Avery grabbed the door handle and opened the door. She tried to ignore the chaos raging inside of her so she could leave. She knew that this would only lead to pain, but her body wanted him so bad. His touch only brought back to mind how no one could ever satisfy her the way Carter did, and she wanted, needed, to be satisfied.

But how could she be such a fool for a man who was so cruel to her?

Carter smiled wickedly as he watched Avery close the door. She looked up at him, and he felt a surge of desire and power race through him. He leaned in and turned the lock on the door. His body pressed against hers as his hands slid up her hips, over her waist, and to her breasts. He watched as her eyes closed in response to his touch.

"Carter," she whispered as his caress began to drive her wild.

Her heart was beating fast, and she felt her body begin to tingle all over. When she opened her eyes, she saw he was looking down at her, and the lustful look in his eyes melted all her resolve. She reached her arms up and pulled him to her, pressing her lips against his with a fervor that matched her body's needs.

When his tongue entered her mouth, he explored her taste and heard himself groan. The potency of her body moving against his was enough to drive him crazy. He ignored every voice in his head except for the one that yelled for him to take her. Take her now.

Avery let out a gasp as she felt Carter wrap his arms under her and lift her up. As he moved her from the door to the sofa, Avery buried her face in his neck and kissed him passionately everywhere. The growing anticipation was making her shiver with desire. As he laid her down on the sofa, Avery looked up at him. Everything was becoming a blur to her, but she delighted in the look of determined passion on his face as he joined her.

Carter could not think of anything but having her as he reached for her shirt and lifted it up. She raised her arms and he slid it over her head and tossed it aside. He was straddling her as his hands caressed her stomach and her breasts. He reached for the clip between her breasts and undid her bra. The sight of her

bare, full, and firm breasts sent tremors through him. He immediately leaned down and kissed them both.

His hands were caressing her outstretched arms when Avery
felt his tongue wrap around her left breast. She inhaled sharply
at the warm touch of his tongue, and her body responded by
moving back and forth. Then his mouth engulfed her breasts,
one after the other, making Avery moan in pleasure and delight.
She wanted him so badly it almost hurt. It was as if nothing had
happened and they had always been here, making love and becoming one.

Carter's patience was leaving him with every second he tasted
her and touched her silky, creamy skin. His heart was booming
in his ears as he trailed kisses down her flat stomach. The sound
of Avery's growing desire only made him harder and more fam-
ished for her. He unzipped her jeans and pulled them, along
with her pink panties, down her legs. He tossed her clothes to
the side and looked down at her body. She was as exquisite as he
remembered her. Her breasts and hips were smaller than they
had been after she had Connor, but she was still curvy and looked
completely luscious.

Her body continued to move, urged by the lust growing inside
of her. The way Carter was looking at Avery made her feel sexy
and womanly. When he looked at her with ravenous eyes, she
wanted to be ravaged. It wasn't because she hadn't made love in
eight months, the last time she'd made love to Carter. It was because of him. No other man could make her feel this way.

He slightly lifted her right leg and leaned into it. He slowly
kissed the inside of her thigh, and the touch was so torturously
tender that Avery let out a cry. As his mouth traveled down her
leg, she could barely breathe. She knew what was coming, and
when his tongue gently teased her center by licking around it,
she couldn't hold it in. She was moaning out loud now as he explored the inside of her with his mouth.

He wrapped his arms around her legs and pulled her body
into him so his mouth could reach farther. She was leaning forward now, and he loved the feel of her hands pulling at his
shoulders and grabbing his head. The harder he savored her,

the more her body moved and the louder she got. It was too much for him. He couldn't take it anymore.

Avery was only able to enjoy the feel of his body on hers for a second. She opened her legs, and he entered her immediately, hard and forceful. They both let out a loud groan as she received him. Avery felt her entire body shudder in delight at the pressure of him completely filling her as far as he could go.

Waves of ecstasy shot through him as he moved inside of her. She was wet and warm and tight, and every thrust sent sensations through him that made him insane. She felt so good, and he told her so over and over again. It wasn't long before he was moving faster and faster, losing complete control of his body. She was meeting him with every advance, her nails digging into his back and her voice screaming his name.

When Avery felt her body begin to shake, the rising storm coming closer and closer, she couldn't take it. She reached up and grabbed the edge of the sofa, digging her fingers in as deep as she could. She wrapped her legs around him tight, her head falling back and her chest arching. Then she felt it and she screamed his name. Her head was thrashing left to right as the delirium took her over for several seconds. She was just coming down as she felt Carter's body jerk in a way that told her he was coming, too, just before he buried his head into her neck and let out a bellowing growl.

All Avery could think of was that she wanted more.

6

Leigh was gazing down at the open suitcases on her bed in her garden-style hotel room overlooking the Indian Ocean. She'd hoped she made the right choices. Packing for Africa's heat while keeping in mind some of the female customs in certain areas could be complicated, but she hadn't had enough time to really think it all through. Downtown Nairobi was a modern city, so she felt confident she could get there anything she had forgotten. After all, they would be there for only a short time.

She contemplated leaving her clothes in the suitcases but then thought that her mother would kill her for something Janet considered low class. Even if one was just staying overnight, she should always unpack her appropriately overpacked suitcase.

As she unpacked her clothes immediately, as her mother had taught her when she was a little girl, Leigh realized that she hadn't spoken to anyone in her family since arriving. She had promised to call her mother as soon as she reached Nairobi and was curious as to why no one had called her at the hotel. She looked around, forgetting where she had laid her purse, but was distracted by a knock on the door.

"Who is it?" she asked, walking to the door.

"Dr. Chase." It was Bem's voice. "It's the senator to see you."

Leigh froze just before she reached the door. What was he doing here, and why was her first thought to look in the mirror covering the closet door to see what she looked like?

When she opened the door, Leigh first thought that the look on Max's face was annoyance because of Bem's reluctance to let him enter the room, but she realized that it was more than that. He was very upset about something.

"I tried to reach you," Max said. "The phones in the hotel, on the whole block, aren't working."

"Let him in," Leigh ordered, and Bem stepped aside so Max could enter.

As she noticed that Bem wanted to enter as well, she held up her hand to stop him. This was going to get tiring quickly. "No."

"What's wrong?" Leigh was getting nervous as she turned to Max, closing the door behind her. Although Kenya was one of the most stable countries in Africa, things were constantly uncertain. But Max's expression seemed more personal.

"Your cell?" he asked, running his hand over his head.

"What is going on?" Leigh asked as she rushed over to the chair where she spotted her purse. When she reached her cell phone, she cursed. "I forgot to turn it back on when we got off the plane," she said while hitting the ON button on her cell.

"It's your nephew," Max said. He reached for Leigh, taking hold of her arm. "Sit down."

Leigh jerked her arm away, feeling panic set in. "Tell me now!"

"Kelly told me that she saw it on the news." Max's eyes brimmed with tenderness and compassion. "Your nephew Evan is in the hospital."

Leigh gasped, her hand gripping her tightening chest. Just then, her cell phone began beeping to indicate she had messages. She opened the phone and saw that she had more than thirty.

"What happened? I have to call my mother," she said.

"You might not be able to reach your mother," he said. "If she's with him, her cell won't work. The news report said that he got sick at the doctor's office with some mysterious illness and is in a children's hospital now."

"Come on, come on," Leigh said as she listened to the phone ring.

"Leigh, he's in a coma."

Leigh's breath drew in sharply just as her mother answered the phone.

"Leigh," Janet said, feeling so relieved to hear from her. "Where have you been?"

"I'm in Nairobi," she said with a panicked voice. "What's going on with Evan?"

Leigh felt complete anguish as her mother told her everything that had happened. Before she could speak again, Leigh was rushing past Max, toward her bags, with her phone tucked between her ear and her shoulder. "Who is his doctor? Dr. Brown? I want to speak to him now."

"No," Janet answered. "His new doctor is Dr. Paris Kent. She is the best, dear. You've heard of her?"

"She is," Leigh responded, but she didn't feel any better. "I want to speak to her, Mother. Is she around?"

"Not right now." This is exactly what Janet didn't want. "I'm not near the room. How did you find out?"

"Senator Cody came to my hotel," she answered. "Phones aren't working. I . . . When will you be near the doctor again? Do you have her cell number? Maybe I can speak with her physician's assistant."

"Leigh," Janet said in her motherly, calming voice. "We have everything under control. You know your father would hold no bars in getting Evan the best care."

"But he's in a coma!" Leigh said. "If his immune system continues to suffer, his condition could get worse. I need to know."

"Now that your phone is working, I'll have Dr. Kent call you as soon as I see her again."

"Leigh," Max said.

Leigh looked up at him. "What?"

"Breathe," he said.

Leigh realized that she wasn't breathing and took a moment

to exhale, trying to calm herself and think. "Mother, I will find a way to get there as soon as—"

"Don't," Janet interrupted. "Leigh, I know you're concerned, but I don't want you to leave."

"How can you say that?"

"It isn't as if flights from Nairobi to L.A. are available every day. The Chase jet is currently in Hong Kong with the head of marketing."

"So? Send it to me," Leigh ordered. "I want to be there!"

Max reached out to Leigh as if to calm her, but she stepped back. "I have to get back to L.A."

"That's not possible right now," he said. "But I'm working on it."

"Mom, hold on a second." Leigh held the phone down, looking at Max. "What do you mean?"

Max gestured for the phone, and Leigh gave it to him.

"Mrs. Chase. This is Senator Max Cody. I've talked to White Star Jets. They have planes in South Africa and can . . ."

"What?" Leigh asked in response to Max's sudden silence. She watched as he listened to her mother, saying nothing.

"Give me the phone!" She reached for the phone, but he backed away, holding up a finger to stop her. This only made her angrier. "I will not wait. It's my phone and she's my—"

"I know you're angry"—Max covered the mouthpiece on the tiny phone—"but don't act childish!"

She was ready to slap him until he started talking again.

"Mrs. Chase, I agree with you completely, but I don't think that Leigh will—" He looked at the phone once more before offering it to Leigh. "She wants to talk to you."

"It's about time." Leigh grabbed the phone.

Leigh did everything she could to protest, but her mother demanded that she stay in Africa at least for another day until they knew more. She promised to have Dr. Kent call her immediately and hung up before Leigh could respond.

Leigh grunted as she threw the phone on the bed. "I can't believe her!"

"She's doing what she thinks is best," Max said.

"What would you know?" Leigh zipped closed one of her suitcases. "I'm going home."

"You'd be surprised how much I know," he answered. "I'm a doctor too."

"What were you telling her about South Africa? How soon can I get there?"

"I promised her not to do that."

"Who are you to make promises to her about me? Why does everyone in my life feel they are better fit to decide what I should—"

"When there is a family crisis," he said, "sometimes the best thing is to not have too many people around so—"

"Too many people? I'm his aunt!"

"And you're a doctor," he responded. "You know that I'm right. Where he is, he can't even have more than one visitor at a time for an extremely short period of the day. Look, Leigh, the doctor is going to tell you the same thing when she calls. There is nothing you can do."

"That's not true," Leigh said. "I can be there."

"You should be here," Max said. "Here, there is a lot you can do. That's why you dropped everything to come along. I was listening to you on the plane. You have an incredible passion for helping these refugees. We're going to a women's clinic tomorrow. Those women have been abused, and they won't want to talk to me. I need you to be there."

Leigh turned away from him, not wanting him to see the pained expression on her face at the thought of what had happened to those girls and what could have possibly happened to her when Nick attacked her last year. It was still fresh in her mind, and it made her so angry every time. She had done research about the neglect of care these women had received since coming here, and it made her even angrier.

"One more day," she said. "But after that, I have to go home to my family."

"Thank you," Max said, smiling widely. "I know this is a hard choice for you, and I appreciate it."

* * *

It was late at night, and the children's hospital was very quiet when Steven and Janet entered and headed for Admitting; however, just before they reached the front desk, they noticed that all of the women standing behind it were staring beyond them at the garden courtyard in the distance. Something had them in a trance, and when they both turned to see what could grasp their interest so intently, Janet gasped and grabbed Steven's arm.

The Family Healing and Meditation Garden was a beautiful circular garden that could be seen clearly through the glass walls of the hospital. It was a relaxing area filled with art made by the patients, allergy-free plants, and various places to sit, but it was hard to see tonight. Tonight it was raining heavily; it had been for hours with enough thunder and lightning to prevent anyone from wanting to be out in the open.

Anyone but Michael Chase, of course, who was standing in the center of the garden, his expensive suit drenched to the core. He was staring straight ahead into space, his hands hanging limp at his sides.

"Steven." Janet's voice trembled with emotion at the sight of her son looking so pitiful, so lost.

She turned to the woman behind the desk. "Has something changed in my grandson's case? Evan Chase."

The woman shook her head, tearing her eyes away from Michael. "No, ma'am. Nothing. He's just been out there for like a half hour. The security guard told him to come inside but he refused."

"I'll get him." Steven headed toward the door, trying to keep it all together. This had been trying in so many ways, but he was the head of this family, and it was his job to keep it together in times of crisis.

Janet followed her husband outside and stood beside him as he called out to their son from underneath the canopied area. The rain was loud, and it took a few calls before Michael turned to them. His eyes were blank as he looked at them, but then he quickly turned back.

"Come inside, son!" Steven yelled.

Michael didn't respond.

"Baby, please!" Janet tried to speak above the thunder. She couldn't stand it. She started out for him, but Steven grabbed her hand and pulled her back.

"Stay here," he told her. He saw the pain of a mother on her face, and his hand went to her cheek. She was so much better at this, dealing with their children's emotions. "This is a father's pain. I'll get him."

When Steven reached his son, Michael didn't look at him, but he could tell, even with the rain covering his face, that Michael had been crying. He reached out and placed his hand on Michael's shoulder, but his son brushed it away.

"You're going to ruin that suit," Michael said, feeling so empty inside that he thought of nothing substantive to say. "That's a Fioravanti, right? But what's ten grand to you?"

"Come inside, son."

"He's not responding to anything," Michael said. "He's just lying with the tubes and . . ."

"You have to stay strong," Steven said. "He needs you to be strong."

"He needs me to have listened to him when he said he was sick!" Michael kicked the stone bench in front of him. It was supposed to hurt, but he felt numb to physical pain. "He told me. He told me. He—"

"Stop it," Steven ordered. "He was acting out at first. You took him to the doctor, and they said he was fine. What more can you do?"

"Sue the hell out of everyone," Michael said.

"We'll deal with that later. Now, come inside. You're no use to him sick."

"I'm no use to him at all," Michael said. "All my life, money has been the answer to every ill. Your money, Mom's society name, my money . . . whatever it was, it was solved. We buried a fucking murder, for Christ's sake."

"This is not the time to talk about that." Steven was still dealing with his own demons over covering up the murder of Kimberly's ex-pimp. He had done what he had to do but needed to move on. He regretted that he allowed that to tear such a rift between him and Michael, because it led to even worse problems. Now especially, Steven felt a disconnect at a time when it was most damaging.

Michael turned to his father. "When is the right time to talk about it? Never, I guess, as long as you say so."

"That's enough, Michael." Steven grabbed him by the arm and began leading him away, but Michael pulled away, swinging around in a circle.

"Why can't you do anything?" he asked. "You're supposed to be king, right? You certainly acted like it. My whole life, it's always been what you wanted. You acted as if your word might as well be written in the Bible. We all obey you, listen to you, fear you and abandoned ourselves to please you, because of what? What is the reward? I spent thirty-one years trying to be your favorite, and I want my reward!"

Steven cleared his throat in an attempt to hold back his emotion. Everything Michael said was true. Steven didn't know why he never thought there would be a consequence for the way he ruled his sons instead of raised them.

"We are going to do everything we can to—"

"That's not enough!" Michael grabbed his father by the lapels of his expensive suit with urgent fists and came to within inches from him. "You've wanted to play God all these years! Now I'm calling your bluff. You have to fix this! Fix it now!"

Steven wrapped his arms around his son and held him tight. Michael struggled against him only a bit. When he stopped, he laid his head on Steven's chest and cried. He cried as he cursed his father and God out loud. Steven didn't say anything. He held his son with the rain falling down on them, and he let him cry, trying hard to keep hold of his own emotions. There had never been a moment in his entire life when he wanted more to be able to say that everything would be fine, that he could take care of it, but he couldn't. There was nothing he could do to guarantee his grandson would get better.

Feeling powerless when your loved ones needed you was worse than death.

* * *

"What do you want?" Carter asked Avery as soon as he opened the front door of his home.

"Can I come in?" she asked.

"Where is Connor?" He stayed in the doorway despite her attempt to enter.

"Are you gonna make me stand out here?"

"Are you going to tell me why you're here?"

"You know why I'm here." Avery pushed Carter aside and walked inside.

Carter closed the door. "Avery, I'm in the middle of a lot right now."

"I know." She turned to face him. "But you aren't going to just sleep with me and then ignore me."

"That's very stalkerish of you," he said. It had been harder than he would ever admit to stay away from her, but Carter had no choice.

Despite leaving her without saying a word after they had sex at Chase Mansion, Carter hadn't stopped thinking of her. It had been a while since they'd been together, and every time was seared into his mind. He wanted her so much, and he hated that he only seemed to want her even more now. He was determined to stay away from her. He knew he shouldn't have done it, but he also knew that having sex with her was what was getting him through this thing with Evan.

"Now I'm a stalker?" Avery laughed, but she didn't think it was funny at all.

Her body was still lit up from their encounter, and she had spent every moment since wanting more. She ignored the rejection she'd felt after they'd made love, because she didn't have the energy to deal with it and didn't want it to interfere with the joy of his touching her, being inside of her. Every moment since, she had tried to tell herself how much of a mistake it had been. She was still married, and Carter hated her, but none of that worked. Her body was speaking louder than reason or right. It ached for that man's mastery over it, and Avery had thought of nothing else.

"I'm not trying to be a problem for you," Avery said.

"You've been nothing but," he responded.

She ignored him. "I know you're going through a lot with your family, which is why I didn't call you out for walking away from me after making love to me."

"Making love?" He smiled. "That's not what that was. It was an emotional release. In fact, I'd say you took advantage of me."

Avery gasped before laughing. "Only you would think that. Your selective memory is impressive."

"Sorry, I can't think to say anything is particularly impressive about you, but I don't think you came here for compliments." He watched her turn, and his eyes went right to her butt—round, firm, and beautiful.

"Like I'd get them from you anyway." Avery made her way to the living room, knowing he was behind her, watching her. She knew what she had come for, and she wasn't leaving without it.

"I share this home with Julia now," Carter said. "You can't just walk around here like it's yours."

"Julia is off with wedding-planning duties, am I right?" She tossed her purse on the cinnabar-finished maple coffee table and sat on the sofa. "She saw fit to blab it to the gossip blogs so someone could show up and take a picture of her picking out silverware."

He looked down at her. "What are you up to?"

He wouldn't let her take control of him, and he had to get back the mind-set he'd lost by making love to her. "What happened the other day was a mistake, and it's not going to happen again."

"It was certainly a mistake." Avery stood up and walked over to him. She stood within inches of him and could feel the kinetic energy from his body make the hairs on her arm stand up straight. "But it will happen again and again. You know that."

Carter could feel his breath pick up. This was unexpected, and he already felt himself slipping. Damn this woman. "Leave, Avery. I'm busy and I don't have time for you."

He stepped aside, but she blocked him, looking into his eyes. Thoughts of getting her hands on him had consumed her to the point of insanity. "I know you hate me, but I know you want me. You can deny it all you want."

"You flatter yourself." Carter spoke quickly so she wouldn't detect in his voice the weakness he was feeling. "I get everything I want from Julia."

"Please," Avery said. "You and I both know what we did, what we've done. Nothing she has given you can compare to that."

She placed her hand on his chest and slowly let it travel up his shoulders. Just as it came to his neck, he grabbed it and pushed it away.

"Do you think you can seduce me?" Carter asked, angry that she knew she could do this to him. She was right. Nothing any woman could do made him feel the way Avery did. That was only one of the damn problems.

"Yes, I do," she answered. "If you need to insult me to make yourself feel better or feel more in control, go ahead. All I know is that I have needs, and I've tried to ignore them. I've tried to place them at the bottom of a list of priorities. But now that we've made love again, I can't. I want you, Carter."

She reached up again, placing both of her hands around his neck. She touched the nape with her fingers, softly, rubbing it gently. When his eyes closed, she felt his body relax and a ripple of heat rush through her.

"What kind of fool do you think I am?" Carter asked with what little shred of dignity he had left. He could feel his groin radiating, throbbing, as he hardened in response to her pressing her soft, curvy body against his.

"The kind," she answered in a seductive whisper as her body tingled all over, "that wants to feel good in a way only I can make happen."

Carter could no longer control himself. He grabbed her around the waist. "I may be a fool, but I won't be your fool ever again."

"Whatever you say," she whispered as she ripped his shirt open.

Sitting at a granite picnic table bench, Kimberly tried to empty her mind as she watched Daniel, only inches away, observe a collection of butterfly paintings. She had spent the whole morning with Evan, reading his comic books to him, because the doctor told her it was possible he could hear her.

Michael had showed up with Daniel in tow, and she took

Daniel to the gardens while Michael spent time with Evan. Kimberly wasn't sure what had happened, but Michael was acting different. He had been completely exasperated in the beginning and so angry that she didn't have any use for him and didn't want him around either of the boys in his state. But for some reason, in the past day, he had been calmer and more positive, hopeful. It made a world of difference to Kimberly, who needed every bit of strength he had to help her through this. Their relationship was still something she struggled to understand and define, but right now she didn't care. She just needed him to help her deal with this, and now that he had calmed down a bit, she felt as if he could.

She didn't look down at the ID on her vibrating cell phone, but as soon as she answered it, she wished that she had.

"Keenan, I can't talk to you right—"

"I heard about Evan."

"Then you know I don't have time to talk to you about anything." Kimberly looked around to make sure no one was close. There was a couple with their ill son sitting in the grass, out of earshot, and no one else was around.

"I'm sorry for your son's condition," he said, "but we have an agreement."

"Are you sorry?" she asked. "Sometimes I think nothing would make you happier than causing Steven pain. You must be happy to some degree."

"I'm sure Steven is fond of his grandson, but you and I both know that nothing matters more to him than Chase Beauty, and I am counting on you."

"Just stop calling me," she said. "I'm focused on my son and getting him well. I don't care about Steven, Janet, or you."

"Have you forgotten the threat they still pose to you?"

"I don't care about that! My son is in a fucking coma, Keenan."

"Then it's a good thing I can keep us focused. Now, I've heard that there were some discrepancies with some distribution centers and a factory in Mexico. I need you to find out more about—"

"Stop it," she ordered. "You want to destroy Steven, do it yourself."

There was a short silence before he responded. "You don't really have the option of backing out of this, Kimberly. I can expose you to them. Once they find out that you conspired with me, what do you think they'll do?"

"You're not listening to me," she said. "I don't care. Besides, you would have to expose yourself to expose me, and you would never give Steven the upper hand."

"Kimberly."

Kimberly almost jumped out of her seat as she heard her name called. She knew who it sounded like, but she was hoping that she was terribly wrong.

She wasn't. As Janet stood only a few feet from her, Kimberly searched her face for an expression to indicate what she'd heard. Had the person she hated most in the whole world just heard her discussing a plot for her destruction? Where had this sneaky bitch come from?

"Hey, Nana!" Daniel jumped and ran over to his grandmother, who knelt down and picked him up.

Janet kissed him on the cheek twice. She could never get enough of any of her grandchildren, but Evan's condition only brought home to her how precious they really were. They were the family's legacy, and they were her babies' babies.

"Janet?" Kimberly slowly stood up, turning the phone off and stuffing it in the back pocket of her jeans. "How long have you been standing here?"

"You should go to the hotel and rest," Janet said in the familiar cool tone she reserved for Kimberly.

Kimberly barely knew how to talk to this woman in any way other than screams and insults, but right now she was so happy that it seemed Janet hadn't heard her that she was temporarily speechless.

"Are you listening to me?" Janet asked

Kimberly looked like Janet felt—exhausted and spent—and despite Janet's intense animosity toward this woman, she had compassion for her. There was something about being a mother that made one ache for any mother who suffered through the illness of her child.

Besides, Kimberly was mostly out of their lives now that Michael had divorced her, so Janet had gotten much of what she wanted. She would never forgive her for the pain she had caused the family, but Kimberly's days as a threat to the Chase family and its legacy were over, placing Janet at ease with the very few times she had to deal with her.

"I'm sorry," Kimberly said. "What?"

"Go to the hotel and rest for a while." Janet placed Daniel on top of the bench next to her but still leaned him into her. "I'll stay with Daniel, and when Michael comes down, he'll take Daniel and I'll stay with Evan for a few hours. Then you can come back having rested."

"That sounds . . . fine." Kimberly's relief that Janet hadn't heard her made her agreeable to anything. Besides, she needed to close her eyes, even if only for a few hours. And she would be sure to check that ID before answering her phone from now on.

When Avery returned home, she wanted nothing but to kiss her baby and head to bed, but Anthony was sitting in the hallway, making certain that this wasn't going to happen. Guilt assailed her the second she saw the angry and suspicious look on his face. She knew what she was doing was wrong, but as she saw her life laid out before her, Avery convinced herself to ignore it. She was paying the price for her mistakes with Anthony, and she saw no escape from them. Carter was her only chance at a few moments of happiness, and she was going to get them.

"Let me stop you." She held up her hand just as he opened his mouth. "I know I'm late, but I had errands to run, and I'm not going to explain myself to you."

"Bullshit," was all he offered back. "Do you think I'm just going to take your lies?"

"What do you mean?"

"How long have you been fucking Carter again?" he asked with a condescending tone. "Or have you never stopped fucking him?"

"That's enough." Avery walked by him, but he grabbed her wrist with a grip so tight it made her scream. He pulled her back so hard that she fell to the floor in front of him.

"What is the matter with you?" she yelled. "Are you crazy?"

"You were at his place," he accused. "I know you were, so don't try to deny it."

Avery looked down at her throbbing wrist, then back to Anthony. As she slowly stood up, she met his eyes with hers. She could tell from his expression that he wasn't being paranoid. He was serious. He knew.

"Are you having me followed?" she asked.

"Should I be grateful that at least you didn't deny it?" Anthony peered into her eyes with contempt. "I'm trying to figure out who you're making more a fool of—me or yourself."

"You don't know what happened," she said, uncertain of where she was going with this. "And I don't appreciate you following me."

"You don't appreciate it?" He laughed. "You cruel-hearted slut!"

"We were talking," she protested, although she didn't figure it was very convincing. The pain in her wrist made her not give too much of a damn. "Do you have any proof anything else happened?"

"You and Carter don't talk," he said. "You either fuck or you fight."

"Things are different," Avery said. "Evan's condition has softened him, and he's being more reasonable."

"It stops now, Avery!"

Avery watched as his hands gripped the edges of his wheelchair. She thought for a second he was going to stand up from the way he was holding on, and when she looked into his eyes, something was there that made her believe that was exactly what he was about to do.

Then he blinked and lowered his head. He looked down at his hands as they loosened their grip. He placed them weakly on his lap, never looking up again as he said, "You can't leave me."

Avery wanted to reach out to him, but she didn't. She had been so sure that he was going to stand up but now realized that he wasn't. He had only forgotten that he couldn't, and it was her fault. He was pitiful and he knew it, which was why he wouldn't look at her. Avery felt awful.

"I'm not going to leave you," she said, because it was all she could say. It was all she could promise.

* * *

"Doctor, please follow me."

Leigh was barely paying attention to Ellen Ogwayo, the diminutive but energetic woman who was giving her a tour of the makeshift refugee camp's hospital two hours outside of Nairobi. It was the first stop on the senator's tour, but Leigh, with bodyguard in tow, stepped away from the scene when she noticed how much press was present. She didn't want to be a part of that.

She had barely gotten an hour of sleep last night after talking to Evan's doctor. Dr. Kent tried to quell Leigh's concerns, but after talking to Michael, Leigh had gotten even more upset—not as a doctor, but as a sister. She changed her mind several times about whether or not to go home, but before she knew it, the morning had come and the bus carrying the senator's entourage showed up.

"As you'll notice," Ellen continued, "we're much farther from the border than our original refugee camps are. Those camps are completely overstuffed, and we're getting there as well. Our camp is a UN camp, but we can't monitor all the camps, and there are complaints of mistreatment at some of them."

Leigh looked down at her cell phone. She still wasn't getting any signal, and it was starting to frustrate her.

"We're trying to keep this section for the women and girls," Ellen said. "There are . . . more sensitive issues they need help with, which is why I asked to take you aside."

"Are you going to do this every time?"

Leigh and Ellen turned around to see Max giving Bem the evil eye as Bem held a hand up to keep him from Leigh.

"Bem, please," Leigh said. "We've discussed this."

Reluctantly, Bem stepped aside and Max approached Leigh with a concerned look on his face.

"It's very nice to meet you, Senator!" Ellen almost giggled the words as she held out her hand.

It took Leigh a second to catch on, but she realized that Max was waiting for her to introduce the two of them. After she did, she ignored their small talk and tried to turn her cell phone off and then on again to see if it would work.

"You might be looking for this," Max said as he held out a small cell phone.

Leigh looked at the phone, confused. "Another phone? None of the cell phones are working. I've tried Bem's and—"

"This one will," Max said. "It's mine."

"I can't take your phone, Senator. You need that."

"You need it more." He gestured for her to take it. "Besides, I'll get to use it as an excuse to stay near you—that is, if Bem doesn't shoot me."

Leigh smiled as she took the phone. Looking at it, she could see it was working. "Thank you. I'm dying to hear from my family."

"I understand," Max said. "And I'm happy you've chosen to stay."

Leigh flipped the phone open. "I should really go call my—"

"Must you do this now?" Ellen asked.

Leigh was sure that Ellen had no idea who she really was or what was going on with her family. The woman was busy trying to help desperately lost people, and Leigh doubted she would understand.

"I will only be a few minutes," she said.

"We have only a few minutes with Katna," Ellen said. She looked nervously at the senator before stepping closer to Leigh. She lowered her voice to almost a whisper. "Katna is a sixteen-year-old refugee who was abused in the Sudan and . . . she has now contracted HIV. She is very reluctant to talk, and I was hoping you could try before she goes back to her family in the camp."

Leigh felt her heart sink into her stomach as she thought of the young girl.

"Leigh?" Max asked, seeming to notice her change in demeanor. "Are you okay? Do you think you can handle this?"

After taking a deep breath, Leigh looked at him. "I'm a doctor. Of course I can handle it. I'll talk to her now."

7

"**D**o you want to talk to Leigh?" Carter asked Michael. "It's not easy to get through to Kenya."

Michael shook his head. "I just talked to her this morning. Nothing has changed."

Sitting in a lounge chair out on the balcony of Carter's condo, Michael stared out at an unusually clear L.A. skyline. He couldn't really take any more questions from his sister, although he blamed himself for not letting Kimberly talk to her about Evan before she left for Africa. He blamed himself for everything.

Carter said good-bye to his sister and hung up. Placing the phone on the table near the balcony doors, he stepped outside. "You should at least eat something. I had a bunch of food brought over from—"

"I'm not hungry," Michael said. "Besides, I have to go back to the hospital."

Carter leaned against the brick wall, wishing there was more he could do. He'd seen Michael take a hit of scotch, but he hadn't seen him eat. "You sure you can drive?"

"I have a driver."

"Well, when you come back, I'll make sure Julia has—"

"I'm not coming back," Michael said. "I appreciate that you're

letting me stay here, because its closer to the hospital than my
hotel, but I'm going to go back there tonight."

"You shouldn't be alone," Carter said.

"Do you love her yet?" Michael asked, finally looking up at his
brother, his best friend.

Carter was caught off guard by the question. "What does that
have to do with anything?"

"I got enough problems," Michael answered. "I don't need to
have to wade through the thick air in this place. I can feel it and
it makes me uncomfortable."

"Since when did you give a damn?" Carter asked. "Nothing
makes you uncomfortable."

"Right now," Michael said, "everything does."

For several reasons, Carter knew better than to let Michael
know that he was sleeping with Avery again. It was Michael who
exposed their affair to the family and to Anthony last year. Michael
didn't approve of Carter's continued pursuit of Avery, and Carter
wasn't interested in the lecture. Most importantly, Michael didn't
need to be bothered with anything right now.

He probably shouldn't have even told Michael in the first
place he didn't love Julia but old habits are hard to break. Growing up on the East Coast at exclusive prep schools while their
family was in L.A., the boys were the only family each other had
most of their lives. They had formed a bond beyond mere brother-
hood. There was nothing they wouldn't do for each other. They
helped each other out when one was in trouble, and they kept
each other's secrets. But lately that had changed. When Michael's
marriage to Kimberly was disintegrating, Carter knew that Michael
was being extremely cruel to Kimberly, but he didn't know to
what extent. Michael was in his own hell, and while Carter, after
Avery left him—again—was willing to spill the beans on his feelings for Julia, he was in no mood to be honest about how angry
he was over Avery.

But right now, none of that mattered. Carter had never seen
his brother, who had a fire inside of him that could be seen miles
away, look vulnerable. Carter hated going to the hospital and
seeing his nephew, looking so small and helpless. It made him

feel powerless, and his grief only made him think of the limits to which he could protect his own daughter.

"I'm sorry," Carter said. "Things are a little tense with the wedding planning and . . . I can talk to her."

"No," Michael said. "I don't want to be pulled into your drama anymore. I'm going back to the hotel."

"What do you want me to do?" Carter asked. "I'm trying to help you, but I can't do anything if you don't talk to me."

"Don't you get it?" Michael stood up, feeling a little lightheaded. "There is nothing you can do. There is nothing anyone can do. Not even King Chase. After all his promises, all that is left is more promises."

"You know Dad would do anything for Evan," Carter said. Carter had noticed that his dad reacted more emotionally to Evan's condition than he had ever seen him in his life. It was weird yet comforting to see this seemingly impenetrable man so openly penetrated. "So would I."

"Dad can pray for Evan," Michael said as the cell phone in his jeans pocket vibrated, "but you can't. All I need is for everyone to pray for him, but you can't pray for my son, can you?"

Carter's atheism was an issue that put him at odds with everyone in his family, especially his mother. When they got engaged, Avery had told him it was the one thing she wanted from him, to give God a chance, and he'd promised her he would be open. Avery seemed convinced that she would bring him around, and he had agreed to let Connor be baptized to make Avery happy.

But he wasn't convinced himself. He didn't believe in much that didn't make sense and couldn't be proven, and he had to admit that the sickness of such an innocent boy made him more inclined not to believe in a God, because why would he let that happen?

While Michael had teased Carter about his beliefs, it had never been a sore spot between them.

"Michael, I—"

"That's my driver calling." Michael turned and walked into the living room. "I have to go to the hospital."

As he watched his brother leave, Carter searched desperately for something he could say or do, but he knew there wasn't anything. It was a fundamental difference that separated him from all those he loved, but this was the first time he really saw it was hurting them, and he felt guilty.

Carter walked into the kitchen with the intent of getting something to eat quickly before he went back to the office, but reaching the refrigerator, he realized that he wasn't hungry. Not for food at least. He wanted . . .

"Carter?"

Carter thought for a second that he was hallucinating when he saw Avery standing in the doorway to his kitchen, but as she walked toward him, he knew he wasn't.

"How did you get in here?" It wasn't what he meant to ask, but it was what came out.

"Michael left the door open."

Avery was so happy to see him again that she couldn't stand it. She knew she was risking a lot by coming here. She had no idea where Julia might be, but she didn't care. Even if all she could do was talk to Carter, it would be enough, but what she wanted was to make love to him, to feel him inside of her.

"I was standing in the hallway," she said. "He walked by without even looking at me. Is Julia here?"

"No." Carter leaned against the refrigerator as Avery walked toward him.

She looked good enough to eat, in a multicolored boatneck dress that loosely hung at her curves and stopped a few inches above her knees. The way she swayed over to him, the dress moving against her skin, made him hungry for her. Tasting her again and again was still not enough. There was a part of him that wished he could get his fill and get her out of his life, but that wasn't happening anytime soon.

"What do you want?" he asked. "I have to go back to work."

"You know what I want." She leaned against him and began unbuttoning his shirt. "You're the one who called me this morning, asking when you could see me again."

"Yes, I remember." Carter slipped away from her and walked to the large kitchen island, where he grabbed a banana from the fruit basket. "Then you told me you couldn't talk, because your husband was rolling into the kitchen."

Avery rolled her eyes. "Is that necessary?"

Carter laughed. "I'm the bad guy? You're cheating on him. I think making fun of his . . . incapacity rates a little lower."

Avery leaned back against the counter. "Well, you certainly have improved your mood-killing skills."

"You're not my girlfriend, Avery." Carter walked over to her, standing just a few inches from her. He loved to see that look in her large, beautiful eyes when he came this close. She gave herself away; she was very aroused. "Stop assuming you can come by when you want."

"We've had this conversation before." Avery leaned into him. She grabbed the banana and tossed it on the counter behind her. She reached up and slid her arms around him. "I know you've missed me and I've—"

"Stop." He removed her hands even though he didn't want to. "I'm going through a lot right now. You're the last thing on my mind. And where is my daughter, by the way?"

"She's with your mother." Avery pushed him back. "You agreed that Janet could take her to a photographer for pictures without telling me."

"I guess I forgot to tell you," Carter lied. "Mom needed to spend time with her. She's very upset over Evan."

"Everyone is," Avery said. She felt her excitement return as Carter came toward her again. She wanted him so bad, but her desire couldn't override her concern for him. There was something in his eyes beyond passion.

"What's wrong with you?" she asked.

Carter grabbed her at her hips and kissed her on the lips. "I'm feeling shitty. Make me feel better."

Avery got goose bumps as his hands rubbed her hips and thighs, but she grabbed them, making him stop. "Carter, I'm serious. Is this about Evan?"

"I don't want to talk about Evan," Carter said as he leaned down and kissed her soft, supple neck. His hands went to her breasts, touching them roughly. "I want to fuck."

"Carter, I . . ." Avery could barely breathe now, but she tried to hold it together. "I just want to . . ."

"What?" Carter abruptly lifted up, separating from her. It wasn't easy; he was hard and felt like his body was a thousand degrees. "I don't want to talk to you about my nephew. You're here for sex, so let's have sex."

Avery was confused. "You still want me to believe that this is just sex for you?"

"What?" Carter asked, almost laughing. "Do you think you're my . . . girlfriend? My lover? You're my piece on the side, Avery. Don't think this is anything more than an affair."

"I told you that I love you," Avery said despite the dagger of his words. "I know you don't love me back, but I am the mother of your child, so don't you ever call me your piece on the side again! I refuse to believe this is just about sex for you. I can feel you, Carter. I can feel what's inside of you. You hate me, but you love me too."

Carter was fuming now. "How dare you tell me how I feel!"

"Fine," she said. "Then I'll ask you how you feel. Do you love Julia?"

"Why does everyone keep asking me that?"

"Do you?" she demanded.

"No!" Carter yelled back. "All right? Are you happy? I don't love her. I don't love you. I don't love anybody!"

"That's my fault, I know." Avery looked into his angry eyes. "Things are beyond our control. But even though they are, we can still have something."

"We have this," Carter said. "And this is all it's going to be. I'm not stupid enough to let you back into my heart."

"Even though I'm stupid enough to let you back into mine?"

As she reached for him again, Carter knew he had no chance against this woman. He reached out and knocked everything off the island. He lifted Avery up and placed her on it. He grabbed her dress at her chest and ripped it open, exposing her breasts. He brought her to him and kissed her hard, wanting to hurt her with the pressure of his lips.

* * *

The less serious pediatric cases in the overcrowded Nairobi Hospital were tended to in the open-lobby area. That is where Leigh had been for the last four hours, trying to help an endless line of cuts and bruises, and no one was willing to tell her where they got them. She had heard reports of abuse by guards in the camps and fighting among the refugees uninterrupted by guards. She had heard that when refugees left the camps to venture into the streets, locals harassed them. With Max's help, Leigh had been able to have some of them transferred to one of the city's hospitals, hoping they would feel freer to talk.

Right now, Richard was the name of the little boy with cuts on his knees that she could readily believe were common injuries of eight-year-old boys, running and falling. He would smile, but he wouldn't talk to her. Leigh could only imagine how insecure he felt in this situation. What had he seen?

"Wanna see something?" Leigh asked.

Richard seemed somewhat curious but was reluctant to respond. He looked around as if he wasn't sure he was safe.

"It's okay," she said. "I have a little present for you."

He very slowly nodded, looking intently into her eyes. When she pulled the present out, his face lit up.

"Batman!"

Leigh feigned surprise as she unwrapped the small cartoon Band-Aid. "You speak English?"

The boy smiled but didn't nod. "Batman!"

"Everyone knows Batman." Leigh applied the Band-Aid to the last cut on his knee. "You like?"

Just as he nodded, Leigh was distracted by a growing noise behind her. She turned around to see Max with his entourage and the press, and it upset her. Every time she wanted to think he was genuine, he did something like this. Looking at him now, basking in the attention as if it was a photo shoot, it seemed clear to her that this was a publicity stunt. While she had seen some of his staff sweating profusely as they volunteered around the camps and other hospitals, she hadn't seen him really working at all.

Leigh had had enough of this. If the senator wasn't going to bring the attention to the real issues, then she would have to make him. Bem didn't try to stop her as she rushed over to Max. She reached within ten feet of him when a member of his staff, a young white man in his twenties with red hair on his sun-reddened, freckled head and wearing a baby blue polo shirt and khaki shorts, jumped in between and held out his hand to stop her.

"The senator is in the middle of a presser right now," he said. "Please wait until—"

"What is your name?" Leigh asked.

"Why?"

"I can call you Lackey," she answered, "but I thought you'd prefer a name."

"I'm Joe," he said, his voice laced with annoyance. "I'm the senator's communications director. Now, if you—"

"What is the topic?" she asked. "Everyone seems to be smiling. I think I even saw them laughing."

"The senator can be very charming." Joe spoke with pride as if it was due to him.

"What was the joke about?" she asked. "The rape victims in the hospital? The hungry orphans wandering through the camp in soiled clothes? I can't think of which one is funnier."

Joe's smile immediately faded. "Dr. Chase, if you'll just step aside."

Leigh didn't move. "No, I think I'll join him. I've got my own set of refugee victim jokes I'd love to share with the press."

Joe stepped in front of her as she started to move. "You can't mention that stuff."

"What stuff?" Leigh asked.

Joe looked around uncomfortably. "The senator is discussing the serious needs of these people, but he doesn't want us to talk about *you know* in front of cameras. It's a sensitive issue and—"

"Rape?" she asked very loudly, garnering a few stares.

Even Max turned his head in her direction.

"That's what you mean?" she asked. "We wouldn't want to spoil the senator's fantastic trip with talk of messy sexual assaults. Such unpleasantness is unbecoming of a future president."

"Leigh!" Max called out, waving her over. "Come over—"

He didn't get a chance to finish his sentence, as Leigh sent him a hateful glare, then turned and walked away, with Bem following close behind.

"I can't talk to you right now, Avery." Carter was looking down at his watch as he stood on his bedroom balcony. He glanced back into the room and was happy it was still empty. Last he heard, Julia was in the kitchen, and he was certain she couldn't hear him talking on the phone.

"Is Julia there?" Avery asked, not bothering to hide her jealousy.

"She lives here," was his answer. "Look, I'll call you tomorrow."

"What are you afraid of?" Avery asked. "We have a child together, remember? We're supposed to talk to each other."

"But we aren't talking about our child."

"She doesn't know. What, are you afraid of her?"

"Please," Carter said bluntly. "I can't talk to you because I'm . . . *we're* going to the hospital."

"Has something changed?" Avery asked anxiously.

"No," Carter said. "But the doctor is giving his update in about an hour, and I want to be there. I wasn't there for yesterday's update."

"You can't be there every time," Avery said. "I know you love your nephew, but you have a business to run and—"

"Avery, do I have to remind you that just because I'm sleeping with you doesn't mean I'm going to discuss my life with you as if we were a couple?"

"When will I see you again?" Avery asked with impatience.

"I have Connor all weekend, so I think next week. I'll call you on Monday."

Carter hung up without saying good-bye. He was angry, not because Avery continued to pry into his life beyond the point he was comfortable, but because the sound of her sympathetic voice made him want to tell her everything. It made him remember the days he came home from work and she was there with a hug and a kiss, with her body to warm and please him. He remembered how, before he met her, he thought he would leave bachelorhood reluctantly, but after they met, he couldn't wait to spend his life with this remarkable girl.

At times it seemed like decades ago, and others it seemed like just yesterday.

Tied up in his own thoughts, Carter was caught off guard when he entered the bedroom and saw Julia standing there with a look of betrayal and disdain on her face.

"Julia." Carter reached out to her, but she slapped his hand away.

"That was Avery, right?" she asked, already starting to cry.

"What did you hear?" he asked.

"You're fucking her again?" Exasperated, she went to the bed and dropped down with a dramatic whimper.

"No," he lied. "It's not what it seems like. She's the—"

"Don't!" Julia yelled. "Don't you dare use that 'she's the mother of my child' line on me again. It worked the last time, but it won't this time."

Carter walked over to the bed and sat silently next to her. He didn't like hurting Julia. Despite the fact that she was a social climber who cared more about superficial things, he had come to care about her and appreciated her ambition. He had led himself to believe that she was more interested in attaining his last name than loving him, because it made him feel less guilty about his feelings for Avery, but times like this she called his bluff. She did love him, and he had hurt her again.

When he started dating Julia, it had been a way to fill his time and it kept his mother, who was always on the lookout for a "proper" girl for him, at bay. Most importantly, it made Avery jealous. He had slept with other women when they started officially dating, but as he focused on winning Avery back, other women made things a little messy. After his affair with Avery ended, he proposed to Julia and hadn't been unfaithful to her at all. At least up until now.

"You know what is so pitiful about all of this?" Julia said, never looking up. "I was hoping it was someone else. I'm so fucking pitiful that I was okay with you sleeping with someone else, but I was just hoping it wasn't her."

"You aren't pitiful," Carter said. "This is my fault."

"You're damn right it's your fault!"

Julia pushed him as hard as she could.

"Julia, things have been so confusing and difficult right now; I just let my guard down."

"She took advantage of you," Julia said, her voice sounding as if she had just made an incredible discovery. "That's it. I could see her seething jealousy over us. She was just waiting for a chance to pounce, and Evan's sickness gave her that chance. That bitch!"

"Stop," Carter said. "This is between you and me."

"But that isn't true, is it? She's always here, isn't she?"

He couldn't deny that, and he couldn't deny that no matter what he wanted or didn't want, people got hurt because of his obsession with Avery. People who now mattered.

"I'll stop," he said. He could see that Julia wasn't buying it, and he was at least honest enough with himself to believe it wouldn't be that easy. But he would try. "I mean it."

"You said that before." Julia wiped the tears from her cheeks. "You said it even when you claimed to hate her. You can't stop, Carter."

"I love you."

Carter was surprised by his own words, but based on Julia's reaction, they had done the trick. They had done the trick on her, but he wasn't so sure about himself. He wasn't sure at all.

Leigh stood in the lobby of the Hilton and reluctantly said good-bye to her mother on her cell phone and promised to call first thing in the morning. The updates on Evan were not encouraging. He wasn't getting worse, but he wasn't getting better, and Leigh knew that she wouldn't likely be able to stay in Kenya for another week, and she felt guilty for it. This was why she agreed to join the senator's people for some drinks in the hotel bar before returning to her own hotel.

Just as she headed for the bar area, where Bem was standing in wait, she heard someone call her name. Turning around, she came face-to-face with Joe, Max's assistant from earlier that day.

"What do you want?" Leigh asked, placing her hands on her hips.

"I want to apologize," he answered.

Leigh was silenced, taken off guard by his statement and the earnest look on his face.

"Senator Cody was . . . I hope you can understand that I feel like I have to do my job."

"What are you trying to say?"

Joe leaned in. "You understand that Senator Cody is . . . special."

"Joe," Leigh said, "CNN isn't here. You don't have to whisper, and, yes, I am aware that he is the golden child of the Republican Party, but that is all the more reason for him to speak up. His words have meaning."

"He knows that," Joe said. "It was my choice not to . . . He just needs to be squeaky clean. You know what I mean?"

"No one is squeaky clean," Leigh said. She was finding herself feeling somewhat sorry for the guy. The Republican Party was pinning its comeback on Max, and with Max being black, there were so many things that Joe and those who were working to get Max to the governor's office had to think about that they might not otherwise. They were paranoid.

"His ability to attack the messy things, the unpleasant things," Leigh said, "is what could make him really great."

"He agrees with you," Joe said. "He saw that you were upset, and I told him why. He was pretty upset to say the least. He really cares about these issues and this trip. He was just doing what comes with it. I worry about him."

"Why?" Leigh asked.

"Because he cares so much about these really important issues, and he doesn't want to play this game."

"That's good, though," Leigh said.

Joe laughed, shaking his head. "No, it isn't. Politics at this level is a well-played game. He has to strike a balance, but he doesn't want to. He wants to get work done and change things, but he won't get the chance if he doesn't play the game first. I guess I get paranoid because I don't want him to look too . . ."

"Caring?"

"Liberal," Joe responded. "I just wanted you to know that what happened earlier wasn't him. It was me."

As Joe passed her into the bar, Leigh felt somewhat bewildered. Her mind wasn't thinking straight these days, and she was so averse to the idea of a relationship that she realized she was probably demonizing every man she met in an unwarranted way. But if it was true that Max did care about the important things, then she owed him an apology for her rejection in front of the press today.

When she found him in the bar, he was standing in a corner with a cell phone to one ear and his finger inside the other to drown out the noise. He looked different than he had earlier that day. He was less formal, and it made him look younger. He looked tired and had clearly been sweating, and it made Leigh think he might have actually put in some work.

Leigh made her way into his line of vision and was surprised at how pleased she was to see the smile that came on his face as soon as he noticed her. He was a really handsome man in both a distinguished and rugged way, and Leigh thought for a second that she would like to explore that further, but then she threw it from her mind. She had made a fool of herself with her assumptions about his feelings all week and wasn't going to do it again.

He quickly closed the cell phone and shoved it in his pocket. "Sorry about that. Work doesn't go away."

"I understand," she said. "I'm a little worried that my clinics are running so well without me. When I checked in today, I'm ashamed to admit I was kind of hoping they would beg me to come back."

"So, you're completely useless to them," Max said, gesturing for a quickly approaching Joe to go away.

Leigh laughed. "Thanks!"

He leaned against the wall. "So, can I take it that you're not mad at me anymore?"

Leigh sighed. "Look, I'm sorry about that. I'm a Chase. I should know better than to think that the press was an avoidable part of the process. You have to do what you have to do."

Max blinked, seeming impressed. "If I buy you a drink, Doctor, can I ask you a question?"

"Leigh," she corrected. "I'll pass on the drink, but you can ask, with no promises to answer."

"A few days ago, when that woman told you about the rape victim that she was hoping you would talk to, your reaction was . . ." He seemed to have a hard time searching for the words. "For a doctor and someone who works with complicated patients and issues, I know you aren't squeamish or nervous about this stuff. But you seemed unusually affected."

Leigh felt anxious and her stomach was tightening. "As a woman, whenever you hear about—"

"That wasn't it," Max interrupted.

He was staring intently into her eyes, and it made Leigh nervous. It was as if he already knew the answer. Why was she eager to tell him, as if it would make her feel better? She hadn't told anyone about what had happened. Only she and her parents knew, and considering how they had handled it from that point on, no one else could know.

"Max," Leigh said softly, "as a politician, you understand that when a lot of your life is public, there are some things you want to keep to yourself."

"And some things," he said, "you can tell people who understand that and can promise to honor that."

Leigh turned her face away from him as she took a second to work up the nerve. Max was waiting patiently. She wasn't sure why she wanted him to know, but she did and she felt safe that he wouldn't talk about it.

"Not here," she said.

They left the bar and found a secluded bench in the courtyard. No one was around, because it was dinnertime and the heat had turned into thick, dense humidity, forcing everyone else inside. Bem and Max's personal security detail agreed to stand close enough to act but far enough not to hear what they were talking about.

It took her a little while, but Leigh finally told him about how she met action superstar Lyndon Prior when he was studying for his role as a doctor who was forced to work in a free clinic in order to inherit his parents' fortune. They began spending time together and started dating. Her parents immediately disapproved. He was white, and, much, much worse, he was an entertainer. For black elites, nothing was less respectable than wealth achieved by entertaining people. Leigh had never cared for their standards of who was or wasn't appropriate for her to date.

Lyndon's life was too fast for her, and it was dangerous. Worse were his friends, and one friend in particular, Nick, gave Leigh the chills from the moment she met him. Then one day, while at Lyndon's mansion, Lyndon left her to go shower and dress. Unaware that Nick was there, Leigh was taken off guard when he found her and came on to her. She resisted, but he got very physical and seemed to enjoy the stark fear he was eliciting from Leigh. She had fought as hard as she could and screamed for Lyndon, but when he came and she was free of Nick, Lyndon only hurt her further by trying to keep her from calling the police, because it might harm his career.

"I felt so ashamed," Leigh said, "and I didn't do anything. I was so angry and so . . . confused."

"But you didn't call the police," Max said.

Leigh shook her head. "I knew that it was . . . I'm a Chase and we don't call the police. We call Mom and Dad, but I couldn't even do that. I was too scared of what Dad would do. My father . . ."

"Is a very powerful man." Max's tone was sympathetic.

"You know my family," she said. "Everyone knows that trouble seems to just disappear. I knew my mother had caught on, from the way I was acting, that something was wrong, but I never told her. I never told anyone. Then one day I read about Lyndon in prison, about the gay relationship with Nick and his confession. I know it was my parents."

"Do you?" Max asked. "Hollywood is a weird place, and I'm not just saying that as a Republican. Actors go to great lengths to hide things. If Prior was gay, he could still be an actor, but not an action star."

"He wasn't gay."

"Well," Max said, "I know this doesn't help, but Steven did what he felt he had to. He's your father."

"I know." Leigh was a little surprised that Max came to this conclusion so quickly, and she wasn't sure if it was a good or bad thing. "We've never talked about it, but that's not uncommon in my family. We tend to act as if unpleasant things just don't happen."

"You have a dysfunctional family?" Max asked. "How odd! You're the first person I've met whose family doesn't communicate."

Leigh smiled. "Fine. Everyone's family is dysfunctional, but mine is dysfunctional on steroids."

"I don't believe that," he said. "Someone as incredible as you had to come from something good."

Their eyes caught for a moment, and while she felt incredibly flattered by his words, something about the spike in her temperature told her that this was trouble. And as his lips spread into a tender smile, she knew she was in trouble.

Max's smile faded as he turned still and serious. "I'm sorry this happened to you, but you know you shouldn't feel ashamed."

"I don't feel ashamed because of what happened to me," Leigh said. "I feel ashamed because of what didn't. These women I've been talking to are healing physically, but emotionally, they are so far from good. I was feeling so sorry for myself, and nothing that happened to me could even compare to them."

"Stop that," he ordered. "Leigh, what happened to you was horrible. It was a terrible crime. Just like any other assault, you were victimized and you have a right to suffer some trauma regardless of how it ended up. You're angry because of what happened and what could have happened, and there is nothing wrong with that."

"I'm not angry anymore," she said. "I was for so long, but now I'm just . . . I don't know."

"I'm not worried about you, Leigh." Max reached out and placed a tender hand on her shoulder, touching her soft skin. "You're strong and you are blessed. You'll be fine, and I know you know that."

Avery felt a warm glow flow through her at his words, and the tension that she felt around him seemed to dissipate. She could feel the bond that had been growing between them since the first moment they met growing strong enough that neither of them could pretend it wasn't there. This was why she didn't stop him as he leaned into her. She closed her eyes when his lips touched hers and savored the kiss. Leigh found it hard to decipher what she was feeling. His lips were sweet and seductive, and were relaxing and unnerving in an unexplainable way. Then that little voice in the back of her head told her to stop trying to figure it out and just enjoy it. Enjoy that little flutter in her belly that was quickly turning into so much more.

Sitting on her bed, researching Evan's condition on the Internet, Kimberly was startled when she looked up and found Michael standing in her doorway looking at her.

"How long have you been standing there?" She hadn't taken his key away, because she knew Michael wouldn't let a lock keep him out anyway.

"I came to get you," he answered, unwilling to tell her he'd been standing there watching her for some time.

He didn't like coming to this house because of its memories, and as he looked at Kimberly sitting in the bed they shared for just a short time after moving in, he was even more reminded of how offtrack his life had gotten.

"Get me?" Kimberly asked. Remembering that she was wearing only a rose silk slip dress, she reached for her bathrobe at the end of the bed.

"Don't," he said without thinking.

Kimberly's beauty was at times painful to see, but at other times, like now, it was just incredible, and it had been a long time since he'd seen this much of it.

Kimberly wasn't sure why she paused for a second before putting the robe on anyway. She had sensed a change in her body's reaction to her ex-husband. Sex had always been great between them, from the first night they met and throughout their marriage. When things were good, they could barely keep their hands off each other. Even after things began to disintegrate, the sex was still fiery and passionate. But his cruel treatment of her at the end changed everything. Not only did she not want him, but also every time he tried to have sex with her, she felt sick to her stomach. She hated him for using their children to keep her prisoner.

She had slipped once. The last time they'd been together, some eight months ago, Kimberly had felt a moment of weakness, because Michael could have died in the jet crash, but she was quickly reminded of her mistake when she walked in on him with his mistress, Elisha, in his office.

"I've seen it all before," he said.

She shrugged off the discomfort his words caused her. "Michael, this isn't your house anymore. You can't—"

"Marisol let me in." Michael wasn't interested in another lecture about how his name wasn't on the deed to this house anymore. That was a piece of paper. He still felt like it was his, because his family lived here.

"What do you think you're doing?" she asked as Michael stepped in the room. "This is my bedroom."

"Do you really want to fight now, Kimberly?" he asked as he kept coming toward her. "I was just at the hospital, and Mother told me that you had left the hotel."

"We had to," she said. "It was upsetting Daniel. He wanted to come home. How is Evan?"

Michael smiled. "That's why I'm here, Kimberly. The doctor said that his immune system is stabilizing."

Kimberly hopped up onto her knees on the bed. "What does that mean?"

"The doctor says it means it's more likely that he'll come out of this coma than not." Michael sat down on the edge of the bed.

"That's it?" Her mind was so erratic that it was difficult for her to understand things. "They have no idea on when this will happen? I was reading that the effects of this disease can last for up to six months. Could he be in a coma for six months?"

"First things first," hc said. "This is good news."

Michael had been on cloud nine when the doctor told him the good news, and while he hugged his mother because she was there, his first thought was to get to Kimberly. He couldn't wait to tell her, and he didn't want to call her. He wanted to see the look on her face. He wanted to see the joy, but that wasn't what he got. Instead, she fell facedown on the bed and broke into tears.

"Kimberly." He reached out with the intent of touching her, comforting her, but he wasn't sure what he should do. "This is good news, baby."

Kimberly cried even more as she felt his hand rub her back. "I know. I know, but it's just so unfair. It's so unreal. How can this be happening to my baby?"

Michael lifted her up and brought her to him. He wrapped his arms around her as she cried into his chest. "I'm sorry. I feel . . . I was supposed to protect you all, and I failed every single one of you. Now I can't do anything for him. I'm so sorry."

Kimberly looked up at Michael and saw something so unusual in his eyes. She had seen him in pain before, but this time he didn't seem to be doing what he usually did, which was immediately directing anger outward or masking it. He was wearing it completely, and he looked like a child, a little boy.

"This isn't your fault," she whispered. "You know that."

"When we moved out of Chase Mansion," Michael said, "into this house, Dad asked me if I knew what it meant to be the head of a household. He said it didn't mean I was in charge. It meant that I was responsible. I failed all three of you, and now . . . I can't go on if he doesn't make it."

"He'll make it." Kimberly felt her hand trembling as she stretched it against his chest. Looking into those eyes that were still lit up, although filling with tears ready to flow, she said, "We can't believe anything else."

Kimberly saw the longing in his eyes as he looked at her and knew she should tell him to leave, but she didn't want to. She was hurting and she needed comfort. As his gaze slid downward, she felt her body react to him.

He reached out and touched her hair, running his fingers through it. He flipped it back, revealing her perfect, long neck. As her eyes closed, his hands went to her bathrobe. He slid it over her shoulders and down her arms. The knot came loose, and the robe fell onto the bed. The touch of her body was so familiar and comforting that Michael couldn't stop. His fingers traced her arms up to her shoulder. He brushed against her neck as her head fell to the side. She opened her eyes and looked at him so enticingly that it electrified the air around them.

Kimberly was surprised at how she was still so captivated by his virile appeal. He was all man, and she could feel, with every touch, the mastery he still held over her body. As his fingers slowly traced her chest to the point between her breasts, she felt her entire body weaken. Everywhere he touched prickled with heat and excitement.

When he finally kissed her, it was sensuous and made her feel as if she were falling under a deep spell. It brought back so many memories that she needed to have right now. As he knelt over her in the bed, Kimberly knew that there wasn't anything else that could make her feel as if everything was going to be okay, even if just for a moment, than having Michael right here and right now.

"I want you," she whispered. "Now."

The fire between them exploded as they began kissing furiously and tearing at each other's clothes in a frenzy. There had always been a madness to the way they made love, and this was no exception. She bit him on the shoulder as he pulled her hair. Like two starving people, they clawed at each other in hunger and an obsessive need to quench their thirst. Flesh against flesh, he was panting as her chest was heaving, and they rolled around wildly as their hands, fingers, and tongues made fiery contact with every part of each other's bodies.

The next time Kimberly rolled on top of Michael, she pushed him down. Straddling his naked body, she pressed against his chest to keep him from raising up. Looking down at him, she positioned herself over his erect tip. This was when she felt the most powerful, just before he entered her.

"Kimberly," Michael begged. "Please."

She moaned in pleasure as she lowered herself on top of him. Her entire body shivered as she felt him fill her up. Slowly she went down as far as she could before lifting up again. He was saying her name because he knew that was what she liked, and as she lowered herself onto him a little faster this time, she stayed for a while and moved around. She leaned back, pulling at her own hair and arching her body.

Michael's hands slid up her stomach and cupped her breasts before reaching behind and bringing her down to him. He felt her hair surround him as he took her lips with his. She was moving up and down now, crying in delight. Her screams stimulated him, and his hands squeezed her butt to bring her down harder as the inferno inside of him raged.

Their bodies molded together as if made for each other, and their very out-of-control movements began to form a frenetic rhythm. They were both bursting with desire and anguish as they delighted each other in crests and peaks before soon they erupted in a release of ecstasy that blew them both away.

8

As soon as Carter entered Hue, Avery felt herself getting excited. He looked great in a dark blue suit. This was an unexpected surprise, and she was eager to see him. The second he saw her, she waved for him to follow her into the back room. The only other person working at the gallery that day, Nina, was on the floor setting up a display.

Avery rushed ahead of Carter into the back room and was confused that he wasn't right behind. When she went to the door and looked out, she saw him walking toward her, but pretty slowly. It disappointed her that he wasn't more eager to see her, but he was coming. That was all that mattered.

As soon as he stepped inside, Avery closed the door behind him and rushed to him. She put her hands on his face and brought him to her to kiss, but he pulled away.

"What's wrong?" she asked. "Nina won't—"

"Stop it," Carter said as he held her hands away. He wanted so badly to kiss her just one last time, but he knew if he did, all his resolve would be obliterated. "I didn't come here for that."

Avery could tell from the tone of his voice that he was anxious. It was easy to detect in a man known for his cool and calm.

Setting aside her desire, Avery looked at his face and saw he was distressed.

"Oh, my God," she said with a gasp. "Evan? Is he . . ."

"No." Carter imposed an iron control of himself, knowing it would be a constant struggle to maintain it. "I came here to tell you that I'm not going to see you anymore."

"How many times have you said that to me?" she asked.

This wasn't going as she'd hoped. Avery knew that Carter still harbored anger toward her, but she felt that as time progressed, he would let go of that hate and even if they couldn't be together the way they both wanted, he wouldn't feel the need to be mean to her anymore.

"This is the last time," he answered, feeling sick with the struggle going on inside of him right now. "It was stupid for us to start this up again. It was understandable because of everything going on, but it makes no sense anymore."

"Don't you think I know that?" Avery asked. "I have tried my whole life to make good choices, to be logical and do the right thing. It didn't work. This may not make sense, but it still feels right."

"It doesn't," Carter answered, stepping back to avoid her attempt to touch him. "I mean it, Avery. Julia knows and—"

"Is she threatening you?" she asked. "Threatening to leave you if—"

"No," he said. "She just cried. I seem to make all my fiancées cry, but this is the last time. Not just for Julia, because I admit I don't love her, but also for myself. Our being together only hurts people, most of all me."

Now it was Avery's turn to feel anxious. A quick and disturbing thought—that he really meant this—flashed through her mind. But he couldn't.

"Carter . . ." She wanted to protest, to say something that would prove him wrong or counteract his point, but he was right. She just didn't care. "This is wrong, I know, but I love you and you—"

"Stop saying that!" Carter yelled, his voice ringing with command to mask his uncertainty. "Stop saying you love me. You never loved me."

"How can you say that?" Avery's chest felt like it was going to cave in from his reaction. "I loved you completely. I can't help what happened."

"That's a lie," Carter said. "You ran away and married someone you didn't love so you could avoid dealing with me. Love doesn't run away. It stays and fights."

"Stays and fights what?" Avery retorted angrily. "The level of deceit you brought to our relationship prevented me from even understanding what I could fight."

Carter took a deep breath, feeling he was about to boil over. It had taken all the strength he had, and a glass of gin, to build up the courage to walk in here and do this. If he didn't leave now, he would take it all back. Seeing her cry and hearing the pain in her voice was just too much for him.

"You'll hurt me again," he said. "Something, anything, will happen and you'll hurt me again. You hurt me every day you go home to that man."

"I tried to be with you!"

"No," Carter said. "You tried to make it okay to be with me. And when you couldn't, you gave up and you went to him."

"You know I don't love him," Avery said. "I love you and I wish that I could be with you."

"That does nothing for me, Avery. I hurt you and you just run away. But when you hurt me, my life stops. I can't let that happen again. I won't!"

"Baby, please." She reached out to him, but he yanked away. She felt panic setting in. "I know we can work something out."

"We have." Carter opened the door, unable to look her in the face. "And it's this. Good-bye."

Avery stood in the back room for several minutes, trying to pull herself together, but it wasn't working. The more she thought about what Carter had said, the more devastated she felt. She finally gave in and fell into a chair, sobbing. She had no right to sob; she knew that. The idea that they could carry on this eternal affair was a joke and a farce. She could hope the day would come when Anthony wouldn't need her anymore and she could be free, but what then? Carter would be married to Julia. The most she could be was his mistress. That wouldn't work. Just as he had wanted all of her the last time, this time, she wanted all of him.

Maybe deep down inside, she just wanted him to stop hating her, and she hadn't even accomplished that. This was hopeless, and Connor was already suffering. Avery was afraid her desire to seek joy for herself may have made it worse for her baby.

Leigh knew she was frustrating Bem by walking in front of him, but she didn't like it his way. She felt like a child following him and still did not believe he was necessary. Today, as they got out of the private car, she jumped in front of him and ignored him as he called after her.

She was already running late for the team's scheduled get-together. After she kissed Max the night before, Leigh pulled away and made an excuse to leave for her hotel. She wasn't sure what she was going to do the next time she saw Max, but despite chickening out the night before, she knew she was looking forward to being with him. It had been a long time since she'd felt excited to see a man. She thought she should feel guilty, lying in her bed touching her lips with her fingers while Evan was still sick and everyone here was working so hard. But she felt hopeful.

While Leigh was nervous about seeing him this morning, she felt the presence of the entire group would alleviate some of the tension. After all their hard work, the last day in Kenya was supposed to be fun. They were to gather in the meeting rooms at eight in the morning and spend the day at the Nairobi Zoo before they had to leave tomorrow. But when Leigh showed up, it was 8:10 and no one was there.

"No," she said, thinking everyone had left without her. "Ten minutes? Do I have the wrong time?"

"No, you don't."

Max seemed to come out of nowhere. Leigh's eyes lit up with surprise. "Where is everyone? You said to meet here at eight, right?"

"I told you to meet everyone here at eight." He stopped in front of her with an indefinable confidence. His expression was a mixture of childish anticipation and determination. "I told everyone else to meet at nine."

"What are you up to?" Leigh asked, not sure if she should be angry or excited.

"Trickery," he answered. "I wanted you to meet me here at eight, because I have a different last day planned for you and me."

"Bem will be here any second," she said.

"I've taken care of that. He's going to be distracted for another two minutes, so we should get going."

"No zoo?" Leigh asked, feeling charged with excitement.

He shook his head. "Have you ever heard of Giraffe Manor?"

"You're not having fun," Peter said as his wife sighed loud enough to be heard by the other customers at the luxury outlet mall in Long Beach, California. "Not that I could tell anyway," he added after getting no response.

Haley wasn't sure what he'd expected. It was his idea to go slumming in Long Beach and have a real outlet mall experience. Why he wanted to come this far from Los Angeles, where they were basically on the border of Orange County, she would never know. He had finally gotten his fill, and that, plus her constant nagging, made him want to call it a day. They were on their way to the hotel where they had valet parked, just across the street from the mall's largest garage.

"Look," Haley said, peering at the time on her phone. "I'm going out with my girls tonight, so I need to get going. I'm taking the Jag. You can get a driver or—"

"Come on," he urged as he followed her across the street. "I don't have any friends here, Haley. I'm tired of following you around like a little puppy doing what you want with who you want."

"No one asked you to even come here," Haley argued. "I'm not adjusting my life for you. Since our marriage became public, my parents have been all over me. I'm supposed to act like I love you, and I can't even date. You want to hang out, then hang out. You don't need me. Throw that Aussie charm on these . . . whatever they're called."

"People," he said bluntly. "You can be an incredible bitch sometimes, you know that?"

"I've always known that," she answered. "Glad to see you've caught up."

Haley could tell from his expression that she upset him. He was so different from when she'd first met him. He was fun and didn't give a shit. He loved to party and spend his family's money. Like her, he wasn't sensitive or sentimental, which was why she was so certain this marriage of convenience would work.

"I want to go home," Peter said, sounding like a ten-year-old boy who had wandered too far from his mommy. "My life and my friends . . . everything is in Sydney. You need to come with me."

"I can't do that." She stopped and turned to him. His homesickness was really starting to irk her and worry her a little. And for Haley to be worried about anything was saying a lot. "My nephew is in a coma! He could die!"

He rolled his eyes, seeming bored with her excuses. "Whatever. I'm tired of sleeping in a guest house and getting evil stares from your father."

"God," she said, looking around the front of the hotel for the valet, who was nowhere to be seen. "I thought I was impatient. We don't have much longer to go. Where is that damn valet? This is what happens when you try to valet in the slums. Chaos!"

"So it shouldn't be a problem," he said. "If there isn't much time, you can stand to come to Sydney. You have to or my uncle won't believe . . ."

He noticed that Haley was no longer listening to him, and she was no longer looking for her red Jaguar. Something had caught her eye, and she rushed to the corner to get a closer look.

"What is it?" he asked, following her.

Haley thought she was seeing things, but she wasn't. A wicked little smile formed at the edges of her lips as she took it all in. Her first thought was wondering if she was seeing right. Her second thought was how she could use this to her advantage. There were so many possibilities.

"Who is that?" Peter asked. "Who is that person you're looking at?"

"No one you need to be worried about," she said as she reached into her purse for her phone. She quickly got frustrated when she couldn't find it, because she was running out of time.

"Give me that," she said as she snatched Peter's phone from him. "How does this camera work?"

"Just"—he reached for it—"let me show you."

"There isn't time!" Seeing the camera icon, she reached up and took a picture as best she could before the chance was lost.

She only hoped she got what she needed. This could be a gold mine.

The Interfaith Meditation Room and Chapel on the first floor of the hospital was open twenty-four hours a day, but this was the first time Kimberly had come down there since Evan was admitted. Now that she was there, she wasn't sure what to do. She was alone except for an elderly woman lighting a candle at a nondescript granite table on the other side of the room.

Kimberly had stopped praying when she was young. After the abuse she experienced at home and the way she was treated as a teenaged prostitute in Detroit, she felt certain that God either didn't exist or he didn't care about her. She felt justified in giving up on him, because he had already given up on her. Then she met Michael and after their one-night stand, she found out she was pregnant. She was a model at the time, and all her model friends urged her to have an abortion. But she had already done that, and it had taken a piece of her away. She vowed to never do it again. She was deathly afraid that Michael would dump her when he found out, believing that she had planned this to trap him. So, for the first time in a long time, Kimberly prayed.

The next night, she told him and God blessed her with Michael, love, and understanding. She prayed a lot over the next six years, because she was so blessed. But in the last couple of years, her prayers weren't prayers of thanks. They were prayers about abandonment and begging for some solution to her nightmare.

Now, she was here to pray for mercy, but she didn't know exactly how to do it, and it was too important to mess up.

"God," she whispered as she knelt down. "In the Bible, you say that your grace is sufficient. I'm placing all my trust in your word for my baby. They say it is a sin to bargain with you, but I'm offering my own soul and a promise to get rid of all my hatred and my quest for vengeance. If you give me my baby back, I will be who I should have always been—grateful for your mercy and grace. Please, give me a sign that you believe me."

Kimberly opened her eyes as she felt someone was near her. She was hoping to feel a spirit but was surprised to see her ex-husband, the man she had recently made love to after having promised herself she would never do it again just days before. How could he be her sign?

"Are you trying to hide from me?" Michael asked as he sat next to her. He could see the serenity she had on her face disappear as soon as she opened her eyes.

"You're the one who left," Kimberly said.

After they'd had sex the other day, neither of them had said anything. It was as if they pretended it didn't happen. Michael asked her if she wanted to come to the hospital with him and she refused, saying she would go with Daniel once he got home from school. And that was that. He left.

"I asked you to come. . . ." Michael sighed. He wasn't going to argue with her. "I didn't want to leave. I felt like we should have said something or talked about it."

"It's okay." She turned to him and forced a smile.

Despite all that happened between them, she knew just from looking at his tender gaze that there would always be a soft spot in her heart for him. She would always love him, and there was no point in denying it.

Michael felt confused by the way she was looking at him. After being married for almost eight years, he had come to know every look, expression, and movement, but that was changing. In these last eight months, she had completely separated from him and was becoming a woman he couldn't so readily understand. He hated it.

"I know what that was—us making love. We share something so pure in those boys and the joy and pain. . . . I'm not making any assumptions, Kimberly."

The truth was, he had left because he was afraid Kimberly would tell him what had happened meant nothing.

Kimberly's eyes widened, as she was somewhat stunned by such a humble statement from the usually cocky, dismissive man. It reminded her of the old Michael, the one who loved her and talked to her with respect for her intelligence and with sensitivity to her feelings.

Kimberly got off her knees and joined him on the bench.

"I j-just . . . ," Michael stuttered nervously. This was new. "I just thought you'd want to know that. Maybe acknowledging that would make it okay for you to talk to me again—that is, if you have anything you'd want to say."

A light turned on in Kimberly's mind, bringing all her senses to life. How could this have been set up easier? She had to do this. She had made a promise, and Evan's life was depending on her following through on it. This was her sign. God was giving her a chance to prove herself true, and Michael had just opened the door.

"Michael." She said his name before swallowing hard. "I need to tell you something, and I hope you can understand and forgive me, but I need to let this go. All of it."

The suggestion that he'd need to forgive her told Michael that this was not going to be good, but he wasn't going to get angry, at least not yet. "Is this about Evan?"

She shook her head. "It's about your father and Chase Beauty."

Michael's entire body tensed at those words. One thing was clear: This definitely wasn't going to be good.

Kimberly told him how she had been curious to find out more about Elisha, his mistress, and about the broker of a purchasing deal for Chase Beauty. Elisha had given her reason to believe that she was more than just another mistress, and Kimberly wanted to see if that was true. She broke into Elisha's bungalow at the Beverly Hills Hotel and found out much more than she expected.

Michael was shocked into silence as she told him that Elisha was using him and was a tool of Steven's estranged brother, Keenan. Michael didn't want to believe this, because it sounded insane. He and Carter had vetted Elisha and dug into her background extensively.

Kimberly explained how she found out that Keenan was holding off on revealing an investigation into the publishing company they wanted to buy so that Chase Beauty would purchase it and thus become responsible for the millions in fines and countless civil lawsuits certain to come from violations that had happened over the previous ten years.

"Michael?" Kimberly asked after his silence lasted a little too long. He was looking ahead, almost blankly. "Are you okay?"

Michael slowly turned his head to her, feeling like a brick had landed in his stomach. "How can you be sure of this?"

"I have proof." She told him about the documents she had stolen from Elisha's hotel room and how she had hired a private investigator. "I still have it. I can show it to you."

"So what you're saying is"—Michael tried to wrap his head around this—"I could have completely destroyed Chase Beauty with that deal. Carter didn't like her and Dad had doubts, but he trusted me. This was the way I was going to get . . ."

"Back into his good graces after what I'd done," she said, finishing what he seemed unable to say.

"Why didn't you let her?" Michael asked. "You hated me and you know that would have been the end of me, the end of everything."

"I'm not sure why I confronted her at the ball. I wasn't really thinking about saving you. I was thinking about saving myself. I didn't know she would crack so easily."

It was that scene—the one of his wife and mistress fighting at the Museum Ball, the Los Angeles social event of the year— flashed on gossip columns and Web sites all over that made Steven decide to kill the deal against Michael's protests.

"Why are you telling me this?" Michael asked.

"I made a promise," she answered. "To God. I'm getting rid of all my anger and coming clean so he'll save Evan."

"But you weren't trying to get revenge. My uncle was." Michael was trying to keep up with his mind, which was racing a million miles a minute. "Can he really hate my father that much? To go through such an elaborate plan that we couldn't even see?"

"He blames Steven for everything in his life that is wrong," Kimberly said. "He thinks Chase Beauty, even Janet, should have been his. He hates Steven for cutting him off almost thirty years ago. It seems like in that time, he had tried to reach out to Steven for money or something else, and Steven turned him away like he didn't even know him."

"My father can be brutal when he thinks someone is his enemy," Michael said. "He is unforgiving to a fault and . . ."

Michael stopped in his tracks as he realized with astonishment what Kimberly was saying to him. "How do you know this? Did Elisha tell you?"

Kimberly took a deep breath. "Keenan told me. That's why I need to tell you, because I was helping him."

"What?" Michael slid away from her on the bench. "How?"

Kimberly told him about how she approached Keenan and offered to help him bring down Chase Beauty, because she wanted revenge against Janet and Steven for trying to buy her children from her for $20 million. She was supposed to try and find out anything she could that Keenan could use against Chase Beauty and Steven.

"How could you?" Michael asked. "What have you given him?"

Kimberly watched with desperation as Michael stood up, every muscle in his body tensing. "Wait, Michael, you have to understand how angry I was. It was all those years of being disrespected and mistreated."

He leaned over her, looking down with a violent anger. "What have you given him?"

"Nothing! I told him that I didn't want to do it anymore. I never really did. I was just so angry at the time. . . ."

"It's been six months," Michael said. "You've told him nothing?"

"What could I tell him?" she asked. "I have no access to anyone in your family anymore. All I care about is Evan and Daniel. I'm telling you because I need the truth to come out. I'm trying to be honest."

"How could you?" he asked again, feeling the knot in his stomach getting tighter and tighter with every second. "You got your freedom and you still wanted to hurt me. And you tell me this now, when my son is in a coma?"

"*Your* son?" Kimberly asked. "It's that kind of talk that turned me against you. You used our children to control me and to threaten me."

"That's the point," he said. "This is never and at the worst time you say this."

"I have to say it now," she said. "I have to clear my conscience so that Evan can get better."

"You sound like a crazy person," Michael said. "The only reason you didn't give him anything is because you didn't have it. Otherwise you would have, right?"

Kimberly lowered her head, unable to answer.

Michael shook his head. "You better hope to God that he doesn't have anything, because if he hurts Chase Beauty, you'll pay for it."

She wanted to call after him as he turned and walked away but noticed she was already getting too much attention from the other people who had come into the chapel. This wasn't the place for it.

Kimberly was scared now. She had wanted to believe she had done the right thing by letting Michael know and letting go of everything, but now she wasn't so sure. She had her freedom and her children, but she was no fool. If the Chase family wanted to go after her, they could destroy her. They could destroy her and take her babies from her. They had the power, the money, the influence, and the cruelty at heart to do it.

She was risking what she had for her son, but she had to convince herself to believe in the power of God over her fear in the power of Chase. It would be enough. It had to be.

Carter was miserable as he sat at his desk in the corner office of Chase Law. He couldn't concentrate on anything but Avery and what he had done. It was over, and while his head told him it was the right choice, his heart was filled with regret. He couldn't stop seeing the pain on her face. He loved Avery and wanted her badly, even more now, if that was possible. He was stuck with the reality of it being over, really over, and it only made him realize how much the last six months had been a joke. He had thought that if he could hurt Avery, he would feel better, but he never did. The second she was back in his arms, he had no choice but to face his real feelings. And, as usual, it brought him pain because he knew he couldn't have her.

No, this wasn't going to work anymore. The only way he was going to get over Avery was to get her out of his life, and with Connor in the picture, there was only one way to do that.

"Carter!" Haley jaunted into his office, shutting the door behind her. "You are unguarded. Anyone could get in here."

"And it appears anyone has," he responded, grateful for the distraction. His baby sis always delivered much-needed entertainment. "You even got past the metal detectors."

"I'm full of all kinds of tricks." Haley sauntered over to the side of his desk and leaned against it. "So how are you? Sulking and angry as usual?"

"You here because you need a lawyer?" he asked. "Or maybe your gay husband needs a lawyer."

"Why do you keep calling him that?" Haley offered a stern-faced expression. "He's not gay."

"Yes, he is," Carter answered. "I'm good at seeing this stuff."

"We have sex all the time." That wasn't true, but even though Haley knew her brother was only teasing her, this persistent theme was getting on her nerves.

"Too much information," Carter said. "And don't . . ." He gave up as Haley hopped onto the desk.

"I need a legal favor," she said, leaning forward.

"I charge five hundred an hour."

"I'm here to make a deal," she said. "It's a very good deal."

Carter leaned back in his chair, entwining his hands in front of him. "Anything to avoid spending money."

"My husband—"

"Your gay husband?"

"Stop!" Haley slammed her hand on the desk and pushed away some papers to add a little flair to her tantrum. "Just listen, you jerk. Peter is getting restless and I need some assurances."

"He'll pay you the money," Carter said. "He doesn't want the Chase family coming after him."

"Well, how could you?" she asked. "I love to throw our last name around to shake some boots, too, but his family is richer than ours, and if he goes back to Sydney, it will be his turf. I have nothing on paper to guarantee that thirty million dollars."

"You have your knowledge of the scam," Carter said. "Which you could reveal and hurt his chances of getting anything."

"I need more," she added. "Preferably on paper."

"That he won't sign."

"That's you're job," she said. "That's why they pay you obscene amounts of money. You make people agree to things they don't want to."

"You make me sound like a thug," Carter said.

"Lawyer, thug, take your pick," Haley said.

"That can be very complicated," he said. "And I am not inter-

ested in playing a role in your scam. I have a law license to protect. Ever heard of the word *ethics?*"

"No," Haley answered flatly. "And if you can find your way
around that, I can tell you a secret that Andy wouldn't want you,
Avery, or anyone else knowing; you could use it to your advantage."

Carter's brows centered in a frown. "Who the fuck is Andy?"

Haley gasped. "Duh . . . Avery's husband."

"His name is Anthony."

"No." Haley shook her head. "It's Andy."

"I think I know what his name is," Carter said. "It's . . ."

"I'm pretty sure it's Andy."

Carter paused for a second, realizing this futility. "Okay."

"Do we have a deal?" Haley held her hand out.

"I will make sure you get your money," Carter said. "What's
the secret about Andy?"

Haley leaned back, folding her arms in front of her chest with
a haughty, very satisfied grin. "He can walk."

Carter sighed impatiently. "Get out of my office."

Haley was shocked. "What? I thought you'd want to know that.
Don't you hate him?"

"Stop playing around." Carter wasn't angry at her but more at
himself for getting excited about an opportunity to do more
damage to a man who was pretty much dead inside already.

"You can blackmail him or something," Haley said. "You can
make him leave Avery, and you can have her."

"I don't want Avery."

"Please," she interrupted. "Save that for someone without two
eyes."

Carter tried to nudge her off the desk. "Anthony can't walk,
Haley. I've had his medical records checked."

"Lately?"

Carter hadn't checked in the last few months, telling himself
there was no point to it. "So you're saying, what, you saw him
walking?"

Haley nodded enthusiastically. "I was in Long Beach with
Peter. Don't ask why I was in that hellhole. Anyway, I saw him in
a garage across from the hotel."

Haley described how she'd seen him wheel himself to the car, and after looking around a little, he slowly stood up. He picked up the chair and placed it in its position in the driver's seat before sitting back in it and driving off.

"I'm not saying he was looking very steady," she added. "But he was standing and walking."

"That wasn't him," Carter said.

"So you're saying there is another crippled guy who looks like Andy and drives that silver piece of crap car that is all hooked up with the driving wheel for people who can't walk?"

"It was a silver Camry?" He couldn't believe he was contemplating this, but the man and the car had to be too much of a coincidence. Wasn't it?

What would Anthony be doing in Long Beach? Going someplace where no one knew him. "Was he alone?"

She nodded. "You believe me?"

Carter stood up, coming face-to-face with his sister, his face only inches from hers. With his most serious tone, he said, "Haley, do not fuck with me on this."

She didn't even blink. "Get me that signed contract and I'll get you proof."

"You have proof?" Carter knew Haley's foolishness too well to believe her, but this was just too much. "Show me!"

"I took a picture with my phone, but . . ."

"Give me your phone!"

"I've already downloaded it," she cried. "I'm not stupid. I want the contract."

Haley let out a little yelp as he grabbed her arm.

"Get me that picture!"

Leigh knew she probably shouldn't have agreed to come to Max's room, but the day had been so incredible that she didn't want it to end. As soon as she was inside, she ran to the window overlooking the preserve. It was amazing.

Leigh had never heard of Giraffe Manor, so she was very anxious to see Max's surprise. But before she could, they had to lose security, both of them. Leigh was very impressed that Max had a plan to distract Bem. He'd been thinking about it all last night. He had ditched his own security just before coming to see her.

Once away, they took a cab to a private air strip and jetted off to Langata, Kenya, home of Giraffe Manor. Leigh was absolutely amazed.

Built in the 1930s, Giraffe Manor was an elegant, exclusive hotel that looked like a very large English cottage, complete with old vines growing along the brown. brick. The manor was surrounded by 140 acres of indigenous forest and hosted all types of animals, but the stars of the show were the giraffes, a herd that was generations from the original two brought to the manor eighty years ago.

Once there, they were taken on a private tour of the grounds and the highland forest. Leigh was amazed at the endless species of beautiful birds and even herds of bucks they saw. They passed dozens of giraffes who would lean down to be touched or just to look. They went by a large pool and ponds full of beautiful flowers. It was like a paradise, and it made Leigh forget about all her worries. She wasn't a Chase and Max wasn't a senator. They were just two people immersed in the romanticism of this breathtaking country.

After a seemingly perfect day, they went to dinner, prepared just for the few guests allowed to stay at the manor. During their dinner, which was at a level fit for royalty in an elegant dining room, a giraffe stuck its head through the window, something they do all the time. While Max passed, Leigh didn't hesitate to feed the giraffe and rub his face. She was breathless at the closeness, those large eyes looking right at her.

They both passed on drinks with the rest of the guests and went to Max's room. There were only six bedrooms in the manor, designed as they would have been in the 1930s, at a price Leigh was sure was too high to ask.

Bem had reached her on her cell, and she told him where she was. Believing that Max had forced her away, he threatened to come get her, but she hung up on him. It was then that Steven called her and forced a compromise.

Max had called for a driver to collect Leigh and take her back to the airport for the short jet back to Nairobi, as she promised Bem she would be back that evening. Max, on the other hand, had rented a room and was going to stay overnight. He offered her a drink in his room before she left, and Leigh didn't want the day to end.

The window from his second-floor bedroom had a perfect view of the peaks of the far-off Ngong Hills. Leaning against the wall covered by bright white curtains, she could hear Max walking on the hardwood floor toward her, and she felt warm inside.

"It's such a shame," Leigh said as he reached her.

"What?" Max offered her a glass of port.

"This beauty," she said. "The beauty of Africa is so immense it's almost overwhelming. It's such a shame that people hardly ever get to see this."

"Well, you certainly took enough pictures for everyone in the entire United States."

Leigh laughed. She had gone a little overboard with the pictures on their driven tour through the preserves, where they stood only a few feet from the youngest giraffe, a one-year-old female Leigh immediately fell in love with.

"Too bad it all ends tomorrow." She turned to him and was surprised to find he had been looking at her the whole time. She had thought he was looking out the window like her. "For you and me at least. Those refugees don't have anywhere to go."

"If you want me to promise my report to the president will be what you want," he said, "I can't do that."

"The people need you," she urged. "I've seen you during the time we've been here, and you have a bigger heart than you like to show."

"If that was all this was about," he said, "that would be enough."

Leigh was hurt when he suddenly walked away. She wasn't willing to let this disagreement ruin their day. It had been too perfect, and she hadn't had a perfect day in as long as she could remember.

"Do you think one of them will stick its head through your window like downstairs?" she asked. "They said they do it all the time."

"Why don't you stick around to find out?"

Leigh turned around to find Max sitting on the flowery cushioned settee at the end of the large canopied bed surrounded by white curtains.

"Is that your line?" she asked, walking toward him.

"That depends," he answered. "Did it work?"

"No." She sat next to him. "The giraffes are keeping me here, not you."

He offered a charming smile. "Leigh, I know you're a cautious woman, and you don't take lightly to relationships."

"Do I sense a 'poor little Leigh' comment coming?" she asked. "Because I'd rather just leave now."

"God, no," he answered. "I look at what you've done with your clinics, and I've watched you here in Africa. You're a very strong woman. If I were to even suggest pitying you, I think you'd punch me in the face."

She tilted her head. "You have to learn somehow."

He exchanged a flirtatious smile with her, then shook his head.

"I would probably be smarter to walk you down to that car waiting for you, but I don't want to. I want to—"

Leigh leaned forward and planted a kiss on his lips, pressing against him gently. His eager response warmed her inside and made her want more.

Max leaned away and with a wicked smile said, "Bem is going to be very angry at you."

"No," she answered as she brought her hands to his face. "He'll be angry at you."

This time, he initiated the kiss and Leigh felt a tingling sensation throughout her body. Her heart began to race as his strong, hard lips coaxed her mouth open, and his hands came to her waist, where he caressed her persuasively, making her body move closer and closer to his.

By the time he eased her down on the bed, Leigh was burning like fire. She was hungry and his lips were tantalizing. He kissed her on her cheeks, her neck, and her chest. As she removed her shirt, he caressed her breasts, his fingers circling her sensitive, hard nipples as his lips seared her soft skin with intimate, slow kisses.

Leigh was tense at first, but her body relaxed very quickly and became eager in response to his touch. He removed her clothes and then removed his own. She could see he was hard but appreciated that he was slow and patient with her. He would kiss her on the lips and then move to another part of her body. As he made a path from her stomach to her breasts and back to her neck, Leigh could feel herself melting. With gratifying touches, sweet kisses, and masterful moves, he was awakening an aching need within her that she had tried to hide. His tongue teased her ear as he told her how sexy and beautiful she was, intensifying the thrill of her arousal. His warm, soft flesh against hers made her body squirm, pleasure radiating everywhere.

He took a second to find a condom and placed it on himself before returning to her. She was sprawled out on the bed, her desire so taut that she felt no apprehension lying there exposed and naked, waiting for him. He leaned over her gently, slowly placing the pressure of his body against hers. She could feel his hardness against her thighs as he took her mouth in his again.

Pleasure radiated through her entire body when he entered her. He was slow and tender as he patiently stoked her fire, letting the passion build within her until it was pounding throughout her entire body. They were moving faster now, their bodies molded together. She was moaning aloud with carnal pleasure as he pleased her, and she pleased him back, bringing each other to the verge of erotic hysteria.

When Janet returned to Evan's hospital room, she was surprised to see Kimberly sitting by his bed. She had left only for a moment to have a cup of coffee.

When Kimberly looked up at her, Janet saw the pain of a mother, and she could feel nothing but compassion. In all of this, while Janet was too preoccupied with concern for Evan to have animosity toward Kimberly, she hadn't until now really taken a look at the woman who had been a source of pain for her for so many years.

Janet had never fallen no matter how many times Kimberly tried to take her down. Yes, Kimberly had caused her to lose her composure and act less than a woman of her standing and breeding should. There were a few times when they actually fought each other. But no matter what Kimberly had thrown at her, Janet had met her tenfold and came out the victor.

She'd wanted Kimberly out of their lives from the beginning and felt a certain sense of relief once Michael finally divorced her, but she hadn't gotten all she wanted. Kimberly was still here, and she had the kids. Janet intended to take a break and focus on the other countless issues she considered a threat to her family, but Kimberly was never far from her mind. She would have to get out of their lives completely for Michael to ever be able to really move on.

That was before Evan got sick and fell into a coma. What else mattered? Everything was about Evan now, and despite wishing she could, Janet could never lay the blame of a bad mother on Kimberly. She was completely devoted to her children, and they worshipped her. But that was never the issue.

As Kimberly was sitting in the chair next to the bed talking to Evan, Janet took the seat at the end of the bed. She reached into her purse to get her BlackBerry and check her schedule. She didn't speak a word as she listened to Kimberly tell Evan about a school project Daniel was working on.

She rearranged her schedule for tomorrow, moving a Chase Foundation meeting back and canceling a luncheon with the Ladies of Distinction Society. She was trying to make sure her day was free to spend with Leigh, who was supposed to come home tomorrow. She hadn't noticed that Kimberly stopped talking, but she couldn't ignore it when Kimberly yelled out.

"Oh, my God!" Kimberly jumped up from her seat. "Evan!"

"Kimberly." Janet shot up from her chair and rushed over to her. "What's wrong?"

"He moved his head!" Kimberly yelled as she frantically searched for the button to alert the staff. "He moved! How do I call the doctor?"

"Stop it." Janet gripped her arm. "That is just a reflex. The doctor told us—"

"Look!" Kimberly yelled. God had answered her prayer!

Janet was already looking, the sudden motion having caught her attention. This was no reflex. Evan slowly moved his head to the left and then the right. Then he let out a soft, almost inaudible sound, a weak moan.

"Thank you," Kimberly whispered to God as her heart caught in her chest.

Without thinking, both Kimberly and Janet turned to each other and wrapped their arms around each other in a big, fat hug.

9

"**B**e prepared," Joe said as he looked back at Leigh and Max. "Lots of press out there."

The Chase jet had landed at LAX just after ten at night with Leigh; Max; Joe; and Max's security guard, Rick, on board. Leigh didn't want to take the jet back and hadn't known that her father had sent it, but after evading Bem, he contacted Steven, who immediately sent the jet to Africa to collect his daughter. Leigh didn't want to break from the group, but she had broken the deal by leaving her security behind. To make peace with her father, she had agreed to take the jet, which would get her home about four hours earlier than the regularly scheduled flight.

Max agreed to come with her, and Leigh was happy. She wanted to be with him. She wondered what he might think of her after last night. Leigh was used to not having sex for long intervals and was surprised at how hungry she was for Max. They made love three times, twice initiated by her. Morning came with a knock on the door and notice of a car ready to take Leigh back to Nairobi.

As happy as she was that Max was coming along, Leigh knew that it would look suspicious if it was just the two of them. That was when Joe and Rick were added to the mix. She and Max flirted and laughed while looking at all the pictures Leigh had taken during their trip.

"Maybe we shouldn't step off together," Leigh said, looking nervously out the window. "They're here for you anyway."

Max frowned. "Are you trying to say you don't want to be seen with me?"

Leigh smiled as she nervously looked down at her feet. "Of course not, but . . ."

"It's too late," he said.

"What's too late?"

"They already know," he answered. "Kelly said someone must have tipped them off about you and me."

"That's not good."

"Sorry to be so embarrassing for you," he said sarcastically.

"It's not you," she assured him. Although now that she was back in the real world, Leigh was worried about another public affair. The last one ended so badly. "It's Evan. It's not appropriate for me to be romancing in Africa while my nephew is in a coma."

"It's not as if you were on vacation, Leigh. You were working incredibly hard for a very good cause. Besides, your brother texted you and told you he's come out of his coma."

Leigh was so happy about that, but she was too experienced with the way the press slanted stories. "But he wasn't when I was in Africa, and that is what the story will be."

"I understand." Max reached out and touched her arm. "I'll make you a deal. I agree to deny romantic rumors and say we're just friends if you agree to have dinner with me very soon."

Leigh was very happy. She had a lot of concerns about many things now that they were back home, but one thing was clear: She wanted to see him again, badly. "Sounds fair."

"Go on." He nodded toward the door, where the flight attendant was waiting. "I'll make a few calls and come out later. I'm sure your family is eager to see you."

"My car is going straight to the hospital." Leigh reached down into her chair and grabbed her purse. "Max . . ."

He pulled her to him and kissed her possessively on the lips. "I know," he said as he let her go. "We're back in the real world."

* * *

Kimberly wasn't sure how long Michael had been standing at the edge of the hallway watching her, but when she came out of her haze and noticed him, he looked away. She had called him on his cell the second she could and was too excited about Evan's movement to remember their last encounter. Now he was here, and she wanted desperately for him to hold her and share in her joy, but he was guarded and kept his distance.

She didn't want to make a bad situation worse, but as time went on, Kimberly couldn't take it anymore. She walked over to him and looked into his angry eyes. She couldn't say she was sorry she told him because she wasn't. She felt certain this was God's mercy, and she couldn't take back what she promised.

"I'm sorry I hurt you again," she said. She wanted to reach out and touch him but wouldn't dare. She was familiar with this cold stance.

"How many doctors need to come in and out of there before they can tell us something?" He glanced impatiently at the door to his son's hospital room, where his mother and both his sisters were sitting and waiting in chairs only a few feet away.

"They said they had a lot of tests to take," she answered. "They don't want to be hasty."

"But he was awake when you went in there?"

Once doctors arrived at Evan's bedside, Kimberly and Janet were thrown out of the room. When she returned, he wasn't awake, but she was told he was conscious and just sleeping. The nurse wouldn't allow her to try and wake him up. More doctors came and she was ushered out again. No one had been let back in for the last couple of hours.

"I didn't see him awake," she said. She had never actually seen his eyes open in front of her. "But he is. I let go of my anger. Don't let it come between us now. They're going to come out any minute, and we can't go in there with this."

"I can't do this," he said. "I just want to focus on Evan now and—" Michael stopped speaking and stood at attention before he rushed past Kimberly.

When she turned around, she saw that the whole family was standing to meet Dr. Kent. When she reached them all, Michael was already demanding answers, and the doctor wasn't pleased. Kimberly placed her hand on his shoulder and squeezed hard. It worked. He stopped and although he didn't look back at her, she could feel him calm down.

"What is going on with our son?" Kimberly asked above all the other voices.

"If you two would like to come in," she answered, "I'll tell you everything we know."

Leigh could see it was killing her mother that she wasn't able to go in the room, but she was a little surprised that she didn't even try. She had been there for only an hour but already sensed something odd in the air between her mother and Kimberly. She had made a practice of steering clear of their insane battles and had become an expert on detecting when the tension would boil over.

"I can't take this," Janet said, squeezing her daughter's offered hand. "Where in the hell is Steven?"

As if on cue, Steven and Carter walked briskly down the hallway, both wearing sharp black suits, as they had come from a business meeting in Pasadena.

Steven immediately rushed to his wife. "I hope these are happy tears," he said as he reached her. "It's still good news."

"They're in there with Michael and Kimberly now," Leigh said as she leaned in to kiss her father. "I'm sure it's going to be good news, right?"

"How sweet," Haley mumbled as she finished off her last text on her cell before slowly standing up. "Everyone is all kisses, hand-holding, and hugs. Too bad it takes a miracle to make it happen."

She sidled up to Carter and asked, "Any update for me?"

"What are you talking about?" Carter was only eager to hear news about his nephew.

"My contract!" she announcement loudly. "I need it now. Really, like now."

Carter took her by the arm and pulled her away from the rest of the family. "This is not the time to talk about this."

"Are you reneging?" she asked. "I helped you out!"

"Please," Carter said. "That very blurry picture you gave me was of an unrecognizable man getting into a car of which you couldn't see the plates. I had to hire my own investigator."

"And I care what you have to do?" she asked. "I did my part. I need my document."

"I'll take care of you as soon as I get proof of what you allege."

"Allege?" She made a smacking sound with her lips. "Why would I lie about this? I don't give a shit about Avery, her husband, or you."

"Point taken," Carter said.

This truth was the only reason that Carter was actually holding on to hope that this was true, but his PI had been following Anthony nonstop for the past few days and had nothing.

"We'll talk about this later," Carter said.

"I don't have much time," Haley said as her brother dragged her back to their waiting family.

It was too early to determine if Evan was suffering from any disabilities yet, but the doctor was encouraged by his fast recovery from the coma. Now that they could test him, they would know what type of medication and physical therapy he might need, if at all. But all the immediate tests they took told them that Evan was going to be among the 50 percent of ADEM children who fully recovered from the disease.

After thanking the doctor, Michael walked over to the bed where his son was sleeping peacefully. For the first time in a while, he didn't feel so helpless and he wasn't so scared for his little boy, who looked so tiny lying in that big bed. He glanced at Kimberly, who stood next to him looking down at Evan. Tears were still falling down her cheeks, and she made no attempt to wipe them away.

Michael felt his heart melt as he watched Kimberly reach down and gently take Evan's little hand in hers. She knelt down and kissed the back of his hand once and then twice before leaning back up.

Without thinking, Michael reached out and placed his hand

over Kimberly's. When she looked at him, he was struck with how completely angelic she looked. Right now she looked beautiful in the purest sense of the word.

"I believe you," he said.

Kimberly let go of Evan's hand but kept Michael's. "Believe what?"

"Everything," he said. "You said you had to tell me to come clean with God, and I can see that now when I look at you. You shine like . . ."

Kimberly's heart caught in her throat as she saw a tear trail down his cheek. How was it that this man could still touch her this way? After everything? She knew how. It was because he was right. With her anger and hatred gone, she was left with nothing but love. Without the animosity, she could see her prince, the prince who he used to be for her.

"I am sorry," she said, turning to him fully.

"No," Michael exclaimed soundly. "Everything you did, you did because you were trying to survive. I brought you into this crazy world occupied by my family and you survived. Very few who connect with this family can do that."

"I loved you," she said. "I loved our family. It was all worth surviving for."

"You shouldn't have had to," he said. "If I had put you first like I should have—like a husband should have—so much pain could have been avoided."

"None of that matters anymore." Kimberly looked down at Evan. "He's all that matters. Him and Daniel."

"It matters to me," Michael said. "And I'm sorry. We're here because of me and I'm sorry."

"You can't still be blaming yourself."

"He's getting better because of you," Michael said. "God answered your prayer because it was said without anger, self-pity, or selfishness, like mine have been. You weren't afraid of the consequences."

Kimberly looked at him with a tender smile. "Oh, there was plenty of self-pity, fear, and anger. And it was all selfishness."

"Well, then," Michael said, "he must just think you're very pretty."

Kimberly laughed as she cried more. "How dare you make me laugh at a time like this?"

Michael shrugged his shoulders. He wanted to pull her to him and kiss her, but he was afraid. Of what, he couldn't be sure, but he was feeling that all-too-familiar powerful hold she'd had on him all those years.

"Do you remember the night you told me you were pregnant?" he asked, looking down at his son.

Kimberly nodded. "I was scared to death. I thought you would ask me to get rid of the baby or just leave."

"I would have never done that," Michael said. "Even if I didn't love you, I wouldn't have asked you to do that or leave. So I guess it was a good thing that I did love you. I should have been scared, but I wasn't. You being pregnant with my baby, it just seemed right."

"It was," she answered. At least it was then.

"Carter!" Avery shouted as she opened her front door.

She was so happy to see him. She had been depressed and heartsick nonstop since he left her at the gallery. Filled with intense regret, her mood darkened as a dream she had told herself wasn't possible a long time ago suddenly seemed impossible for real. It was only news of Evan's condition that lifted her spirits.

"I heard the news. I'm so happy! How is Kimberly? I tried to call her, but . . ." Carter's staid expression made her stop, made her worry. For a second, she had hoped the good news had softened his heart and that was why he was there. It clearly wasn't.

"Is he here?" Carter asked, stepping inside without an invitation.

"Anthony?"

"Do any other men live in this house?" he asked sarcastically.

"No," she said. Her mood fell from the top of the sky to the ground in seconds. "He's not."

"Where is he?" Carter asked. "Jogging?"

Avery frowned, confused. "Why aren't you happier? You hear that Evan is awake, and your first reaction is to come over here and make fun of my paralyzed husband?"

It wasn't his first reaction, Carter thought. When he heard the news, he first thought of Avery as he always did when he felt any overwhelming emotion. Whether it was happiness, sadness, or frustration, his mind still went to the woman who once comforted him in a way only she could. But he fought that emotion and instead sought comfort in his fiancée.

"Where is Connor?" he asked, looking down the hallway.

"She's sleeping in the . . ." Avery rushed after Carter as he stormed through the house. "What are you doing? This isn't your house!"

"Isn't it, though?" he asked as he turned to her. "You pay the mortgage with my child support, don't you?"

Avery fumed. "You are such an asshole. Just leave."

As soon as he entered the living room, he saw Connor. She was sleeping on the sofa, and Avery had placed pillows on the floor near the edge in case she rolled over. He walked over to her and looked down at her, his little princess. Since hearing of Evan's improving condition, he wanted to kiss her, hold her. He was tempted to wake her up, but he knew Connor turned into the spawn of Satan if she was awakened prematurely. So for now, he satisfied himself with a gentle touch of her tiny hand, loving the softness of her skin.

"Carter," Avery whispered as she stood in the entryway to the living room. She gestured for him to come toward her. "Don't wake her up."

"Where is Anthony?" Carter asked as soon as he returned to the hallway.

"He's at the physical therapist. Why?"

"Where is he, really?" Carter asked. "Because he sure as hell isn't at the physical therapist. He hasn't been to the doctor's office in two months."

"He goes two days a week." Avery was trying to decipher where he was going with this, but she was clueless. "Why do you—"

"He's lying," he interrupted. "I know for a fact that he stopped going to physical therapy two months ago and hasn't been to his doctor in almost three months. Why don't you know that?"

Avery gave him a hostile glare. "Snooping again, Carter? Do you ever learn your lesson? What right do you have to—"

"I have every right to protect my daughter from crooks."

Avery gasped. "How dare you?"

"Why don't you know this?"

Avery was searching for an explanation that didn't sound so pitiful. She didn't want to tell him that Anthony had shut her out of his care. "He must have changed doctors."

"No, he didn't," Carter said. "And don't try to fool me, Avery. Clearly I know more about this than you."

"Which is what?" she asked.

"Anthony can walk."

Avery stared at him for a few seconds before saying, "You're crazy."

"Doesn't change the facts. I've been having him followed for a few days now."

"Which only proves you're sick," Avery retorted.

"After this." Carter pulled the photo Haley took out of his jacket pocket and handed it to Avery.

She snatched the object and unfolded it. She looked at it for a second. "What is this supposed to be?"

"Are you gonna tell me you can't recognize your own car?"

It did look like her car, and it did look like Anthony, but . . . "This is too blurry. I would expect you to do a better Photoshop job."

"If it was Photoshop, it would be better." Carter snatched the photo back. "This was taken in Long Beach. I've been trying to get a picture for myself but haven't been able to. My PI should be calling me any moment to tell me where he is now."

"This is sick." Avery went to the front door and opened it, trying to fight her own doubts. Emotionally, she couldn't handle any more right now. It had to be a lie, another attempt of his to make her miserable. "Is this your new game? You already dumped me. What more do you want?"

"For you to see the truth." Carter approached her. "And if you can't, then . . ."

"Then what?" Avery's eyes flashed outrage. "Anthony hates being disabled. It has destroyed his life. If there was any chance he could walk, he'd be running."

"So would you," Carter said. "If he could walk, you'd be running too."

Avery swallowed hard as she was hit with the irony of his words. "To what? You? You've made your feelings clear. Besides, you don't know how Anthony feels. He blames me for this, and if he could take care of himself, I know he'd want to do it."

"Part of me feels sorry for him." Carter's eyes were cold, matching his biting tone. "I know what it's like to keep a secret from the woman you love just so you can keep her, knowing she doesn't love you enough back to forgive you and stay. I learned my lesson."

"Apparently you haven't," Avery said. "Which is why you're here pulling this stunt."

"Stunt?" Carter shrugged. He could see it in her eyes. There was doubt and still she stood by that liar. "Why the fuck would I bring this to you if it wasn't true?"

"Why would you do any of the things you've done to me in the last year?" she asked. "I'm still asking myself that. Maybe you can tell me because I feel like it's been your mission to hurt me, and this is all you have left."

"Is that what you think?" Carter smiled wickedly. "Baby, you are way wrong. I have a lot left."

Avery watched as she saw Carter look toward the living room. "Leave her out of this and just go."

"No, Avery." Carter slowly walked toward her, hatred blazing in his eyes. "I'm not going to leave her out of this. She's my daughter, and I'm not going to have her living in a house with a criminal. Insurance fraud is a crime, you know. And you just might be an accessory."

"Bullshit!"

"You certainly can't say you don't know anymore." He headed to the door. "You've made your choice. Now I'm making mine."

"You're bluffing," Avery spat out. "You don't think for a second—"

"Have you forgotten who I am?" Carter asked. "Have you forgotten what I can do? If I want her, she'll be with me and you'll be lucky to see her once a month. And I don't need to prove any crime to get that. I just need to call in favors."

Avery knew he wasn't lying, and the look in his eyes, a combination of outright hostility and contempt, told her he meant every word. "You would take Connor away from her mother just to hurt me?"

"You think everything is about you, don't you?" Carter asked as he stepped outside. "Do you think you can really afford to be such a self-centered bitch anymore?"

"You think I'm a bitch now?" Avery asked, her eyes sparking. "You try and take my baby away from me and I will turn into something you have never seen."

Just after she slammed the door in his face, Avery pressed against it to hold herself up. She would run away with Connor if she had to, and she thought she just might. No matter how good a mother she tried to be, she was no match for Carter in a courtroom; if he was intent on taking Connor, he would get her.

She regretted everything about the way she had just handled that, but the feeling of apprehension that Carter's accusations caused frightened Avery to death. She had thrown her own doubts out of her head, because it just made no sense, but why was she so quick to dismiss his accusation about Anthony? She feared that it may have been her angst about being alone. If Anthony was lying to her, she couldn't stay with him and Carter didn't want her anymore. The thought made her cringe, but Avery didn't have time to think about that. She had much more important things to do.

"Mom, please." Leigh leaned away from her mother's fussing as they walked down the hallway of the hospital toward the gardens. "Enough with the kissing."

"I'm just so happy you're back." Janet took hold of her daughter's hand. "You've had a couple of days to adjust, so now we need to have lunch and—"

"I have to go back to the clinic," Leigh said. "I can't stay away from there. Now that Evan is getting better, I should go back to work."

"Oh, for Pete's sake." Janet was tired of the workaholic martyr in her daughter. "Can you stand to enjoy yourself for even a minute? For me at least? These past few weeks have been hell, and I need your compassionate ear."

Leigh slowed down and smiled at her mother. She did want to

tell her about her wonderful day in Langata, but she couldn't do that without giving away how she felt about Max, and she didn't really want to give away that much.

"I guess I could really go for something fattening and creamy."

"That's what I want to hear," Janet said. "We can go for lunch and maybe a spa day at the Four Seasons."

Leigh turned to her mother, who had let her hand go and stopped walking. Janet's attention had been taken by something on a bench they had just passed. It was an issue of *What's Hot,* a weekly local gossip paper with a picture of Leigh coming off the Chase jet at LAX.

Leigh grabbed the paper and read the title out loud. "'The Senator and the Socialite!'"

"It's a slow week in the gossip business." Janet took the paper out of her hand and tossed it back on the bench. "It's meaningless. We can issue a press release tomorrow."

"No, Mom," Leigh protested.

Janet could read her daughter's expression easily. She had done it all her life, and she was surprised that she hadn't noticed this one sooner. "Did something happen?"

Leigh nodded. "Nothing really, just . . . well, yeah."

Janet smiled and clapped her hands together joyfully. "This is wonderful! Leigh, do you know what this could mean for you?"

"Yeah," Leigh said, pointing to the paper. "That, and it's exactly what I don't want. We're telling everyone we're just friends for now."

"That's fine." Janet couldn't hold back her excitement. Her mind was always on what was good for the Chase family name and image, but nothing was more important to her than her children's happiness and success, whether in their careers or their personal lives, and Leigh deserved it more than anyone.

"Wow," Leigh said as soon as they reached the doors to the garden.

Janet was looking at the same thing she was. Michael and Kimberly were standing near a fountain along the far edge. They were only inches apart, facing each other and looking into each other's eyes. Janet read their body language; anyone could have figured out what was going on. They weren't speaking to each other, just looking into each other's eyes. Then slowly, Michael lifted his hand to meet hers, which were at her sides. He took her hand in his and leaned forward.

Janet turned away just as they began to kiss. "We shouldn't disturb them."

Leigh looked away from the touching scene to her mother. "Mom, are you okay?"

Janet held her chin high with a confident smile. "Of course. Why wouldn't I be?"

"I know you can't be happy to see that," Leigh said.

Janet would never tell Leigh or Haley all she knew about Kimberly. They were both aware that she brought Paul Deveraux, the French designer who'd had an affair with Janet thirty years ago, to View Park to break up their marriage, but they knew nothing of David and his death, nor did they know about Kimberly's true past. They only knew that Michael and Kimberly's marriage had fallen apart, but both blamed Michael because all they could see was how badly he had treated Kimberly.

"It looks like they're . . . together again," Leigh said. She wasn't surprised, being a doctor who had seen what a sick child can do to two people. It either tore them apart or brought them closer than ever.

"We don't know if it's permanent. They've gotten together before only to hate each other more." Janet found the courage to look into the garden again and see them kissing. This time he had his arms wrapped around her and was holding her tight. She expected to be livid, angry that all she had done to get this woman out of their lives was for nothing. But she wasn't. Something had changed inside Janet, and she wasn't sure how to deal with it. "But it could be."

"You're okay with this?" Leigh asked, thoroughly confused by the peaceful expression on her mother's face.

"As long as Evan gets better," Janet said, "I'm okay with anything."

"Come in," Steven yelled from his Chase Beauty office. He was curious to see who else was working late on a Sunday evening.

When he saw Michael enter, dressed in jeans and a polo shirt, he was a little confused. "What are you doing here? Is everything okay with Evan?"

Michael nodded. "He's being moved out of the special care unit. He's going to be there a while."

"Your mother and I will be visiting him tomorrow before visiting hours close. You know, I said you can work from the hospital if you want."

"I needed to talk to you about something." Michael dreaded this conversation, but he knew he needed to have it.

"Sit down." Steven gestured toward the leather chair across from his desk and watched his son apprehensively sit down. "I think I know what this is about."

"I don't think you do."

"Kimberly," Steven said. "Your mother told me she saw you two together."

Michael leaned back in the chair. "We're always together, Dad. Our son is sick."

"You know what I mean," Steven said.

Michael nodded. "But that's not what I'm here to talk to you about."

"Do you want my opinion?" Steven asked. "About you and Kimberly—do you want my opinion?"

"No," Michael said. "I have my own."

Steven paused at his son's response. It was as unexpected as his own reaction to it. For a man who generally demanded obedience from all his children no matter how old they were, he was eerily proud of his son's verbal slap in the face.

And for the first time in a long time, Steven didn't feel as if the rejection of his guidance was made out of anger or spite.

"Things certainly have changed," Steven said.

"I'm glad you see that," Michael added after a moment. "I love you, Dad, but . . . things are never going back to the way they were."

"I guess it's about time. So what's your news?"

"You aren't going to like this," Michael said. "But you need to know it."

"That seems to be the theme today." Steven took a deep breath. "Hit me."

Reluctantly, Michael told Steven everything that Kimberly had told him, reminding Steven that he had not confirmed any of it but that he believed it completely. His father seemed to be taking it well for a man who had just found out that his brother had tried to completely demolish him and had come so close. Then again, his father was an expert at either not feeling affected or looking as if he wasn't.

Michael paused for a few moments while he waited for Steven's response, but his father said nothing. He simply looked past Michael, as if his mind had ventured beyond this conversation. Michael could tell he was already thinking of what he would do next.

"I've been trying to locate Elisha in New York," Michael said. "I didn't let on what I want to talk to her about."

"Have you contacted Keenan?" Steven finally asked.

"Of course not," Michael answered. "There would be no point without a plan."

Michael was startled when Steven abruptly and angrily pushed away from his desk and got out of his chair. He walked to the floor-to-ceiling windows overlooking downtown L.A. from his office high atop the 777 Tower.

Steven's mind was racing hundreds of miles a minute. "What did I do wrong?"

"He's always hated you," Michael said. "He's jealous of you and blames you—"

"Not with him," Steven snapped back. "With this deal. How could I not have seen this?"

"None of us did," Michael said before clearing his throat and adding, "but I was supposed to."

Steven turned to his son, his nature urging him to chide Michael for his irresponsibility, but he wouldn't dare do that now. Besides, there would be nothing gained. Michael made it clear to him that he no longer had the power over his son that he used to, so a tongue-lashing wouldn't have its desired effect. The publishing acquisition deal was dead anyway.

"Go ahead," Michael said. "I can see you want to. Blame me for almost taking down Chase Beauty again."

"I want to talk to Kimberly." Steven leaned over the back of his chair, looking intently at his son. "I want to talk to her now."

"Not a chance," Michael quickly responded. "I'm not letting you attack her. She's not helping him anymore. In fact, she hasn't helped him at all, and she's going through too much with Evan."

"I'm not asking!" Steven demanded. "I'm not looking to attack her. I want to ask her for details. I need to know everything so I can get someone on this."

"On what?"

"I want to find out if Keenan really had the capability of doing what he and Elisha were threatening to do, and I need to know what he's up to now." Steven was already thinking of his best people in D.C. who could investigate this discreetly. "We should have found this out during our due diligence. The fact that we didn't makes me wonder how much power he really has."

"Not enough," Michael said. "Dad, I know this was my responsibility, but I can't get Kimberly involved right now, and I can't be a part of this revenge. With Evan—"

"Don't worry," Steven interrupted. "You're making the right choice. You're making the choices I didn't."

Michael was so surprised to hear that, it made him fall back into his chair after starting to get up. "What?"

"You're picking your family over work." Steven was nodding. "It's the right choice. I know how much you love this company and how much you want to be CEO after I leave. You have drive and ambition like my own, but you don't let it run your life like I let it do to me."

"That wasn't always the case." Michael tried to control his reaction to his father's praise. It came so infrequently, and this time it meant more than any good report or cost-saving acquisition. "I put this company and you ahead of everything, and I lost my wife and hurt my kids. I broke my family."

"That's just it," Steven said. "I had the same warning signs that you did. I had the same regrets, but I still made the same choices again and again. I can see the price I've paid by not being the father I should have been. You've learned from regrets, and because of that, you'll be a much better father than I ever was. You already are."

Michael couldn't think of the words to show a measure of what he was feeling right now, so he simply stated, "Thank you."

* * *

"Have either of you seen my cell phone?" Leigh asked as soon as she entered the kitchen where her mother and sister were having breakfast. "I can't find it anywhere."

"Good morning to you too," Janet said as she wiped the edges of her mouth with her napkin.

"Sorry." Leigh stood in the middle of the large kitchen, looking around. "Morning. I'm just going nuts. I called it and I didn't hear anything. I have to get to the clinic. I was in the kitchen last night and thought maybe I left it here."

"Here." Sitting at the table across from her mother, Haley tossed the phone at her sister.

Leigh jumped forward and grabbed it after juggling it a bit. "Why do you have my phone?"

"I'm trying to help you out," Haley said. "You have to play hard to get. You go on one jaunt to Africa with this man and you're all his."

"You don't know what you're talking about." Leigh scrolled the call history to check the calls she missed.

"I was in your bedroom this morning and . . ."

"Why?" Leigh asked.

"I was stopping by to borrow your laptop, 'cause I broke mine throwing it at my stupid husband yesterday."

"Why did you do that?" Janet asked.

"Anyway," Haley continued, ignoring her mother. "You were in the shower, and your phone was ringing. I noticed that you've already put him on your contact list, because his name came up."

Leigh stuffed the phone in the back pocket of her pants. "He did that."

"That was quite bold," Janet interjected. "Putting his number in your cell. Was it with your consent?"

Leigh hadn't said no when he took her phone and input his private number. She was flattered that he initiated such a gesture, even though it was pretty presumptuous. "It's no big deal. We just don't want people talking about us, so it's better if I not call the office."

"So you are still seeing each other?" Janet asked, unable to hide the excitement in her voice.

"I guess." Leigh turned to Haley. "And stay away from my phone and out of my room."

"He's called you twice already today," Haley said, ignoring her sister's warning. "If you had the phone, you would have picked up. I just know it. You have to play these powerful men right. I can teach you."

"I don't think I want to hear this," Janet said.

"You can't be nice to them," Haley continued. "They can't stand that."

Leigh grabbed a half of a bagel from her sister's plate. "I'm not taking romantic advice from Mrs. Marry for Money."

"I'm just looking out for you," Haley said. "Have you been on the Net? The gossip blogs are all about you two. They're talking about how lucky he is to marry a Chase and how that will be his on-ramp to the White House."

Leigh grumbled.

"That's foolishness," Janet said. She knew how much it upset Leigh to be gossiped about because of her last name, but there was no avoiding it, not this time. "And it's insulting to your sister."

"How is it insulting?" Haley asked. "They're saying he's lucky, which is a compliment to her. They're saying you could be First Lady."

"That's enough, Haley." Leigh headed for the fridge to get some juice. She really didn't want to hear this.

"You deserve that," Haley continued.

Leigh's head shot up from the fridge. She and Janet looked stunned at Haley before turning to each other. Neither was sure they heard right.

"Did you just give me a compliment?" Leigh asked.

"Don't jinx it by asking," Janet urged.

Haley smirked. "Ha. Ha. Ha. You're both so funny. I was just saying that you would make a good First Lady. You care about people and crap like that. Also, you've had sex with like, what, five guys your entire life, and at least one of them was gay so—"

"At least one of them?" Leigh asked.

"Can you be so sure about the others?" Haley asked. "I think every guy you've dated has been suspect. Until now, of course."

Leigh took a sip of orange juice before saying, "Well, I'd prefer you say I would make a good president, but I'll accept First Lady, since I know how hard it is for you to say something nice about anyone."

"It's Evan!" Janet said joyfully. "He's got everyone in a good mood. Even Haley is acting human."

"Hey!" Haley was not amused.

"You know what I mean, dear." Janet turned to Leigh. "And, Leigh, I hope your good mood won't be broken by my confession."

"What have you done?" Leigh felt her stomach tightening. Her mother's involvement in her private life always led to disaster.

"I called his office and invited him to dinner tomorrow night." Janet cringed at the astonished look on her daughter's face.

"How could you do that?" Leigh asked incredulously. "Without asking me first?"

"I thought you would say no."

"Mom," Haley chimed in. "You're ruining everything. This is not in my plan. Now he's going to run away from her."

Leigh wondered what the damage the mixed message would cause. She was telling him to take things slow and not go public while Janet was inviting him to a family dinner. "I would have said no. It isn't like that between us, Mother."

"What is it like?" Janet stood up.

Leigh shrugged. "I don't know yet. I'm focused on getting the clinic back on track, and he has to put together a big report for the president. We're both focused on work. I haven't really allowed myself to think about a real relationship."

"Well, I have," Janet said. She patted Leigh on the arm as she passed her on her way out of the kitchen. "Don't worry. We'll lock Haley in the guest house."

"You can try!" Haley yelled out. "Nothing is keeping me from this dinner."

"There isn't going to be a dinner," Leigh said. "I'm calling to cancel."

"You shouldn't," Haley warned.

"More advice from Mrs. Marry for Money?"

"The sad thing," Haley said, "is that you think that name bothers me. All I'm saying is that this family is bat-shit crazy, and maybe his reaction to the crazy will tell you whether or not you want to allow yourself to think about it, whatever that means."

Leigh couldn't believe she was thinking it, but Haley was right. Africa had been like a fantasy, and both Leigh and Max knew that. It was probably why they had little more than texted each other since coming back. They wanted to keep the fantasy. But the real world wouldn't wait, and there was nothing more real than a dinner with the Chases.

There would be no point in thinking of seeing Max again if he couldn't handle the Chase clan. If it turned out he could handle them just fine, well . . .

10

Leigh handed a glass of red wine to Max as he leaned against the standing bar in the backyard.

"I didn't ask for any wine," Max said, taking the glass anyway.

"Trust me," Leigh said. "You'll need it. Dinner is starting any minute now."

Looking at the lights reflecting from the pool, he said, "This must be nice for throwing parties."

"You would be surprised how many fake people with lots of money you can fit into this backyard."

Max turned to her. "Why do you do that?"

"Do what?"

"Make assumptions about people with money," he answered. "You know you're talking about yourself, and you're talking about the people who keep your clinic going."

"What happened to your sense of humor?"

"It's a little distracted by that sexy dress you have on." He slowly looked her up and down. "That is not a meet-my-daddy dress. It's a take-me-home-right-now dress."

Leigh laughed, blushing. She had gone over in her mind what to wear and decided that since this was the first time they had seen each other since Africa, she would kick it up a notch. For that, she had to raid Haley's closet, but it was worth it. What she came up with was a black spaghetti-strap sheath dress, just at the edge of classy and sexy, with Miu Miu platforms that made her legs look a mile long.

"You'll have to watch that dirty smile of yours," she said. "I like it, but Daddy won't."

"Don't tease me," he said with a wink. "I've met your dad, and he seems to not want to kick me out yet. I bet your mom likes me more than you do. That was the hard part, wasn't it?"

"Oh, you poor baby." Leigh placed her hand on his arm and rubbed it, feeling his muscles. She wasn't wearing a take-me-home-right-now dress for nothing. "Just think about the most painful political dinner you've been to and take it up a few notches. That's what this will be like if you're lucky."

"Let's make a deal." Max stood up straight as Janet made her way toward them. "If I survive this, you have to—"

Leigh pressed her index finger to his lips. "Let's see you survive, and then we'll talk about deals."

"Maya is bringing dinner in," Janet said as she stood with an excessively approving smile.

Standing in the hallway, Avery took a deep breath and tried to brace herself for what was to come. She had gone for a long walk with Connor in her stroller. She spent it crying and talking to herself. She wanted to call her mother but couldn't. She had to handle this herself and deal with whatever came out of it. She had to stop avoiding the truth and making other people open her eyes for her. She couldn't be afraid to be alone. She had practically been alone for months now.

When she finally turned and walked into the dining room, the sight of Anthony sitting at the table eating leftovers made her angry. He was sitting there eating as if he didn't have a care in the world. She reminded herself she had to keep this civilized. Her baby was sleeping down the hallway, and although the bedroom door was closed, Connor seemed able to hear anything. No screaming.

Then she saw it. On the table next to him was a prescription bottle of medications he took. He had to take it with dinner every night, and it looked like he had.

"Hi, baby." Anthony looked up for only a second as Avery walked to the other end of the table and gripped the chair with her hands.

"Anthony, we have to—"

"Have you been crying?" Anthony asked as he looked back up with a frown. "Your eyes are all red."

"I see you found the pills," she said, pointing to the bottle.

Anthony looked at it for a second, before taking another bite of his Greek chicken.

"You were looking for them earlier today," she said. "Where did you find them?"

He didn't look up as he answered. "I don't know. In the kitchen I think."

"I looked everywhere in the kitchen." Avery tried to keep her voice from giving her anger away too soon. "Where were they?"

He stopped eating but didn't look up. He shrugged his shoulders. "I can't remember."

"Are you sure you didn't find them here?" she asked. "In the dining room?"

This time Anthony looked up, and Avery could see he was trying to look nonchalant, but the anxiety in his eyes gave him away. "Um . . . probably. I'm not sure. I was preoccupied and I just saw them."

"I saw them here too," she said. "Just before I left. I saw them on the edge of the curio right next to the window. Then I placed them on top of the curio, so I'm curious—how did you get them?"

Anthony's fake smile went flat as he realized what she was doing. "I . . . I just reached up and got it."

"You can't reach that high on your own." Avery felt if he was going to insist on continuing his lie, she could play this game too. "You would have had to stand up to get that."

Anthony swallowed hard. "What are you saying?"

Avery placed both hands on her hips. "I just said what I'm saying. You would have had to stand up to get that, so how did you get it?"

Anthony seemed speechless for several seconds before adding, "I had to push the curio a little and it fell off."

"I put it in the middle, Anthony." She pointed sharply at the curio. "You would have had to tip the curio over to get it to fall off, but all the china would've fallen off too. How did you avoid that?"

Anthony sighed, looking down at his food. "Avery . . ."

"You stood up, didn't you?"

"You must have been mistaken as to where you left it. It was on the edge."

"I wasn't mistaken at all," she said calmly. "You see, I specifically put it there, because I knew you would have to stand up to get it. In other words, I set you up."

Anthony's face held an injured expression as if she had wronged him. "Since when did you become so devious? Oh, yes, that's right. Probably back when you started cheating on—"

"Give it up," she said in a controlled tone, trying to hold back her outrage enough to keep her composure. The truth was, up until this moment, she believed—wanted to believe—that it was all a lie. She wanted to be proven wrong. There was no going back now. "I know you can walk, you asshole."

"I admit that sometimes I get sensations in my legs, but—"

"I have pictures," she lied. If he asked to see them, she would tell him they were hidden somewhere.

"Pictures?" He was clearly astonished.

"You look as if you couldn't believe I would ever do such a thing," Avery said as she took a few more steps into the room. "As if you thought you could fool me forever."

"Where did you get pictures?" he asked. "Carter? Was it Carter who did this?"

"Stop it!" She was glad to see him startled by how loud she yelled. He had to stop the bullshitting now. "I just want you to get out."

"Fine." Anthony slowly stood up. He seemed wobbly but clearly was on both feet. "But it's not as if I'm fully—"

"Did I ask you to explain this to me?" Avery asked. "I just told you to leave."

"It's still hard for me to walk!" Anthony yelled as she left and went into the kitchen. "I'm not completely faking it. I wanted to be able to fully walk before I—"

"This would have been effective if you hadn't already showed me how much of a fool you think I am." She kept her back to him. "You want to confess? Go ahead and confess. If that's what you need to make you leave."

Anthony needed the counter to keep upright. "When I started feeling sensations, I—"

"This is why you didn't want me to come to your doctor's appointments?"

His voice was shaky and uncertain. "No, I didn't want you . . . to come to the doctor's because . . . I got sick and tired of seeing that look of pity on your face. You looked so fucking pressed to even be there."

"That was all in your mind." Avery turned to look at him. It was odd to see him standing, even though he didn't look strong. "You created this scenario where I . . . I'm not going to do this. You were trying to deceive me, lie to me."

"Don't you want to know why?" he asked.

"I just want you to leave."

"It was to keep you!"

Avery stared impatiently and was disgusted by the self-pitying look on his face. "Save me the sob story, Anthony. You lied to control me."

"I knew if I told you, you would leave. We both know the only reason why you're with me is because of my legs."

"I tried, Anthony." Avery leaned back against the sink, her hands gripping the edges. "I was wrong to cheat on you. I felt guilty, but I stayed because I wanted to be a good wife. I believe you get married once, and I wanted us to make this work."

"If that isn't a load of bullshit, I don't know what is," Anthony said. "You were waiting for me to walk again. The only time you acted even remotely interested in my care was when the doctor talked about possible recovery."

Her laugh was filled with derision. "I wanted you to get healthy again for all of us! I wanted us to be a family again."

"We were never a family," Anthony said. "I was the filler for the void Carter left."

"Stop talking about him!" Enraged, Avery grabbed a plate and threw it across the room. "I don't want to hear his name come from your lips ever again!"

"I don't deserve to lose you!"

Avery was utterly confused. "What in the hell does that mean?"

"I've earned the right to have you, Avery!" Anthony slammed his fist on the counter. "Out of all of this—"

"You could at least have me? That's what you're going to say, right? I should be your going-away or thank-you-for-playing gift."

"You should be my wife," Anthony said. "You should have been my wife and you never were."

Avery's guilt made her calm down a little. "You're right. I should have been your wife, and I never really was. I hurt you and I betrayed you. I was a horrible wife to you, and maybe I deserve to be deceived, but I'm done taking the blame for all of this."

Shit happens, she thought to herself. She screwed up, tried to fix it, but the game was over. She had lost her marriage and the man she loved, and she would not be anyone's consolation prize.

"What you've done here," she said, "has only made it clear to me that this is over and that it never should have been!"

"Because I can walk?"

"No," she answered. "Because I was the coward who ran from my own heart, and you're a liar who feeds off of other people's guilt."

"Avery, please." He walked gingerly toward her with his hand out in a plea for sympathy.

Avery held up her hand to stop him. "You and I both know what insurance fraud is, but I'm going to give you a chance to leave and never come back."

"What about Connor?" he asked. "She's my—"

"She's your nothing! You are never going anywhere near her again."

A stone-cold expression transformed Anthony's face. Gone was the victim in search of pity. Consuming bitterness had replaced him. "He won't take you back."

"Get out." She knew what he meant, and the pain it caused in her chest only made her angrier.

"He doesn't want you anymore," Anthony continued. "I'm the only choice you have."

Avery laughed. "Is that what you think? So you must be a liar and an idiot."

"You don't care if you're alone?"

"I'm not alone," Avery said. "I have my baby, and I don't need you or Carter."

"But I need you," Anthony said. "I won't make it without you."

"You don't have a choice." Avery reached up and opened the cabinet. She searched the back, behind the box of baking soda. She grabbed the bottle of scotch and pulled it out. She took a second to observe the look of surprise on Anthony's face, surprise that she had found the bottle he thought he'd hidden from her.

"This is the only thing you really love anyway."

She tossed it to him without warning, and he leaped forward to grab it.

She was full of despair when she finally got Anthony to leave. Running to her baby's room, she watched her sleep peacefully, and it calmed Avery down. She had told Anthony she didn't need him, and she meant it. She told him that she didn't need Carter, and she only hoped that could be true. It needed to be.

She had gone from Alex to Carter to Anthony and then back and forth, and that was enough. She still loved Carter and believed she always would, but she didn't need him. What she needed was to focus on Connor and make sure no one could take her away.

"Haley!" Janet's terse tone reverberated throughout the dining room as her daughter asked the senator yet another inappropriate question. It was the third of the night, the only chink so far in an evening that had gone as well as Janet could have hoped.

Despite her desire to not have Haley join them, there was no stopping the girl, who dragged her husband out of the guest house at the last minute, knowing that Janet wouldn't make her leave in front of Max. Other than that, it was just Janet and

Steven, and Janet had been able to control the dinner, at least up to this point.

"It's a legit question." Haley leaned away as Maya took her plate. "It's not like you haven't been asked before. It's pretty simple. You know the thing that always destroys a politician's life. Is there a dead girl or a live boy in your past?"

Leigh turned to Max, who was studiously and politely smiling as he sat next to her. "Feel free to ignore her. We all do."

"No, Haley is better company than I've had in a while." Max placed his glass of wine down. "I'm with politicians all day. They walk around the block to get across the street. A straight question is a nice change of pace."

"Who cares," Peter said.

"So he speaks." Max turned to Peter. "You haven't said a word all night."

Peter shrugged and stuffed a piece of filet mignon in his mouth. "You Americans are so uptight. You do all kinds of shit, but then act all holier—"

"What did I tell you about language at my dinner table?" Steven stared the boy down.

"You just proved my point." Peter sat up in his seat, seeming to finally find something to be interested in. "I hear you curse all the time, but you—"

"This is my house," Steven announced firmly. "Something you seem to not get after several months of being told so."

"Steven." Janet's tone was completely calm as she eyed her husband. He had promised to behave.

"I ask," Haley continued as if never having stopped, "because there are quite a few dead girls—and dead boys—in our past."

"Stop it," Leigh ordered.

Max turned to her, and she tried to make it seem as if it was nothing, but she knew it wasn't possible.

Max cleared his throat. "I'm aware of what papers say, but I can say firsthand that you can never believe what you read in the papers."

"That is certainly true," Janet added with a nervous laugh.

"I get that it's your house," Peter said. "You try to remind me every day. This is your house. That's your guest house. This is your daughter and—"

"We can continue this later," Steven said.

Ignoring both men, Haley leaned forward. "Well, Max, most of what you read in the papers about us is true, and if it isn't, it's because we put it there to hide what really is true."

"Stop being rude," Leigh ordered sharply.

"And it's Senator Cody," Janet corrected.

"I don't mind," Max said. "She can call me whatever she wants."

"Don't say that," Leigh whispered to him.

Suddenly, Peter pushed away from the table, making his glass of wine and Max's glass, which was just across from his, spill over into Max's lap.

"Oh, no." Leigh reached for her napkin as Max slid back in his seat.

Peter stood up briskly. "I don't give a damn that this is your house. I'm tired of being treated like a boy."

"You're twenty-three," Haley said. "Trust me. You could be forty-three and he'd still treat you like a boy. It's how he treats everyone."

"That's enough," Steven said.

Janet had gotten up and was at Max's side. "I am so sorry. I can get Maya to—"

"It's fine," Max said, pushing Leigh's fussing hands away.

Leigh could tell from his tone that he was annoyed.

"You're excused from this table." Steven was looking at Peter.

"I don't need to be excused from this table," Peter said. "I'm leaving this table, this house, and this damn country. And I'm taking Haley with me."

Haley almost choked on the water she was swallowing. She looked up. "Peter! Not now."

"What do you mean?" Janet had been halfway to the kitchen but swung around now.

"I told you I didn't want to go." Haley grabbed Peter's hand and tried to pull him back into his seat.

"You're my wife," Peter said. "You have to go with me."

"Haley isn't your wife," Janet said. "Not really, and she isn't going anywhere."

"What is she talking about?" Max whispered to Leigh.

"If you go upstairs," Leigh said, trying to distract him, "I'm sure I can find some of my brother's pants."

Peter turned to Janet, breaking free of Haley's grip. "If she wants her thirty million dollars she is."

"That money is mine!" Haley stood up, getting in Peter's face. "And if you go back without me, your wife, your family will know that this is all a lie and you'll get nothing but a measly allowance. Trust me, I know firsthand that that isn't worth it."

"Haley, please." Leigh could tell from Max's expression that he was taking it all in, and that wasn't a good thing.

"You're both excused," Steven said calmly, but his tone warned that he was only a second from exploding.

"Whatever!" Haley exclaimed. "Let's go."

"Haley." Janet went after Haley, who followed Peter toward the hallway.

"Janet," Steven called to her. "Please take a seat."

"She can't go," Janet said.

"I'll take care of it." Steven gestured toward Max and Leigh. "We have guests."

"Oh." Janet couldn't believe how quickly she had forgotten Max was even there. The thought of Haley leaving had upset her so much. "I am so sorry, Senator."

Leigh was hoping Max would say something like *It's okay* but he didn't. He simply accepted a napkin Maya handed him and placed it on his damp lap.

"Haley is a little high-strung." Janet reclaimed her seat at the other end of the table. "She doesn't like it when anyone at the dinner table gets more attention than her."

"That young man is her husband, right?" he finally asked.

"Yes," Leigh hurried her answer. "It's a long story, but she is married to him."

Max's brows drew together, showing an uncertain, cautious frown.

"I would love for you to meet our more well-behaved children." Janet smiled but could see from Max's expression that Haley's explosion had made an impression on him. "We're having a birthday dinner for my son Michael at Tulips in Wilshire Plaza next week."

Max hesitated a moment before saying, "I would . . . I . . ."

"I don't think so, Mom." Leigh's eyes shifted nervously between Max and her mother.

She had thought she was doing Max a favor, but when she looked at him, the expression on his face made it seem as if he was offended. It was confusing, but Leigh was too disappointed in the turn the evening had taken to understand what it meant. All she knew was that Max had gotten a taste of dining with the Chases, and she thought to head off an additional invitation before he would decline and embarrass everyone.

Kimberly was surprised at how she felt when she rang the doorbell to Chase Mansion. Standing outside the giant double wooden doors, she normally felt a tightening of her stomach and anxiety creeping up the back of her neck. For so long, she feared that every time her babies were brought here, she would never see them again or that Janet was waiting for her with some evil plot and no one would ever see Kimberly again.

She was there to pick up Daniel, who had been spending a fun day with Michael, something to get his mind off of how much he missed Evan. Michael usually dropped them off at her place, but today he had told her his hectic schedule made it impossible and asked her to come here.

Kimberly would be lying if she said she still didn't fear coming to this house. As a matter of fact, she had been feeling queasy all day, but she felt calmer than ever now. It almost made her laugh to think of how much stress she let go of when she wanted to.

"What are you doing ringing this doorbell?" Maya asked as soon as she opened one of the doors. She stepped aside to let Kimberly in.

"Hi, Maya." Kimberly stepped inside. "I'm not really welcome here anymore."

Maya made a smacking sound with her lips. "Most of the people who live here aren't welcome here. Your baby is upstairs in his room. He's exhausted."

"Kimberly." Michael made his way down the double staircase.

Kimberly loved it when he "went rugged," a term she used when he wore jeans and a T-shirt. He rarely wore anything but an expensive suit or pricey European casual wear. A pair of Levi's and a Columbia Business School T-shirt made him look like a college boy and accented his best attributes—his muscular arms and flat stomach.

"He's actually sleeping right now," Michael said as he approached, wondering what that gleam in her eye was. It excited him, but he tried not to show it. "But I need you to do something first."

"What?" Kimberly asked as Maya left them alone.

Michael looked down the hallway toward the east wing of the house, where both of his parents had their home offices. "I had to tell him."

"Tell who what?" Kimberly asked.

Michael waited as Kimberly figured it out for herself. "I had to. He should know what is coming at him."

Kimberly rolled her eyes. She couldn't get out of there fast enough. "So how many threats did he make against me?"

"None, but he wants to talk to you."

Kimberly laughed. "Funny. Can I just get my son and get out of here?"

"It's okay." Michael placed a hand on her arm comfortingly, wishing he could do more. He wasn't sure what to do with her now that they had slept together again. "I've talked to him. I promise you, he just wants to talk."

"And Steven always keeps to his word, right?" Kimberly moved her arm away, because she was too affected by his touch. Maybe it was the exposed arms or how well his jeans fit. "I won't come out of there alive."

"Kimberly." Michael tried to speak in as assuring a voice as he could muster. "I promise you, he will not hurt you. I made him promise me."

"I'm not your wife anymore, Michael. You don't get to make bargains regarding me without my consent."

"I'm very well aware of who you aren't," Michael said. "Dad

has a right to hear firsthand what you have to say. You were trying to bring him down."

"I did what I did because he tried to buy my children from—"
Kimberly stopped herself and took a deep breath. No more.

Michael felt compassion for the pain she had experienced
when his parents tried to buy the kids away.

"I know he's hurt you, but you said you wanted to come clean.
You knew it would be hard. Look, I'll go with you, and I won't let
him do anything to you."

She was still hesitating, looking very worried. Michael gazed
intently into her eyes and said, "I will never let anyone hurt you
again."

He could see her relax as her lips curved into a tiny, tepid
smile. He wanted to kiss her, but when he moved in, Kimberly
leaned away.

"What's wrong?" Michael asked, smarting from the rejection.

"Michael, we need to be clear about what is going on." Kimberly took a step back, hoping that this would lower her body
temperature a bit. She had really wanted to kiss him, but her fear
of Steven was too prominent in her mind. "We were . . . intimate
because of Evan."

"I wasn't under the impression you were mine again," he said.
"I know thinking that is what made me lose you in the first place.
But what we did was about more than Evan."

"Maybe." Kimberly shook her head regretfully. "My emotions
are all over the place. This has all been too much for me to deal
with. All I am clear on is that this menacing summons from King
Chase reminds me that I don't want anything to do with this
family again."

"What about me?"

Kimberly hoped to find the courage to say what her logical
mind told her to instead of what her heart was saying. "Let's face
it, Michael. You can't extract yourself from this family, because
you can't extract yourself from Chase Beauty. It has always been
the one you loved most."

Michael lowered his head shamefully. "I know. This has been
true, but—"

"I'm sorry," Kimberly said. "I'll go talk to Steven because you're right. Coming clean doesn't mean just coming clean to people I pick and choose. But that's it. You will always be the father of my children, but I can't have any connections with the Chase family and especially with Chase Beauty."

She turned to leave but then turned back. "And I'll go alone. I don't need you to protect me anymore."

"You're a different woman than I remember," Michael said. He was conflicted and hurt by her rejection but was impressed with her independence.

She smiled. "I think we've all changed."

As he watched her walk down the hall toward his father, her words were swirling around in his head. He was distracted by the confident sway of her perfect hips and the way her long hair bounced behind her. It wasn't enough to make him forget her feelings. She didn't hate him anymore, but she didn't need him either. It only made him want her more.

But she was right. They had gone too far to go back—at least back to the way they had been. Michael would have to take drastic measures to get her back and keep her so he could make up for all he'd done wrong. And he knew what that drastic measure was. He would just have to build up the nerve to make it happen.

11

"Carter!" Leigh was surprised to see her older brother enter the house as she was coming down the stairs. "Did you bring the little munchkin?"

"Hey, Leigh." Carter closed the door behind him. "Why is it that after you have a kid, people treat you like you exist only to bring them by?"

"Everybody loves a baby." Leigh stopped at the bottom of the steps.

"Speaking of which," Carter said, "I'm looking for the kid. I have some legal papers for her. She here?"

Leigh rolled her eyes. "I don't want to talk about Haley. Sometimes I wish she would go back to Australia."

"That's right," Carter said. "You had the Red Team's senator over for dinner a couple of nights ago. He get out alive?"

"Barely." Leigh looked down at her watch. "I'm on my way to meet Max for lunch now and apologize."

"You didn't apologize that night?"

"I wimped out." In actuality, Leigh hadn't really gotten the chance to apologize.

After things calmed down at dinner, she was able to get Max away from the rest of the family and into the rarely used library, a massive, dark leather and cherrywood decorated room filled with oversized, leather-bound books, first editions behind protective glass cases and antique furniture. Her hopes of ending the night on a good note were squashed when Max suddenly got a text from Kelly informing him that the head of the Republican National Committee would be making a surprise visit to L.A. in the morning.

She believed Max when he said that he had to leave because he needed to prep for the meeting; he intended to get the RNC to have its next convention in L.A. in the year he would be running for governor. What she didn't believe was him saying he felt horrible for having to leave and wished he could stay longer. The relief with which he spoke of Kelly's call told the real truth. He couldn't wait to get out of there and barely took the time to kiss her before rushing out.

"What, exactly, do you intend to tell him?" Carter asked. "Are you going to lie and say that was an aberration? That this family really isn't a nightmare?"

"I don't think it would make any difference," Leigh said. "Either way, I have to get this over with. I was going to put it off until our date this Friday, but since Avery canceled on me, I took it as a sign to just deal with this."

"Avery?" Carter asked.

"We were going to have lunch today, and she canceled on me, so I saw it as a sign—"

"Why are you having lunch with her?" he asked angrily.

Leigh placed her hand on her hip. "Possibly because she's my friend. Don't expect me to hate her just because you do."

"I don't hate her," Carter argued.

"I know you don't hate her," Leigh agreed, leaning in. "You love her, and if I was a psychiatrist, I'd have a word for whatever this is you're doing."

"But you're not, so . . ."

"You need to take it easy on her now," Leigh said. "With everything she is going through, she doesn't need you making it harder on her."

"Avery brings trouble on herself," Carter scoffed.

Leigh made a smacking sound with her lips. "You ought to be

ashamed of yourself. It isn't as if you didn't have a hand in ending her marriage."

Carter frowned, confused. "What are you talking about?"

Everyone in the family knew that Anthony's accident was a result of Avery telling him she was leaving him.

"Just back off of her," Leigh said. "If not for her sake, then for Connor's. This situation is hard enough on the baby. A divorce—"

"What divorce?" Carter asked, shocked.

Leigh's body stiffened as she realized what she'd done. "Oh . . . I thought you knew."

"What are you talking about?" Carter's tone belied his desperation. Had he heard right?

"She canceled on me because she was too upset. She said that her marriage was over and that she had left Anthony."

"She said that?" Carter asked her tentatively, as if giving her one last chance to take it back. "She is leaving him. She . . . Why?"

"She didn't want to tell me why," Leigh said. "And the fact that she didn't tell you tells me I better stop talking."

"I have a right to know what is going on with my daughter," Carter insisted.

Leigh started for the door, not sure what she had just started. Before leaving, she said, "She just said she and Connor are going to live with her parents in Baldwin Hills."

Carter wasn't sure what he was feeling as he stood alone in the foyer of the house. She left him. She left him! She had listened to him and must have gotten Anthony to tell her the truth. She was leaving him! Carter couldn't stop the thoughts from racing through his head, but they were all too far away to grasp and make sense of. The only thing that seemed firm in his mind was that he had to talk to her, had to see her.

He wasn't sure how much time had passed before he reached into his pocket for his cell. For whatever reason, before he pressed the speed-dial button to reach Avery, it struck him where the number was. She was still number one. After all this time, she was still at the top of his speed-dial list, and although he had changed phones a few times since putting her there, he'd never moved her down. Julia had never gotten above number two.

Why did something so trivial and insignificant bother him all of a sudden? Why did it anger him that he hadn't been able to remove her from that spot? He knew why. It was because he knew, without having to check, that he wasn't number one on her speed dial, and he hadn't been for a while. Why hadn't she called him? Why did he have to hear about this from Leigh in passing?

Carter knew he had to stop this, all of it. He had to stop running to a woman who only seemed to hurt him, and he had to stop making it his purpose in life to hurt her. This game was over and everyone lost. Things had gone too far to go back and too far to start over. The only thing to do was move on.

No, it wasn't Avery he needed to call. It was Julia.

Lunch at Cecconi's was not going very well for Leigh and Max. When she'd arrived, she was disappointed to find Kelly was already there. Max spotted her and waved her over. She reluctantly approached and was met with a brief smile as Max kept his attention on his phone conversation. Kelly had already ordered a selection of cicchetti, which the waiter placed on the table just as Leigh arrived. Despite the dirty looks Leigh gave him, Max seemed reluctant to get off the phone, only holding up a finger to beg her patience.

Leigh tried to engage Kelly in small talk, but the woman clearly didn't want to talk to her. Leigh had the feeling that her presence here was a threat to Kelly, but she didn't really care. She just wanted her to leave so she could have a real conversation with Max. After he finally got off the phone, Max infuriated Leigh by engaging in small talk with her and political talk with Kelly. It wasn't until dessert arrived, which Kelly had also preordered, that Kelly excused herself from the table to return to the office.

"You look lovely," Max said, reaching for his fork to dig into the panna cotta. "You should wear red more often. It's a very attention-getting color."

"You seem to be immune." Leigh met his glance with a terse one of her own to match her tone.

Max smiled. "I'm sorry, Leigh. It's very busy these days. The campaign is about to gear up. I hope you understand."

"Why was she here?" Leigh asked.

Max paused and lightly sighed as if he knew an argument was coming. "You're the one who wanted us to appear as just friends. Kelly makes a good buffer and an excuse to say this was policy related."

"Or maybe it was to avoid talking to me."

Max casually tugged at his sharp blue tie. "I'm talking to you now, but I can see that fact isn't going to soothe you."

"This is about my family, right?"

"I was only complying with your request to make it appear as if—"

"I'm not talking about that and you know it." Leigh leaned in. "I'm talking about what happened at my house and how you've been avoiding me since."

"It's been two days."

"Why did I have to call you?"

"Why wouldn't you have to call me?" he asked. "Do you expect me to be the only chaser here?"

Leigh frowned in exasperation. "Don't you dare. This is not about chasing and romance. This is about you being scared shitless about my family."

Max made a dismissive frown. "Is that what you think?"

"I understand that my family can be a real turnoff," Leigh said, "but you could at least—"

"Do you think I'm stupid, Leigh?"

Taken off guard, Leigh wasn't sure how to respond. She leaned back, trying to study the flat expression that took over his face. "I didn't call you stupid."

"Wouldn't I have to be if I didn't know what your family was like?" he asked. "Granted, the show that was put on was a bit much, but I don't scare that easily. It appears, however, that you do."

"You want to explain that to me?" She leaned back in her chair, crossing her arms over her chest.

"I can explain it to you as soon as you explain to me why you told your mother I wouldn't be coming to Michael's birthday dinner."

Leigh laughed to cover her annoyance. "I was just certain that you wouldn't want to—"

"I can speak for myself," he said sternly. "You know that, so I assumed you spoke out to keep me from doing so."

Leigh could have tried to find excuses, but she wasn't good enough at lying to pull it off, and from the look on Max's face, he didn't have the patience anyway.

"I think you did it because the idea of me coming to Michael's dinner meant that this was real, that our relationship was no longer an extension of some vacation romance."

Max's cell, lying on the table next to his plate, began to vibrate, and Leigh wished he would be rude and answer it. Instead, he reached over and turned it off, never taking his eyes off her.

"It wasn't your idea to have me come over for dinner that night, right? It was your mother. If it was up to you, I wouldn't have even met your family yet."

After a moment's pause, Leigh finally said, "You're right. But you have to understand that you and I becoming an 'us' is more than just an 'us.'"

"I know," Max said. "It's more than a relationship, and that is why I was willing to keep its status a secret from the public, but I didn't know you were going to keep it secret from me too."

"I was only hoping we could navigate this between the two of us before any families got involved."

"No, Leigh. You were hoping you could navigate this by yourself before you got involved."

Leigh's mouth opened in protest, but nothing came out. She was hurt by his words.

"I'm in love with you, Leigh."

Leigh's eyes widened in surprise and shock. "What?"

Max's expression was starkly serious, his eyes holding hers with an intent strength. "I'm in love with you, and I haven't allowed myself to feel that since my wife. I knew going into this that you aren't the kind of woman a man can just date. And although I understand what you've gone through, and I'm just as concerned about the public consequences of our relationship, I'm willing to work through that. I know what your family is, but I don't care. I know who you are and you're what I want."

Leigh was affected deeply by his words, and by the strength and determination in his tone. He just didn't understand.

"How can you know so soon?" she asked.

Leigh could tell from Max's reaction that he was disappointed in her response. She was making a mess of this and she knew it, but she was scared. She was just so scared and confused as to why he wasn't.

"I don't want you to think I'm not happy that you feel that way about me, but I'm just not as brave as you."

"Bullshit," he snapped back. "I wouldn't let myself fall in love with a woman who wasn't at least as brave as me."

"You have to know that I feel strongly for you," Leigh said. "I had vowed to stay away from men at least for now, but I couldn't stay away from you. I wouldn't have ever . . . shared myself with you if I didn't have feelings."

"But?"

She sighed. "I just need more time to know if this is something I want or something I'm supposed to want."

"You need time?" Max asked. "Well, I'm going to give it to you."

"I just need a few days to—"

"You'll get more than that." Max raised his hand for the waiter to approach. He asked for the check before turning back to Leigh. "I'm leaving for D.C. tonight."

Leigh couldn't hide how much that upset her. "Why? The session doesn't begin for another couple of weeks."

"I have a lot to do." Max picked up his napkin from his lap and placed it on the table. "And, frankly, I need to leave L.A. if I'm going to stay away from you."

"Why do you need to stay away from me?"

"I'm already in love with you, Leigh. If it turns out you don't feel the same, it's going to be very hard on me. I need to prepare myself for that possibility."

"I don't want to—"

"So it's best," he interrupted, "if I just not see you. I'm looking at you now, and I want to take you on this table."

Leigh felt a tingling sensation run through her at the deep look in his eyes as he said this

"So you see," he continued, reaching into his pocket, "I think leaving L.A. is the only way I can stay away from you."

Max stuffed a few bills in the billfold and handed it back to the waiter as he returned. He stood up from his chair, looking down at Leigh. "Call me when you know what you want."

* * *

Walking down the hallways of the private wing in the hospital, Carter was getting ugly looks from the nurses, and he knew why.

"I have to go," he said into his cell. "I'm not supposed to be on the phone in here, but make sure the meeting with Borst is rescheduled for—"

He was only a few feet from Evan's room when the door suddenly opened and Avery stepped out. Their eyes met and Carter froze. It was the first time he'd seen her since finding out that she had left Anthony and since threatening to take Connor away. During that time, Carter had made some big changes in his life that he was still dealing with, but mostly he had tried his best to keep from calling her. No matter how much he tried to distract himself, he couldn't get her leaving Anthony out of his mind—and even more so the fact that she still had not told him. It was yet another obsession he had that centered around Avery, something he was trying desperately to stop.

It was his weekend with Connor, so he knew he would have to deal with her in a couple of days, but he'd wanted to be more prepared so he could manage his feelings. He wasn't used to having to manage his feelings, but Avery made him angry, excited, and nervous like no other woman could, so although he was no longer interested in hurting her, these surprise encounters could cause him a lot of trouble.

Avery was jolted by this chance meeting too. She had timed her visits to the hospital to avoid anyone in the Chase family except Kimberly, whom she needed to get into Evan's room. The degrading state of her relationship with Carter made it awkward for her to be around any of them. Kimberly had promised her no one was due until 4:00 p.m. Carter, the workaholic, was the last person she expected to see at noon.

So much of her life had changed since she last spoke to him, when he had threatened to take Connor away from her. The threat was still fresh in her mind, and she had expected to hear from one of his lawyers or be served with some papers any day now. She lived in fear of this, because his last threat seemed so much more real than any of the others. Her response, harsher than any others, had made it even more serious. She couldn't take it back because she meant it, and even if it was another empty threat, this had gone too far to play nice.

Then there was the dissolution of her marriage and everything that she had ahead of her to deal with. Now here was Carter standing in front of her, not looking as angry as usual, but clearly not pleased to see her. No, the last thing she needed right now was to say anything that could escalate their drama. So what was she supposed to do? Trying to be civil had done nothing in the past, and she couldn't ignore him. And then there was still that little part of her that wanted . . . She had to stop that thought before it finished.

"Hello, Carter." She spoke quickly as she passed him.

"Avery." Carter turned around. "Stop."

Avery took a deep breath and turned around. "I was just leaving. Kimberly said I could see him."

"I don't care about you being here," Carter said impatiently. "I wanted to know when you were going to tell me about your separation from Anthony?"

Avery sighed, looking away. She had not yet rehearsed this conversation, having so many other important things to think about. She had been dreading his reaction, based on how he'd been treating her.

"Why would I tell you?" Avery asked. "So you could throw an I-told-you-so in my face? You were right. He can walk."

"Why are you acting as if this is my fault?" he asked.

"I'm not," she answered. "This has nothing to do with you."

"Considering I'm the one who made you aware of this, I think it has to do with me." Carter shoved his cell in the jacket pocket of his suit. "You could have told me."

"You would have found out eventually," she said. "Besides, I'm not giving you any ammunition against me."

"Ammunition?" Carter shrugged, confused. "For what?"

"For Connor. You think I don't know what a disadvantage being a single parent against a married couple is in a custody battle? I don't care if I'm single or you're married to Julia or anyone else. I'm still not going to let you take my—"

"I don't want to take Connor away from you," Carter said. He could see the look of disbelief on her face. "I was angry."

"You're always angry." Avery was trying to figure out how many grains of salt she should give his words. "Every time you get angry, you threaten to take her away from me. You can't keep doing this."

"I won't do it anymore," Carter said. "No matter what has happened between us, I know you're a great mother. I would never take Connor away from you."

Avery was touched by his words despite the voice in the back of her head telling her she couldn't believe him. "All I've ever wanted to be was a good mother to Connor. You've been making it so hard."

"And I won't anymore," Carter said. Humility was hard for him, and this was making him feel guilty on top. "Look, Avery . . . I'm trying to move on with my life. For Connor's sake, we'll find a way to get along."

"That's all I've ever wanted," Avery said, knowing it wasn't entirely true. Even now, with all the madness her life had become, she still wanted him. She didn't need him, but she wanted him.

That was the problem, Carter said to himself. If only that could be all he ever wanted, too, things would be much easier. "Where should I pick Connor up from this Friday?"

"My parents' house," Avery answered. "We're staying there until I can get my own place."

"Then I'll see you Friday." Carter quickly turned and walked away.

The haste with which he walked away from her only served to confuse Avery more. She was hopeful that he'd meant what he said, because although there had been lulls in his quest for vengeance, he had never gone so far as to praise her. On the other hand, the way he had just walked away from her told her that he didn't want to spend a second more than he had to in her presence.

"Maybe it's an improvement," she said to herself as she started off again.

"Maybe what's an improvement?"

Avery turned back to see Kimberly only a few feet away from her. "How long have you been standing there?"

"I just came out as Carter walked in." Kimberly pointed to Evan's room. "Are you talking to yourself?"

"He can't stand to be near me," Avery said, "but I guess it is an improvement from wanting to be near me just so he can hurt me."

"Disregard can be more painful than cruelty to some people," Kimberly said. "But I thought things were changing now."

"We'll see, but even if he still hates me, at least he won't use Connor to hurt me anymore."

Kimberly frowned, confused by Avery's response. "We aren't talking about the same thing, are we?"

"I'm talking about Carter saying he wants to move on and stop threatening to take Connor away from me every time I make him mad. What are you talking about?"

"Wow." Kimberly looked around before stepping closer to Avery. "Don't you dare tell him you heard this from me. I'm dealing with enough now. I don't need Mr. I Love Making People Miserable on my ass."

"Do I want to know this?" Avery asked cautiously.

Kimberly smiled as she answered. "He broke off his engagement to Julia."

Avery's mouth flew open. She didn't know what to say. She wasn't sure what to believe. "How can you know that?"

"That whole family is running in and out of here, and I overheard it." Kimberly shrugged with a gleeful smile. "Not only did he call off the wedding, but he also broke up with the snobby bitch altogether."

Avery didn't even know where to begin. "Did he say why?"

"I thought it was because of you," Kimberly said. "You know, because someone was saying that you and Anthony are done."

"I had nothing to do with this," Avery argued.

"Please," Kimberly said. "You have everything to do with anything Carter does, and you know it. Maybe he thought you left Anthony for him?"

"No," Avery said. "That was completely separate. It's not—"

"I was so sure." Kimberly looked curiously disappointed. "I'm thinking for Avery to leave her husband, a man in a wheelchair, it had to be for Carter."

"My life doesn't revolve around Carter," Avery said defensively. "I don't need him or any man. I left Anthony for reasons I just don't want to get into now. Not for Carter."

Kimberly flipped her hair back and looked Avery up and down. With a smirk, she said, "You expect me to believe that you leaving Anthony and Carter leaving Julia within a week of each other isn't related?"

"Believe what you want," Avery said. "Carter and I aren't together. I left Anthony for my own reasons, and I don't know why he left Julia, but I can assure you it wasn't for me."

"Well," Kimberly said. "Could it be eventually?"

Avery looked toward the door, finding it curious that he was so upset she hadn't shared her news, while at the same time not sharing his.

"Sorry, Kimberly, but that ship has sailed. Whatever the future holds for me and Carter, it's not us being together."

Avery just hoped that one day, this realization wouldn't hurt as much as it did right now.

Leigh was staring at the cell phone on her desk at the clinic as if she could will it to ring. She knew she should call Max. He had been gone for a couple of days, and she had yet to call him after he walked out on her in the restaurant.

Leigh found it odd how scared his confession of love made her. She knew that she held on to some baggage because of what had happened in the past with Lyndon and Richard, but what woman didn't want to hear a man who made her feel the way Max did tell her he loved her? And although it felt good to know he loved her, what came next was what frightened the hell out of her. Leigh wasn't sure she had the strength to survive another heartbreak, another public heartbreak at that.

Her first objection had been to the idea that they be together because it was expected, a good union as her mother would call it. It was good for the family socially and good for Max politically. But the truth was, Leigh wasn't really concerned about that. The night they'd spent together in Africa made it clear to her that their attraction was genuine. The fact that she wanted more nights in his bed told her it was more than genuine. And that was her concern. She would let her guard down, let herself fall in love and then . . . it was always the same.

"Come in." A knock on the door broke Leigh from her trance.

Alicia, one of the doctors who helped Leigh build the clinic and one of her best friends, poked her head in and asked, "Is it safe?"

"What do you mean?" Leigh waved her in.

Alicia entered, closing the door behind her. "You've been in a bad mood all day. I didn't want to get in the line of fire."

"I'm sorry," Leigh said. "I have a lot on my mind, but I would never take it out on you. As a matter of fact, I'm still trying to think of a way I can reward you for running this place so well while I was gone."

"Don't even think about it," Alicia said. "This is our dream, and we've done a great job here."

Leigh smiled at the thought. She began this clinic with Alicia and Richard almost four years ago, and it had grown beyond her dreams. "Can you believe we're going to open a third clinic?"

"We're going to need it." Alicia sat down in the wooden chair across from Leigh's small, cluttered desk. "Did you see the *L.A. Times* today?"

"No." Leigh reached out and pulled her laptop closer to her on the desk. "Do I want to?"

"Um . . . no, but yes."

Leigh laughed as she typed. "That's helpful."

When she got to the Web site for the newspaper, she didn't need any direction to find what Alicia was referring to. In the top right column, in black letters, was the headline:

SOURCES SAY STATE HEALTH CARE PROGRAM IS NO-GO

"'Aides to Governor Sand,'" Leigh read aloud, "'tell the *Times* that a recent report submitted to the governor by Senator Max Cody, a rumored candidate for the governor's seat next year, recommends that, due to budget concerns, he not implement the proposed version of state health care, California's own version of universal coverage.'"

"From the look on your face," Alicia said, "I take it you didn't know about this."

Leigh's anger was only compounded by what she read next.

"'This comes on the heels of what Capitol Hill sources say is a recommendation by Senator Cody that the president also reduce some aid programs to Africa.'"

"How could he?" Leigh slammed down the top of her laptop in an act of rage that satisfied nothing.

"The bill has been out there for a few months," Alicia said. "You aren't the only person who lobbied for it, but you know Republicans."

"This isn't about him being a Republican," Leigh said. "It's about him being a liar. He told me he wasn't going to shut down the entire proposal but might make some cuts."

"When did he tell you that?" Alicia asked. "Were you in an . . . intimate setting?"

Leigh gave her an agitated look. "Are you saying he only told me that to get me in bed?"

Alicia lurched forward, her eyes wide. "He's gotten you in bed? So it's true. You two are—"

"Don't start." Leigh reached for her cell phone. "I think I know what this is about."

"You think it's about you?" Alicia asked.

"It better not be." Leigh wouldn't be so vain as to suggest that her refusal to return his profession of affection had anything to do with it, but that didn't change the fact that he went back on what he had said he would do.

"He's not getting away with this." Leigh waited impatiently for someone to pick up the call. "Hello, Mom? It's Leigh. Has Dad left for D.C. on the jet yet? Good. I'm on my way to the airport to join him."

"I'm not going to tell you again," Kimberly warned Daniel as he tried yet again to climb up onto Evan's hospital bed.

"I wasn't doing it," Daniel insisted.

"He can come up," Evan offered.

"No," Kimberly said. "You're already excited enough just having him here."

Kimberly couldn't stop smiling at the sight of her baby sitting up in his hospital bed. He was thinner, but the color was coming back to his face, and he was well on his way back to normal. Looking at him now, she couldn't believe that she once thought he was about to die. The memory made her shudder.

"Can I have my PSP?" Daniel asked as he came around to the other side of the bed.

"No." Kimberly patted him on the head. "You're here to visit your brother. We have to leave soon, so talk to him."

"There's nothing to talk about." Evan sighed to relay his boredom. "I want to go home with you guys."

"Any day now." Kimberly patted him on the leg. "Mommy, Daddy, and Daniel can't wait!"

Evan's eyes widened in surprise. "Daddy's home? He's back home?"

"Um . . ." Kimberly hadn't thought about her words before speaking them. "No, I meant . . . No, just that we'll all be happy you'll be at home with me and Daniel."

"When is Daddy coming home?" Evan asked. "I want him to be there when I get home."

"We've discussed this," Kimberly said. "Daddy will bring you home with me and spend time with you, but he has his own house."

"Stupid hotel room," Daniel said. "He won't even take us there."

"That's because it's not the right place for children." Kimberly really didn't want to discuss Michael, but she knew that the best way for them to work through it was to ask the same questions over and over again until they were satisfied. "He takes you to Chase Mansion because you need space, but when he gets his own place, you'll be going there."

"We should just be in the same house!" Evan said.

"Calm down, sweetie." Kimberly stood up from her chair and leaned against the bed. She ran her hand over his head softly. "You don't have the energy to get so upset."

"Then I want Daddy to come home," Evan said. "I won't be upset if he comes home."

"I don't want him there," Daniel said. "He was mean when he was there."

"Not anymore," Evan said.

"No," Daniel said. "But I don't want to go back to that. Daddy was mean there, Mommy. Don't let him come live there again."

"Daniel," Kimberly admonished with a look, urging him to calm down. "Your father was having a hard time then, but he's not anymore. He won't be mean to you no matter where he . . ."

Kimberly realized she had lost her son's attention to something behind her, and when she turned around, she felt a stab in her heart to see Michael standing at the door. She could tell from the look on his face that he had heard what Daniel said. He tried quickly to cover, but it wasn't fast enough. She could tell how hurt he was, but he swallowed hard, pasted on a smile, and walked toward them.

Kimberly felt sorry for him but admired him for trying to hide it from the children. She knew that, of all his regrets, the harm the end of their marriage caused their children was the greatest. They both had a lot of makeup to do with the boys.

It was an unusually quiet afternoon in the Baldwin Hills neighborhood where Avery's parents, Charlie and Nikki Jackson, lived. Usually, the well-to-do suburban street was full of young kids playing outside, but it was the middle of the day, so Carter guessed they were all at school. If it wasn't for the quiet as he approached the front door of the modest two-floor brick home, he probably wouldn't have heard voices in the backyard—his daughter's voice.

Relishing the opportunity to avoid Avery's parents, he chose to walk around the side of the house to the gate to the backyard. He wasn't sure if they were home, but he avoided any opportunity to run into them. The Jacksons had never liked Carter from the beginning. Charlie, when he was View Park's chief of police, always complained about the favors the family called in when any of them ever got in trouble. There was also the fact that his sister Haley had made the life of their middle son, Sean, a living hell after he broke up with her a couple of years ago. Haley also tried her best to implicate their youngest daughter, Taylor, in a murder scandal out of spite, which almost got Taylor killed.

Most of all, they distrusted Carter and blamed him for everything bad that had happened between him and Avery. They made life hard for him when he'd tried to find Avery after she'd left, and they tried to help her keep Connor a secret from him.

For his part, Carter couldn't stand any of them. He didn't know or care about Taylor, but Sean, Charles, and Nikki had always been on his shit list since the beginning. But clearly things had reached an unsustainable level after he decided to make Avery the focus of his wrath. Now they didn't even pretend to be cordial. They didn't speak at all.

The wooden gate to the back of the Jackson home was chest-high, white, and unlatched. Carter opened it, and as he walked down the side of the house, he smiled at the sound of Connor's laughter getting louder and louder. Just as he reached the edge of the house and was about to turn the corner, he stopped.

Avery was sitting on the bench of a wooden picnic table with Connor sitting on the table in front of her. She was adorable in a little pink jumpsuit and was twisting and turning as Avery tickled her everywhere. She was very ticklish and was hysterically happy. Carter stood where he was and watched this scene for a few moments more. His baby's joy always made him smile, but he couldn't help but feel bad as well.

They were all supposed to be together. That had been the plan a little over two years ago. Avery would marry him and they would have children. They had decided on three. He had imagined them being a family and being happy. He was a realistic man, so he knew it wouldn't always be butterflies, but he was certain that the love he and Avery shared for each other and would share for their children would get them through the harder times.

He was supposed to be there on that bench with his wife and his little girl, but he was standing away, watching as if from the outside. He didn't belong there at all and was astounded as to how this came to be. There had been so many mistakes and so many chances, and he was tired—tired of trying and hurting. He only wished he could be tired of wanting. He wasn't.

Avery was beginning to have trouble holding Connor up and tickling her at the same time. She was twitching and jiggling all over the place. She was big enough to sit up on her own, but when she jerked around like that, Avery had to hold her to keep her from falling down. She just didn't want to stop because she loved this so much. Her baby's joy was her whole world and her whole focus.

She felt the burden of a pending custody battle lifted from her shoulders, at least for now. She still had a separation and a divorce to deal with and imagined it would be hard, considering Anthony's refusal to talk to her now that he realized she wasn't going to change her mind. It bothered her and worried her, but Avery had all she needed. She had Connor.

She'd wanted more, of course, but her heart had broken enough. It was hard. Every time she felt levity and thought she could enjoy her life, she would think of Carter and everything that could have been. It was odd to her that she wished that would stop but also wished it wouldn't. She would miss how just the thought of him would warm her inside.

Getting a weird feeling that Carter was with her, Avery turned her head. She was surprised to see him even though she'd felt him there. She managed a tiny smile as she turned back to Connor, who, out of curiosity as to what had made her mother stop tickling, looked and saw her father too.

"Dada!"

"How's my little princess?" Carter walked over to the bench and dropped down only a few inches to Avery's left. He reached out and grabbed Connor, kissing her on the cheek, and he wasn't sure why it made him sad.

"Mommy," she cried out. "Dada!"

"I know," Avery said with her baby voice. "I see Dada."

Connor leaned away from her father and said, "Dada. Look. Mommy."

Carter nodded. He was well aware Avery was next to him. He was always aware of her when she was this close. He could smell her body wash, and the hair on his arms started to rise.

"I know I'm early," Carter said as he turned to Avery.

Connor grabbed his hand.

"It's okay." Avery continued to look at her daughter, wishing he wouldn't sit so close. "You'll be happy. She's been crazy all day and will probably sleep well tonight."

"Mommy," Connor pleaded, "give me."

Avery offered her daughter what she was requesting—her hand—and finally found the courage to look at Carter. "So I guess you'll bring her back on . . ."

Avery hadn't been paying attention to what Connor was doing until it was too late. With her tiny hands, she had managed to take her father's right hand and her mother's left hand and bring them together.

"Mommy! Dada!" She placed Carter's hand on her lap and Avery's hand on top of Carter's, looking very pleased with herself. "See!"

Carter and Avery looked at their hands touching on their daughter's lap, and they both smiled for what they told themselves was for her sake. There wasn't the usual sexual tension that existed whenever Avery and Carter touched. This was different, and Connor's involvement made it so. Instead there was the tension that exists when two people are thinking the same thing at the same time.

How good it could have been.

Avery was the first to remove her hand as she laughed nervously to play it off.

Carter took a moment to get it together before standing up from the bench. "I guess we'll go," he said as he picked up Connor and held her in his arms. "I'll . . . bring her back Sunday night."

Avery nodded but didn't look back at him. She smiled at the sound of Connor talking gibberish as if she was having a conversation as they walked away. But this wasn't funny. No Anthony, no Julia to stand in their way. How was she going to do this?

And why had he still not told her about Julia?

The Palisades was an upscale area of Washington, D.C., with beautiful homes surrounded by greenery that would put any suburb to shame. It was quaint with a lot of character that included various styles of old and new homes.

Steven was standing at the black double doorway to a three-story gray brick Federal-style home when the ruby-red Lexus drove up the short black driveway. The door to the garage began to lift, but the car stopped abruptly before entering. Steven's stoic expression didn't change as the driver noticed him, turned the car off, and got out.

Steven waited until he got closer before speaking. "Hello, Keenan."

This was the first time in almost twenty years Steven had seen his brother, the last being at their father's funeral. Things were so bad by that time that Keenan even blamed Steven for their father's cancer. Everything in the world had become Steven's fault, and Steven had stopped giving a damn. Cutting Keenan out of his life was better than dealing with his hateful envy.

"What are you . . ." Keenan stopped at the bottom of the doorsteps with a cautious and angry expression. "What are you doing at my house?"

"I thought it would be better to tell you face-to-face that your plan with Kimberly won't work," Steven said.

He observed that his brother had not aged as well as he'd expected. He was about fifteen pounds overweight and had gone almost completely gray.

"Better than over the phone or in a court of law," he added.

Seeming to take his defeat in stride, Keenan stood tall. "I don't know what you're talking about, but you weren't invited, so you can leave now."

"Kimberly told me everything," Steven said. "Going all the way back to Elisha and how you planned to destroy Chase Beauty."

"You can't prove anything," Keenan said. "But I guess that doesn't matter to someone like you. If you don't have evidence, you buy some."

"I could have," Steven said. "I could have put together any plan I wanted to that would make you pay for coming after my company. I thought about how I could punish you, but what would be the point?"

"I'm a very high-ranking government official," Keenan said. "I'm not like those nobodies you walk over every day."

"I don't waste my time on nobodies," Steven said. "What I meant was what would be the point, because you've punished yourself by holding on to this hatred and unwarranted jealousy."

"Unwarranted?" Keenan laughed bitterly. "Since as far back as I can remember, you tried to upstage me at every chance. As a child, a teenager, and an adult; no matter what, you took from me."

"I was better than you," Steven said. "It wasn't a plot. It was reality. I was smarter, faster, keener, and more determined."

"You were ruthless," Keenan said. "You took from me. You took Dad's praise, Mom's love."

"You're insane," Steven said. It was true that their parents had played favorites, but Steven wasn't to blame for that. "You've created all of this in your mind."

"You took Janet."

Steven paused, unwilling to take that any further. His brother's claims had always annoyed him, but the idea that Janet had belonged to Keenan really did make him angry, and he didn't want to get into an argument. That was not what he'd come for.

"Why don't you let me in?" Steven asked. "We can have a civil conversation."

"You're not getting into my home." Keenan stood firm, as if defending a fort.

"Have you heard about my grandson?"

Keenan looked away for an instant as if he considered caring, but then turned back with a cold stare. "I don't care about your family."

"He's your family too," Steven said. "And he almost died. He's better now, and that is a blessing."

"I guess you're lucky," Keenan said. "You always seem to be lucky."

"If only you knew," Steven said. "My life has been full of turmoil, but you don't care about that, and I don't need you to. I intended to make you pay for what you've tried to do, but because of my grandson, I'm here to suggest a truce between us, possibly the chance to have a relationship. I can forgive and forget. Can you?"

Keenan looked astonished that Steven would even suggest such a thing.

"Do you have a response?" Steven asked impatiently.

"I'm trying to figure out what you're up to," Keenan said. "What is this fake play of peace a prelude to?"

Steven sighed, realizing what a waste of time this was. "This is not a game, not a ploy, Keenan. Family is everything, and you have to understand that—"

"I don't have to understand anything!" Keenan yelled. "I don't give a damn about you or your grandson. Why would I let you back into my life? So you can rub my nose in your success from close up instead of afar?"

"I want to start a clean slate."

"Get off my property," Keenan ordered. "Now, or I'll call the police. You're not top dog in D.C. I have more clout here than you."

After a second's pause, Steven started slowly down the steps. "I know this is a lot to take at once, so I'll give you time. I'll try again or you can contact me. I'm open to welcoming you back into my life, and I hope you're open to welcoming me back into yours."

As he reached the bottom step, only inches from his brother, Steven looked him dead in the eye and said, "But if you ever try to come after Chase Beauty, me, or anyone in my family ever again, I will demolish you. Brother or not."

12

When Leigh burst into the senator's office in the Hart Build-ing on Capitol Hill, all eyes shot up and everyone in the room stopped working. She imagined they were intrigued by the furious look on her face, but she didn't care. Without a word, she walked right past a nervously smiling woman who greeted her politely and headed for Max's office. She heard someone ask her to wait and then another person demand she stop, but she didn't. When she swung the door open and stepped inside, she saw an empty chair behind an immaculate desk.

"He isn't here."

Leigh turned to her right to find Kelly standing near a win-dow overlooking Constitution Avenue with a stack of folders in her arms.

"Hello, Kelly."

"Do you always just burst into rooms without knocking first?" she asked. "Or even having an appointment?"

"I wasn't aware I needed an appointment to see Max," Leigh said. "I'm not here as a constituent."

Kelly seemed to get her meaning and glared disapprovingly in return. "Either way, he isn't here."

"Do you know where he is?"

"I always know where he is," Kelly answered flatly.

Leigh didn't have patience. "What is your problem? I haven't done anything to you."

"I don't know what you're talking about." Kelly turned her attention to the top file in her hands.

"I want to speak with him," Leigh said. "Now."

Kelly looked up with a sarcastic smirk on her face. "He's having lunch with the president's chief of staff. Should I call the White House and let them know they'll have to cut it short because the senator's girlfriend needs his attention?"

"Fine." Leigh sat herself on the sofa at the other end of the room, slamming her purse down next to her. "I'll wait for him."

"He's got a very busy—"

"I'll wait," Leigh repeated.

"Can I know what this is regarding at least?" Kelly asked.

"No," Leigh answered. "You can't."

Kelly walked over to the desk and placed the folders down before turning to Leigh. "You can't do this."

"I might regret asking this question," Leigh said, "but what, exactly, is it you think I cannot do?"

"What you've come here for," she answered. "It's about the health insurance plan, isn't it?"

"I'd rather discuss that with Max, if you don't mind."

"I do mind," Kelly responded. "I don't think I need to impress upon you the plans that are set for the senator."

Leigh held up a hand to stop her. "Spare me. I've heard it a million times. So many people are placing their hopes in Max for the White House."

"But it takes only one person to ruin it all," Kelly said. "This recommendation is going to be unpopular with some Independents, people he needs for the next election. You getting involved will only give it more publicity and keep it in the news longer."

"I will keep my conversations with Max between him and me," Leigh said. "If you stay out of it, who would know about our . . . disagreements?"

"Everybody knows everything that happens on the Hill, and if you add the name Chase to it, that only makes it worse."

"What does my last name have to do with policy?"

"Nothing," Kelly said, "but when your last name is mentioned, people forget about policy. They focus on you and that . . . that family you have."

Leigh shot up from the sofa. "I beg your pardon? Do you have something to say about 'that family' I have? My family?"

Kelly paused, seemingly to reserve herself. "No offense, Ms. Chase."

"It's Dr. Chase," Leigh corrected, "and it's too late for that."

Kelly seemed uncertain as to whether she wanted to continue. "I'm only saying that there is a lot of activity that comes along with your family that is not conducive to a successful election."

"People have the sense to know that what they read on gossip blogs is just that, gossip."

"But what about the things they don't read on gossip blogs?" Kelly asked with a noticeably louder voice. "What about your sister's marriage for money?"

"What?" Leigh couldn't believe it. Did Max tell her about Haley?

"Ms. Chase, an in-depth investigation into your family's dealings has brought to light some personal—"

"What are you talking about?" Leigh took a step forward and could tell that Kelly was intimidated. She tried to keep a cap on her anger. "You investigated my family?"

"There are a lot of people determined to protect the senator, and you should—"

"Who?" Leigh yelled. "Who is doing this? I want their names! If they have a question about me and my family, they should at least have the—"

"Ladies." Max entered the office looking very upset. "I can hear you from outside."

Both women backed away from each other as Leigh turned to Max. She didn't care that he was upset but regretted not maintaining her composure.

"We need to talk," Leigh said bluntly as she returned to the sofa.

"Senator." Kelly followed Max as he walked behind his desk. "We have to discuss your afternoon meeting with the health workers association."

"What would be the point?" Leigh asked.

Both Max and Kelly turned to her, and Leigh was expressionless in return to their offended glares.

"You're already running behind," Kelly continued. "You have to get ready to—"

"Leave us, Kelly."

Leigh watched as Kelly reacted to Max's sudden dismissal of her. Her eyes widened and she briefly looked shocked, but she covered it up quickly. She opened her mouth as if to protest but seemed to change her mind. She turned to leave without looking at Leigh or saying a word.

"I'm disappointed in you, Leigh." Max got up from his desk and started for the sofa. "I would expect a woman of your class to be able to control herself in a professional setting."

"Fuck that," Leigh said sharply.

Max froze just as he was about to sit down on the sofa. Leigh was pleased that she got his attention. "People like to take advantage of me, because they think I'll be sweet and well behaved."

"I know you too well to think that." Max sat down, unbuttoning his suit jacket.

Leigh couldn't believe it, but despite how angry she was at him, seeing this small gesture turned her on a little. It was just the way he carried himself that distracted her so much.

"When were you going to tell me you had my family investigated?"

"I wasn't," he answered. "Because I didn't."

"Kelly just told me—"

"Kelly did it without my permission, but she was just doing her job. And before you get on your high horse, you can't possibly expect me to believe that your family didn't do some undercover snooping on me and my family."

Leigh couldn't argue that. Her parents were notorious for doing extensive background checks on anyone their children dated, which was why she had always made a practice of keeping her boyfriends secret from her parents for as long as she could.

"That's what I thought," Max said.

"You are so smug." Leigh wanted to punch him in the face.

Max smiled self-assuredly. "You traveled all the way to D.C. to compliment me?"

"I traveled here to ask you why you lied to me."

Max's smile disappeared. "I don't take kindly to being called a liar."

"Well," Leigh said, "then you shouldn't lie."

"You're talking about the health care program," Max said. "And before you get started, I did not lie. On the plane ride home from Africa, I told you I would give the state program serious consideration and do what was best for—"

"The people of California," Leigh interrupted. "You said—"

"No." He held a hand up to stop her. "I said I would do what was best for California. To suggest we, as a state, are broke is the understatement of the year."

"So the poorest of our state's citizens have to suffer?"

"Everyone is suffering," he said. "It isn't as if I'm taking away something they had. I'm just recommending we not enact a proposed program. We can't afford it. That is something you liberals can't seem to get through your heads."

"Now I'm a liberal?"

"You're not?" Max asked. "Look, I appreciate social programs that are effective, but the truth is, most are not and even those that are can bankrupt a state if we can't pay for it."

"You see, Max, that is where I think you are wrong," Leigh said confidently. "The money is there, but it's going to something that doesn't deserve it, because lobbyists have their tentacles around you."

"What do you think you are?" he asked. "You're a lobbyist, too, Leigh. You're also a business owner, and you make decisions every day that you don't want to. You can't serve everyone. You can't help everyone who comes to you and deserves it. You can only do what you can do. That is all government can do too."

The strength of his argument made her pause, but only for a moment. "Good speech, Senator, but I haven't done all I can do. I can protest and I plan to. I plan to protest this proposal here and in California."

"Good for you." Max stood up and walked over to his desk.

Leigh was trying to figure out what he was up to. "What do you mean? You think it's good that I'm protesting you?"

"The first amendment is my favorite of them all." Max turned and leaned back against his desk. "It won't change my mind, but I applaud and encourage you."

Leigh stood up with a squint in her eyes. "Is this a trap? You can't be happy about that. Kelly said your people will not—"

"Ignore Kelly," Max said. "I do it all the time. I like your passion and assertiveness. You have a fire for what you believe in. We don't have to agree on everything to love each other."

"Excuse me?" Leigh asked, astonished. "Love each other. I didn't say—"

"You don't have to," Max said. "You could have called me. You know I was waiting for your call. You came all the way out here, because you wanted to see me."

"Your arrogance is astounding," Leigh said. "I'll have you know, my father was already coming out here, so I just—"

She leaned away as he tried to kiss her, but he was persistent. He placed his hand behind her head and pulled her to him. She moved her head to the left as he tried to kiss her. She tried to evade him again, but he caught her mouth and pressed his own against it. His steamy kiss heated her up immediately as his hand worked the small of her back.

"How long is your father staying in D.C.?" he asked, breathing heavily.

Leigh could barely speak as she whispered, "Uh . . . um, he's leaving . . . leaving today."

"Will you be joining him?" He leaned in and this time planted a quick, sweet kiss on her lips. "Or will you be coming home with me?"

"Where is Daddy?" Evan asked as he sat with his legs crossed on his hospital bed.

"He's outside." Kimberly packed the last piece of clothing that had been in the dresser of the private room. "He was just here a few minutes ago."

"I thought he left."

Kimberly stopped packing and turned to her son. "He's filling out all of the paperwork. Now, is there anything I forgot?"

Evan looked around the room. "No."

Just then, Janet entered the room with a harried look on her face. "I was so afraid I'd be late. The traffic out there is ridiculous."

"What are you doing here?" Kimberly asked.

"I wasn't going to miss this." Janet walked over to the bed. "My little grandson is coming home today."

"I'm coming to Chase Mansion?" Evan asked.

"No," Kimberly insisted. "You're coming home."

"You feeling okay?" Janet asked him in a tiny, sweet voice.

"I just want to go home." Evan leaned forward so she could kiss him on the cheeks as if it was a duty.

"Well," Kimberly said, "we're ready. It's the middle of rush hour, so it might take a little while to reach Hollywood Hills. Go use the bathroom before we go."

As Evan slowly got off the bed and went to the bathroom, Janet turned to Kimberly.

"I know everything," Janet said.

Kimberly zipped up the bag full of Evan's things before looking in Janet's direction. She didn't need to ask what Janet was talking about. When she last spoke to Steven about Keenan, he made it clear to her he intended to tell his wife.

"Spare me your derision," Kimberly deadpanned. "Today is about Evan coming home, and I've already heard it."

"I think," Janet began, "I would be within my right to be angry that you attempted to destroy, once again, everything Steven and I have worked so hard to build. But I am also aware that it could have been worse if you hadn't stopped Elisha or seen the error of your ways with Keenan."

Kimberly realized that was the closest she would ever get to a compliment from Janet and somehow found it humorous.

Janet took a deep breath. "I know I don't deserve anything from you."

"So please don't ask," Kimberly responded.

"I have to," Janet said, "because something terrible has happened."

"I don't want to hear bad news today." Kimberly grabbed her

purse, slinging it over her shoulder. "Evan will be coming out of there soon, and—"

"Michael quit Chase Beauty."

Kimberly turned to her, shocked. "When?"

"Two days ago."

"I'm sure it is just like before," Kimberly said cautiously. "A few days ago, he realized that the kids are still feeling some residual effects of our breakup, and he's probably decided to take another leave of absence."

"It wasn't a leave of absence," Janet said as the toilet flushed in the bathroom. She had to be quick. "He quit. He said it was because he needed to prove to you that your family means more to him than our family and Chase Beauty."

Kimberly wasn't sure how to react to such a statement, especially considering she was hearing it for the first time from someone other than Michael. "I'm not interested in talking to you about Michael's career or my family."

Evan came out of the bathroom.

"Did you wash your hands?" Kimberly asked.

He frowned before turning around and going back in.

"Look, Kimberly." Janet had to remember how much she needed Kimberly right now and had to stay polite. "To suggest that you and I could ever be friends is a waste of time. But we don't have to be enemies. I think what we've experienced with Evan has shown that we can coexist peacefully."

"My relationship with Michael is no longer about you," Kimberly said, feeling increasingly uncomfortable at Janet's attempt at humility.

"This isn't about me," Janet said. "This is about Michael and his future. He has made the gesture, Kimberly. Now it's your turn to make him take it back."

"I'm not going to do that."

"You have to," Janet insisted. "Steven is very upset over finding out that his brother was trying to destroy him. Now he's lost Michael. He can't take it."

"He won't lose him," Kimberly said. "He'll just not be working with—"

"I'm ready," Evan said with glee as he came out again, holding his hands up.

"Good." Kimberly smiled wide. "Let's go home."

"Kimberly."

"This is between Michael and Steven." Kimberly held her hand out to Evan. "Let's just leave it between them."

"Have you read my report?" Carter asked his father.

Steven was looking out the window of his home office, which faced the front of the house. The large half-circle, black driveway was empty except for Carter's Maybach.

"Dad," Carter spoke up.

Steven turned back to his son. "I got you that car when you joined the board of Chase Beauty."

"What about the new advertising agency?" Carter asked. "I'm concerned about some of their insurance policy terms."

"Do you have any regrets?" Steven asked.

Carter leaned back in his chair, trying to figure out what was going on. "I regret coming over here to discuss business with you when I could be out by the pool with my daughter."

"Will you be bringing Connor over to Kimberly's house to see Evan?" Steven asked.

Carter shook his head. "Kimberly just wants it to be a very low-key dinner. He's still on bed rest. Connor being there will just get him excited."

Steven sighed, taking a seat in his chair. He folded his arms across his chest. "I have a lot of regrets."

Carter's brows furrowed, as he found this very odd. Was Steven Chase admitting that he wasn't perfect? Was this one of the signs of the apocalypse? Studying his father's distracted expression, Carter tried to figure out how to gauge him. He was clearly upset over something.

"What's wrong, Dad?" he asked quietly.

"I was very happy when you agreed to join our board," Steven said. "I had both of my sons a part of my dream. Of course, I hoped the experience would make you quit your firm and decide to come work for us full-time instead of just being our lawyer."

"I already told you that wasn't going to happen," Carter said. "Chase Law is my dream in the same way that Chase Beauty is yours."

Carter felt at least that was one dream that he could make happen even if his most important dream never would come to fruition.

Steven nodded. "It's taken a long time, but I accepted that Chase Law would be yours and Chase Beauty would be Michael's. So now what do I do?"

"What do you mean?"

Carter was shocked as his father told him about Michael's resignation. He went over the scene, which had taken place in this office only days ago. Steven shot down any suggestion by Carter that it was more of the same from last year—just a leave of absence for Michael to get his head together. He relayed his own pleas for his son to change his mind. This was particularly troublesome to Carter, because he could never imagine his father pleading with anyone for anything. The fact that he had done so meant that Steven knew this wasn't temporary. Michael was really leaving.

"I'll talk to him," Carter said. "He's just going through a lot."

"No," Steven said. "There is nothing you or I can do. You didn't see the look in his eyes, Carter. It was as if he was . . ."

Carter was extremely affected as he watched his father pause. He had never seen the man look so helpless. He was just human, after all.

"He said," Steven continued, "that of all the regrets, the one he couldn't live with was losing his family. You see, he said that because he doesn't think of me as his family."

"That's not true, Dad. He worships you."

"He worshipped what I promised him," Steven said. "Chase Beauty and I are the same thing to him. If I had been a better father, that wouldn't have been the case."

"That doesn't mean he wouldn't have quit," Carter said. "His decision is about Kimberly and the kids."

"The point is," Steven said, "if I had been a better father, he wouldn't have had to quit to keep his family."

"He'll get Kimberly back," Carter said, even though he wasn't sure of that. Although they had been best friends their whole lives, Carter and Michael had grown apart in the last year. He no longer knew absolutely everything there was to know about his brother. Despite that, he was shocked Michael hadn't told him about quitting.

"He's got some shit to work through," he continued. "And when he does, he'll come back to you. It's just hard for him to concentrate on big things when he has Chase Beauty on the brain. It will just take a while. Probably a lot more time than any of us would want."

Steven laughed softly.

"What's so funny?" Carter asked, confused.

"That's what I've been telling myself about you," Steven said.

"Michael and I aren't the same, Dad. I thought you would have figured that out by now."

"You're more alike than you think," Steven said. "Look at where your families are. Michael and Kimberly and their kids and you and Avery and your—"

"Don't," Carter said. "This is about Michael, not me. Most importantly, it's not about you."

Steven nodded. "I take it you don't want to talk about Avery or Julia."

"Julia is gone," Carter said. "Avery is . . ."

"The mother of your child," Steven said. "The woman you love."

"Not anymore," Carter said. "It's too hard to love her."

"Does this mean you intend to continue on your quest for easy love?"

Carter smiled. "No, but I'm not on a quest to get hurt over and over again either."

"So you're giving up?" Steven asked. "Do you really want to do that?"

"This isn't about what I want," Carter said. "I have to get on with my life."

"Can you do that without her?" Steven asked. "I mean, if you didn't have to see her or hear from her, you probably would get by. You'd have to make sure you don't date anyone who looks like her, reminds you of her or—"

"What are you trying to say?"

"Of course, none of that matters because you have Connor, so you won't be able to do that. This means you'll have to get on with your life with her in it. Can you do that?"

"I can do whatever I have to."

"Exactly." Steven's lips spread into an accomplished smile. "You can do whatever you have to. You're a Chase. The question is, what do you have to do to get on with your life?"

Carter didn't quite understand the question, but he stopped himself from thinking about it more, because he wasn't prepared to answer it when he did understand it.

"I'll talk to Michael," he said. Yes, that sounded a lot easier.

Leigh was no fool. She wasn't about to get excited about how well the night had gone so far. After all, she remembered a little over a week ago how her family dinner started out so well. She didn't want to press her luck, but as she sat in the living room with Max and his parents, Eva and Douglas Cody, she was pretty pleased.

That she was going to stay in D.C. for a little while was a settled matter after Max kissed her. She was still upset with his decision, but Max was hard to resist, and she agreed to stay overnight. Her father's jet would pick her up in the morning.

This night almost hadn't happened. Eager to continue what he had begun, Max canceled the rest of his day and quickly took Leigh to his Capitol Hill luxury high-rise apartment, where they made love for two hours. It wasn't until they had showered together afterward that Max informed her they would be having dinner with his parents in their Silver Springs, Maryland, home.

After persistent pleading, and proof these plans had been made well before Leigh showed up in D.C., Max convinced Leigh to come along. He promised no pressure, even though for Leigh that would be impossible. She was nervous, but as soon as she arrived at the large colonial-style home, his family made her feel right at home. His father, Douglas, was a thin but distinguished older man with nutmeg-brown skin. He had the same dark, intense eyes that Max had but was more mild in temper. He asked very few questions and spent most of the night telling Leigh stories about Max's misspent youth. Now retired, Douglas used to run a very successful investment banking firm, which was behind the family's wealth.

Although she wasn't born into privilege, Max's mother, Eva, reminded Leigh so much of her own. She was a beautiful, bronze-colored woman in her early sixties, who had not a hair out of place or a wrinkle on her very expensive designer dress. She was excessively gracious, beautiful, and classy, and almost all of her questions revolved around the Chase family, its members, its charity, and its social club distinctions. As her questions persisted, the feeling of comfort Leigh had was replaced with trepidation. The questions made her incredibly uncomfortable, and she was appreciative for the times Max interrupted his mother and attempted to change the topic. This continued after dinner, as they all convened in the living room for a drink.

"Mother," Max interrupted again as he sat on the sofa next to Leigh. "Leigh doesn't want to talk about Carter's engagement. It's a personal issue."

"Not anymore." Eva was sitting up straight on the sofa across the coffee table from them. "The young woman, Julia, is blabbing it to . . . well, certain people who don't have the respect for privacy they should."

"That's usually because people keep asking them," Leigh said. "I respect my brother's privacy too much to talk about it."

"Of course." Eva smiled as if she had just been complimented. "But we won't have to worry about that with you two, will we?"

"What do you mean?" Leigh scooted forward on the sofa.

"She only means," Douglas said, while standing near a large mosaic painting that was twice as large as he was, "that you have both handled the gossips very well."

"I do think it is time to make a formal announcement," Eva said. "I was thinking we could coordinate with Max's office on a press release and—"

"Mother." Max held up a hand to stop her.

"There isn't going to be a press release," Leigh said. "This is a relationship, not a merger or a political campaign."

"It's more important than either of those," Eva said. "Which is why—"

"Why it won't be treated like them," Leigh interrupted.

"What Leigh is saying," Max said, "is that what we have is just for us."

"You can't keep it secret," Eva said.

"There is a difference between trying to keep something secret," Leigh said, "and not making it public."

"I agree with Leigh," Douglas said as he approached his wife. "Right now is not the right time. The campaign will be starting at the first of the year. We should announce it then."

"Of course!" Eva clapped her hands together in excitement. "Once it is announced, everyone will want to see you two together, and they'll pay whatever it costs to attend fund-raisers so they can see you."

"You can't be serious?" Leigh asked her. She turned to Max, who was just shaking his head. "She isn't serious, is she?"

"Unfortunately," Max said, "she is. Mother, we won't be using our relationship for political gain."

"The election is next November," Eva said, as if she hadn't heard Max. "We should announce an engagement in June. Everyone will want to see a wedding at the Governor's Mansion."

"Mother, enough!"

Eva paused, raising her chin in the air. "I'm sorry. I get a little ahead of myself. I'm just very excited about what this partnership can do for the both of you."

"Partnership?" Leigh asked angrily. "You talk as if we're already engaged."

Max placed a hand on Leigh's lap. "It's okay, Leigh."

"No, it isn't," she said. "We should get something straight from the beginning. Max and I are in love with each other. There are only two people in this relationship, and only those two people will decide how this relationship goes."

"For such a sophisticated young woman," Eva said, "you are quite naïve. You act as if you are just two people in love. You are a Chase, and he is a senator and future governor. You cannot—"

"I'm leaving," Leigh said, getting up from the sofa.

"Leigh." Max stood up and took her by the arm. "It's okay. Mother gets a little carried away."

"I didn't mean to offend," Eva said, looking up at Leigh. "But I consider myself very realistic."

"Realistic?" Leigh asked. "It sounds more like opportunistic to me."

"Okay." Max stood between Leigh and his mother, looking down at Eva. "This has been a nice evening. Let's not ruin it."

"Too late," Leigh said. She freed her arm from his grip. "I'm leaving. I can call a cab or you can come with."

Max called Leigh's name once, but she didn't turn around. Feeling almost unable to breathe, she couldn't get out of there fast enough.

"She's still not there!" Janet complained as she slammed the door to the master bedroom behind her.

Drying his hands on a towel, Steven came to the doorway to the bathroom of the massive room, which took over most of the second-floor east wing of the mansion. "I told you not to go down there."

"Why aren't you worried?" Janet walked through the ornately designed room, past the Victorian bed and into the sitting area. She sat on the French-stitched settee in front of the massive window overlooking the front of the house.

"About what?" Steven asked. He tossed the towel on the counter and walked through the bedroom over to her. Sitting down next to her, he reached over and rubbed her thigh. "Haley not being in the guest house? She's never there."

"She isn't home," Janet said. "It's almost midnight, and she isn't answering her cell."

Steven smiled. "And how is this different from every other Saturday?"

Janet didn't appreciate his sarcasm. "Because this is the Saturday after the Sunday she said she's leaving for Sydney."

"First of all," Steven said, "she didn't say she was going back to Sydney; that idiot husband of hers did. Secondly, I believe I remember her saying that she doesn't want to go back."

"She wants that money," Janet said. "Steven, I'm really scared. I have a bad feeling about this."

"Like?"

"Like she might not come back."

"Don't be silly," Steven said. "Haley is accustomed to a wealthy, indulgent American life."

"She'll be richer in Sydney than she is here," Janet responded.

"But you'll be in View Park." Steven gently cupped his wife's chin in his hand and lifted her face so their eyes met. "Haley loves money, but she also loves you. She couldn't give a damn about the rest of us, but she won't want to stay away from you for long."

Janet smiled and closed her eyes as Steven kissed her on the forehead. His words soothed her. "I think you're right. I just wish this could be over with. Do you think there is a way to . . . I don't know. I want to make it so Peter can't—"

"No," Steven said. "No more interfering with that. Our interference in our children's lives is something we have to stop. It's not working."

"Haley isn't the same as Michael," she argued. "Our interference in her life has saved her life more than once."

"But maybe it's the reason why we keep needing to interfere," Steven said. "Look at Michael."

"Michael is just trying to find his way," Janet said. "His son almost died. It's normal for him to review his life."

"He has," Steven said, "and the solution he's found is to leave me."

"He's not leaving *you*," Janet said. "He's leaving Chase Beauty and only for a short while. He'll be back."

Steven shook his head. "Janet, I—"

Janet placed her hand on his chest. "I'll talk to Kimberly again. I think she's the way that we can—"

"You've been talking to Kimberly? Since when and why would she help? She hates us."

"Things change," Janet said.

"You putting your faith in Kimberly," Steven said. "That's more change than I'm willing to believe in."

"It will take time," Janet said. "But we'll be there for Michael. We won't interfere. You won't be his boss. You'll be his father, and when he figures out things with Kimberly, you'll be there when he's ready to come back."

"You sound like Carter." Steven laughed. "You realize that his figuring this whole thing out is likely to include Kimberly coming back into the fold. Can you deal with that?"

Janet let out a deep sigh. "I'm tired of fighting. I just want our children to be happy. If Michael's happiness—if his return to Chase Beauty—requires Kimberly to be in our lives again, then I'll be fine with it."

Janet wanted desperately to believe what she was saying, and when Steven leaned across to kiss her on the lips, she promised that she would pray for it to be true. Something inside of her told her that her family was at a turning point. It wasn't just Haley's threat to leave or Michael's quitting Chase Beauty. It was about Steven finding out his brother had just tried to destroy him. It was about Carter ending his engagement to Julia. It was about Leigh dating a man who could put the Chase name in the limelight more than ever before. A limelight that, in its current state, this family was simply not strong enough to stand in.

13

As soon as Avery opened the front door to the Jackson home, Connor began jumping in her father's arms. She was screaming for her mother to look at the tiny stuffed elephant in her hand.

"Wow," Avery said, feigning excitement. "That's amazing. A new toy from Daddy . . . again."

Avery looked at Carter, who shrugged and smiled. They had argued often about how Carter bought Connor too many toys and gave in to her every demand.

"I felt bad," Carter said as he entered the house. "I can't bring her to Evan's homecoming party, so I bought her a stuffed animal."

"She doesn't know you can't bring her there."

The second Carter placed her the floor, Connor waddled into the living room and sat on the floor, playing with her elephant while her parents stayed in the foyer.

"They aren't here," Avery said as she watched Carter look around the house. "You're in luck."

"I'm not afraid of your family," Carter said.

"Please," Avery said. "You can't fool me."

"I just prefer not to have someone answer the door with a loaded gun in their hand."

"Daddy hasn't done that in almost six months."

"That isn't something you forget," Carter said.

"Give him a kiss for me," Avery said.

Kiss? Carter was sure he'd heard her wrong. "Kiss? What?"

"Evan," Avery said, laughing. "Kiss Evan for me, please."

"Oh, yeah." Carter felt stupid and awkward. Now that he had let go of his animosity for her, Carter was back to the way it used to be. Avery made him nervous. She was the only woman he had ever met in his life who could make him nervous.

"I wanted to give you this." Carter reached into his pocket and took out a business card. "Charles Elysian is one of the best divorce lawyers in the country."

"Then I can't afford him," Avery said.

"You can," Carter said. "I mean, he won't . . . He'll be somewhat reasonable."

"Because you're paying him?" Avery asked, shocked by his altruistic gesture.

"Will you take it?" Carter asked, holding the card out.

"No," Avery answered. "I've already contacted a lawyer who I can afford. She's very good."

"Who is she?" Carter asked. "I know the best lawyers in—"

"Carter." Avery held up a hand to stop him. "What are you doing?"

"I'm trying not to be the same asshole I've been for the last almost nine months." Carter stuffed the card back into his pocket, frustrated. "I know that some legal referral isn't going to make up for the way I've been acting, but I thought—"

"You don't have to do anything to make it up, Carter," she said. "You just have to stop doing it."

"I have."

Avery couldn't help but feel hopeful. It might have been a mistake, but her heart urged her to believe him. "Then we're good."

"You can't tell me you don't hate me after all I've done," Carter said.

"I've never hated you," Avery said. "I told you that. I love you, Carter. I always have."

"Avery." Carter backed away from her as if it could halt the emotion that her words were bringing on. "Don't do this."

"Don't do what?" she asked.

"I have to go," he said, ignoring her question. "Good luck with . . . with your lawyer."

"Don't you walk away from me," Avery ordered as he turned.

Carter turned back around. Was she giving him an order? "I can do whatever I want. I tried to help you and you didn't want it."

"Would you prefer that I hate you?" Avery asked. "You seem so uncomfortable with the opposite."

"You call me the callous one," he said, "but you're the one who never cared about how much it hurt to hear you tell me you love me and then go back home to your husband."

"I knew it hurt," Avery said. "How do you think I felt knowing you were sleeping with Julia every night? I told you I loved you because I couldn't stand you not knowing."

"Why?" Carter asked. "So it could hurt more?"

"I thought it would make it hurt less," Avery said. "You're the one who wanted to hurt me more, but I still love you."

"Stop. I don't want to talk about this."

"Is that why you didn't tell me about Julia?" Avery asked. "You seemed offended that I didn't tell you I left Anthony, but you didn't mention Julia to me."

"It's public knowledge," Carter said. "Besides, you don't give a damn."

"You know that isn't true," she asserted. "This whole vendetta you've had against me is because you knew that I gave a damn."

"Well, that's over," Carter said. "None of it matters anymore."

"You're wrong." Avery was surprising herself with what her heart was telling her to say, but she couldn't hold it in. "It will never be over between us, and I'm not just talking about Connor. I will always love you, and I think you'll always love me."

Carter was shaking his head. "What good can come from you saying this?"

"Because we have to stop pretending it isn't true," Avery said.

"I'm fine on my own. I can do this now. I can be a mother to Connor and try to build something with my life without you, but I will always love you."

"Stop." Carter felt his chest tightening. She was making this impossible.

Avery stepped closer to him. "I know you've made up your mind about me, and I know that's my fault. When you love someone, you should be with them. I tried, but—"

"Avery, please don't cry." Carter knew he was going to lose it if she started tearing up. He had to get away from her. "I can't take it. It's too much. It hurts too much to see you cry, to see you with someone else, to see you standing there and not be able to . . ."

"Touch me?" she asked.

"Yes," he answered. "Not being able to touch you because I'm so sick and tired of waiting for you to hurt me again."

Avery looked away, wiping the tears from her cheeks. "I know, and that is why I never hated you."

"A part of me died inside when you left me that first time," Carter said. "Even though I deserved it. Then you came back and rejected me again. It killed me to have to watch you be a wife to someone else. Then you came back to me, and we were going to be a family. I had been waiting so long for that to happen. I tried to be patient, and my dreams, what I thought were our dreams, were coming true."

"Then I left you again," Avery said.

Carter paused, looking away. He hadn't wanted to do this, but he couldn't stop now.

"You have no idea how much that destroyed me. It killed a part of me. Everything that has happened in these past few months has shown that I have to get over it. I have to grow up and move on. I'm doing it for myself and especially for Connor. I will not set myself up for this pain again. It isn't worth it."

"What isn't worth it?" Avery asked. "Me? Us? Do you remember what it was like?"

"Of course I remember."

"No," Avery said. "I'm not talking about a couple of months ago or last year. I'm talking about before I left and before all this madness started. Do you remember that?"

Carter didn't answer, afraid he'd be unable to control what he might say. He felt himself losing the grip on his emotions and was helpless to stop it.

"You do," Avery said. "I can tell that you do. That, Carter, is that not worth it?"

Carter looked down at his feet. "No, it isn't."

Avery didn't think she was strong enough to hear that. She wanted to drop to her knees but couldn't. "I understand. I do, but I want you to know that if you ever decide it might be, I will be here."

Carter didn't have time to protest before she approached him and took his face in both her hands. He could have protested when she pulled his face down to hers, but he didn't. The taste of her lips sent a sweet current of pleasure through him, but he knew he had to be stronger than this.

"Please, Avery." Carter separated himself from her, taking a few steps away. "I have to go."

Avery stood in the foyer for a few minutes after he left, trying to regain her composure before walking into the living room. Connor wasn't paying her any attention as she shared her focus between the elephant and the baseball game on TV.

"It's me and you, baby," she whispered as she sat on the sofa. "It's just me and you, and we'll be okay."

They had to be, Avery thought. She only prayed that someday she would be able to get beyond the regrets of everything that cost her the love of her life and be satisfied with the memories of what they once had. She didn't see it happening, but she had to hope for her own sanity and for Connor.

Leigh had just grabbed her keys and was opening her bedroom door when she came face-to-face with Janet, poised to knock.

"Morning, sweetheart." Janet smiled, lowering her hand. "On your way out?"

"I have to go to the clinic," Leigh answered. "I'm sorry, Mother. I am very busy."

Janet stepped aside as Leigh passed her. From her daughter's mood, Janet knew she was right to suspect something had gone wrong in D.C. She hurried after her.

"Can I talk to you before you leave?" Janet asked.

"I'm not really in the mood." Leigh kept walking.

"It will only be a few seconds," Janet added.

"You have until however long it takes me to reach the front door." The last thing Leigh wanted right now was a heart-to-heart. She wanted to focus on putting together her protest group and getting started.

"It isn't fair to walk at cougar speed." Janet sped up to keep pace with her daughter as they hurried down the west-wing hallway. "I am twice your age."

Leigh stopped and turned to her mother with a curious smile. "This must be serious. You just gave away your age. You only do that when you're panicked."

"So I'm thirty-nine," Janet said. "Big deal."

Leigh smiled. "Thanks for the laugh, Mom, but I have to go."

"Did something go wrong between you and the senator?" Janet stayed side by side with Leigh as they traveled down the stairs.

"There is no me and the senator," Leigh responded.

"I figured as much."

Leigh stopped as she reached the bottom of the staircase. "I'll probably regret asking, but why?"

"When the driver who was to take you to the airport checked in, he said you'd changed the pickup location from an apartment on Capitol Hill to the Mayflower Hotel."

Leigh rolled her eyes.

"And before you start in on me," Janet added, "I didn't check. He volunteered the information, because hotel pickups have a different fee."

"I decided to sleep at a hotel." Leigh started for the door, trying not to think about how badly things had gone the previous night.

While Max had followed her out of his parents' home, they continued to argue in the car over what had taken place. After Leigh told him to drop her off at the hotel, not another word was spoken.

"That," Janet said, "as well as your mood and refusal to discuss your dinner with the senator's parents would tip even the worst of sleuths."

"Stop sleuthing, Mother!" Leigh opened one of the large French doors to the front of the house. "This thing with Max isn't going to happen."

"Oh, Leigh, I only ask because this is such an opportunity and—"

"You sound like his mother," Leigh said. "You'd both get along very well, and that is not a compliment. A relationship is not an opportunity. Do you want me to be like Haley and marry for something other than love?"

"Why do the two have to be mutually exclusive?" Janet held out her arm to prevent her daughter from leaving. "You know what I think, Leigh? I think you've fought so long to not be the privileged little princess with a perfectly preplanned life that you're willing to deny yourself something that you genuinely want and that could make you happy just because you know it would fit into that plan."

"That's ridiculous," Leigh said, even though she knew it wasn't.

"Do you love this man?" Janet asked.

Leigh reluctantly said, "Yes, I think I do."

"You think you do?" Janet asked. "I didn't raise wimps. Do you love this man or not?"

Leigh nodded.

"So you're willing to forgo a chance for happiness that, let's face it, you damn well deserve, just because you know it's what superficial high-society schemers like myself would exactly want for you?"

"Mom, you don't know how much pressure this all is."

Janet laughed out loud. "What are you, new? I've been living under that pressure since the day I was born. Unlike you, I loved it. I wanted to live up to all of it, except for one thing."

"Marrying Daddy?" Leigh asked. She had known that Dad's middle class upbringing made him fall short of what her grandparents had planned for her mother.

"I still married the man I wanted and turned out as my parents expected. The truth is, like it or not, you're a Chase and you will always be around people who have expectations of you that you may or may not like. You can't let your desire to prove you aren't ruled by it keep you from being happy. Even if it is my dream, or his mother's dream, to see you two married and him in the Governor's Mansion, it doesn't mean that it can't be a real dream that you would want for yourself even if nobody else wanted it."

"So what are you telling me to do, Mother?"

Janet gently touched her daughter's cheek. "I'm telling you to do what I want you to, but you better do what you want to and nothing else."

"Please, Mommy, please, please, please."

Kimberly looked down at Evan as he lay back in the lounge chair. He had already thrown the small blanket she had put over his legs onto the ground. "We aren't going over this again. You aren't strong enough to swim."

Evan pouted, looking over at the pool in his backyard where his brother, who was the best swimmer in his age set at the country club, waded while tossing a ball in the air.

"Then he has to get out."

"Daniel can swim as long as he wants." Kimberly walked around the lounge chair to the other side and picked up the blanket. "You keep this on or you go back inside."

"I don't need it." Evan pushed at the blanket as Kimberly tried to place it over him. "I'm not cold. I'm not a baby and I don't—"

"Listen to your mother," Michael said as he stepped onto the back patio.

Kimberly found herself smiling at the sight of Michael because of the timing of his appearance. She had been thinking about him, because he was the missing link. She was sitting on her back porch, smiling at one son in the pool and thankful to God for the other sitting next to her. The only thing missing was her husband, and, God help her, she wanted him there. And now he was.

"What are you doing here?" she asked.

"I need to talk to you." As he approached her, Michael made an attempt to read her face but decided not to bother. She was a different woman now. He just didn't know her well enough anymore to be able to predict her mood.

Evan turned around in his chair. "Daddy, can I swim?"

"No." Michael leaned over and kissed his son on the forehead. "Mommy will know when it's time to swim again."

As his son moaned his displeasure, Michael turned to Kimberly. "Can we have a little privacy?"

"Marisol isn't here tonight." Kimberly looked toward the pool. "I don't want to leave them unattended."

"You don't have to." Michael walked toward the house and stood in the patio doorway. He looked back and waved Kimberly over.

Kimberly walked over cautiously. "What is going on, Michael?"

Before she could think, Michael took her in his arms and kissed her desperately on the lips. When he pulled away, the look of her, breathless, filled him with the confidence he needed. "I understand why you wouldn't want to be with me anymore."

"Michael, I—"

"Please," he said, "let me tell you why. Everything has been my fault."

"That isn't necessary," Kimberly said. "I told you that I've let go of my anger and have forgiven you for everything."

"But that doesn't mean you want to be with me."

Kimberly was uncertain how to respond, but from the way he was looking at her, she had to say something. "Forgetting is different from forgiving, but—"

"I know," Michael said. "I can see that. Instead of being willing to stand by you and everything about you to my parents, I started our relationship off with a lie, and when it came back to me, you were the one who got hurt."

"I should have told you about David."

Michael shook his head. "No, Kimberly. I gave you every reason not to. You were right. I put my father ahead of my family, our marriage, and I gave you no choice but to try and keep it from me. I shouldn't have put the burden of my father's approval on your shoulders."

"But I put you in that position," Kimberly said. "After what I tried to do to Janet by bringing Paul to L.A., that was what led to her so-called overdose and rehab stint, and it hurt you in your father's eyes."

"How can someone so beautiful be so stupid?" Michael smiled

as Kimberly seemed uncertain whether to be angry or confused. "First of all, you didn't make my mom take those pills with her wine. We all know her issue with prescription drugs started well before Paul came to town."

"I made it worse," Kimberly said.

"So did Leigh's decision to blame Mother for Richard's death and cut her out of her life. So did Haley's decision to date that asshole of a club owner. So did her decision to keep from Dad what had happened with Paul in Paris and the abortion."

"Why are you doing this?" Kimberly asked. "Why are you saying these things?"

"I can't say exactly," Michael said.

It was the truth. He had come there to confess his undying love and to proclaim the sacrifice he had made for his family, but he realized once he'd gotten there that it wasn't enough.

"What I can say is that what happened between you and Mother back then was my fault. If I had listened to you and put our family first, we would have moved out of Chase Mansion years before."

Kimberly was stricken with an unexplained joy at hearing him say the words that had kept her sane all this time. Despite the fact that her life had been falling apart ever since David had come back to L.A., the only thing that kept her from hating herself for all her mistakes is that she wasn't completely to blame. But Michael had never believed that. He had only told her how much she had ruined his life, how this was all her fault. He had said it so many times that she had almost believed it.

"I know," Michael said. "I know it's too much to ask you to just settle back into my life, and I know I have no right to ask to settle back into your life, but what if we did neither?"

"How could that happen?" Kimberly asked. She couldn't believe it, but she found herself really wanting to know. Was she crazy?

Michael reached down and took her hands in his. "We start a new one."

"A new what?"

"A new life," he whispered. "I left Chase Beauty, Kimberly. For good. You and I can take the kids and move to another state. Fuck that, we can move to another country. As far away from Chase Beauty and my parents as you want."

"Do you really think that would work?" Kimberly could feel her heart beating wildly.

"Think about it," Michael said. "Besides these last couple years, our marriage was great, wasn't it?"

"It was like a dream come true," Kimberly answered.

"We were so happy," he said. "And that was with all the bullshit I made you deal with. Just think, if we started over without Chase Beauty or Dad or Mom, what we could have."

Kimberly turned to her sons, trying to stay grounded in reality for their sake. "It can't be real if its safeguarded from the rest of the world. We could go to another continent, but you're still Michael Chase and the boys are still Chases. That company will still be your destiny and your right."

"I only want my family, this family."

"You don't get it," Kimberly said. "You just told me how none of this was my fault, but your solution is to leave everything behind for me. That would be my fault."

This was what Michael had feared. He had offered everything and it wasn't enough.

"We can't do that," Kimberly said. "But—"

"But?" Michael's head shot up.

"This time," Kimberly demanded, "I'm building our house from scratch."

"What?"

"And I'm going to college," Kimberly added. "I'm getting a bachelor's degree and probably a master's. Or a JD. And I decide which family events we go to and that includes the children."

Michael was too busy laughing to interrupt as Kimberly went down a list of demands signifying the way things would be from now on.

"Regarding money," she added, "I have my own accounts, and I don't have to ask permission to do anything. If you even so much as—"

"Can I make one request?" Michael interrupted.

Kimberly placed both hands on her hips and looked him up and down. "I'll consider it."

"A daughter."

"I've been meaning to ask you about your storage space, Mr. Chase."

Patrick Cello, the work manager in Carter's condo building, led Carter down the hallway of the basement, where all the storage units for the condos were located. It was a dimly lit warehouse-style place with tall cages, each about fifteen by fifteen and stocked with shelves and flood guards around the bottom edges. All but two cages. At the very end of the hall were the storage units for the two penthouse apartments, one belonging to Carter. They were twice the size of the others.

Carter stopped as they reached his unit. "I'm sorry about needing you to let me in. I just can't find my key."

"No problem." Patrick, a cordial, cushiony Italian man in his midforties, with salt-and-pepper hair and large, dark-rimmed glasses, unlocked the unit. "Did you vote in favor of electronic locks?"

"What are you talking about?"

"The condo committee put out a vote to upgrade all the storage unit locks to—" Patrick stopped, realizing Carter didn't care. "Anyway, you can always get your spare in my office."

"Thank you." Carter stepped inside, looking around.

"I was saying," Patrick continued, "you have a lot of space now that . . . well . . ."

"Ms. Hall took her things," Carter finished for him. "It's okay."

Patrick shrugged uncomfortably. "Well, anyway, I have some residents who need more storage room and will pay to rent some of your shelves. Of course, they would have to go through me to get access and—"

"Patrick." Carter stopped him from going on. "Sorry, but, no, and I'll be fine from here."

"Okay." Patrick seemed disappointed as he turned and left.

Carter looked around his unit, which was full of discarded items and pieces of furniture that didn't fit with a design or no

longer appealed to him but he was too lazy to get rid of. It wasn't
junk. There was a sofa from India. The pool table was bought at
a luxury movie studio auction. There was the sculpture from
Greece that he actually liked, but Julia said it frightened her so
he put it in storage.

When Julia left, she had taken her things, and the place seemed
a little empty. Only a little. It was odd to Carter that Julia, who
had been so eager to move in once they were engaged, had not
made that much of an impression on his home. In contrast, Avery
had changed it significantly. Carter offered very little protest as
she did her redesign. Once he had passed the fear of making
such a permanent commitment, he easily acquiesced to her demands.

When Avery left, Carter made no changes because he assumed
she would be back soon. Once he realized that wasn't happening, he became enraged and destroyed some of her things. He
went through phases over the six months she was gone, fluctuat-
ing between doing anything it took to find her and bring her
back and claiming to hate her and wishing she would get run
over by a truck. In one of his latter phases, he had sent what was
left of Avery's things to her parents, which he'd immediately regretted during one of his former phases.

The place looked very empty after Avery's things were gone,
and it only worsened Carter's depression. On the other hand,
Julia's absence was purely superficial. Despite how angry she had
been when he told her the engagement was off—all the screaming and pleading and yelling—she had done little to lay claim to
his place while she'd been there. Luckily for Carter, the majority
of the items she smashed and destroyed in her fit following the
breakup were hers.

There was one exception: the wall in the hallway between the
entrance to the condo and the living room. The wall on both
sides was painted a dark blood red. After a coat closet, the left side
was adorned with an oversized, ornately detailed, three-panel
antique Camilla mirror positioned above an English console table.
A few feet away was a pair of hanging handcrafted leather tapes-
tries on brackets, which Carter had purchased while visiting Paris.

On the right side, there was nothing now. It had always been bare before Avery moved in. She had placed one of her mother's large paintings on the wall, and Carter had sent it back to her parents. When Julia moved in, she had replaced it with an iron and tole wall medallion that Carter found archaic and dull. Julia would only remind him that it was very expensive.

For some reason Carter couldn't explain, now that the wall was bare again, he needed to cover it. He figured it was possibly just an excuse to preoccupy his Sunday with something other than thoughts of Avery's kiss and the painful tears in her eyes as she proclaimed her love for him. Since then, he had been sleep-walking, figuring out how he could coexist with Avery as a parent to Connor but forget what she had told him.

He grunted as he pushed a stone-carved sundial pedestal out of the way to reach the collection of paintings that were leaning against the wall. He quickly flipped through the group of mainly abstract paintings he had purchased during the course of trying to be more cultured, mostly while visiting Europe. None of it was too expensive, nothing more than $5,000. He would have to pick one with streaks of color that didn't stand out or clash with everything else, and he wasn't good at that.

"This is what you pay decorators for," he said to himself. "They all look the same. . . ."

Carter stopped in his tracks as he reached the last painting against the wall. He thought he was seeing things, so he removed the plastic covering and tossed it aside. He wasn't.

He was certain he had sent this painting back to Avery's parents, but clearly he hadn't. As he looked at the large painting on white canvas, Carter felt himself getting emotional again. Damn her!

The familiar hand-painted oil image of black, white, and silver tones flowed violently together in what Nikki Jackson had titled *The Night Storm*. Before she started Hue, Nikki had been a somewhat successful local artist, and although Carter would never admit it, she had done great work.

Looking at this painting now brought back memories Carter would rather forget. He thought of the day Avery brought the painting to his house unexpectedly. She stood at the door, invisible behind this block of canvas that had to weigh almost as much as she did. Carter told her there was nowhere to put it, but she pointed to the wall behind him and asked him to go get a hammer.

After about five minutes of teasing Carter for being an elitist who didn't own a hammer, Avery told him the story behind the painting and won him over. He had always been so affected by how easily she showed her emotions. It was a sign of trust that she hid nothing from him, and even then, he had only wished he could offer the same.

"This is now officially our house," she'd said.

Carter had to admit the painting was beautiful, and he liked seeing it when he passed it every day. It was his reminder that he was no longer a "me"; he was a "we," and that was how it would be from now on.

Carter took his hands off the painting and turned to leave, but he couldn't move. He turned back and cursed out loud as he reached for the painting again. He couldn't escape the feelings that it brought back. He had been so happy, and even though he knew that he was keeping a very big secret from Avery about how he'd stolen her away from her then-fiancé Alex, he was full of hope. He had retired his black book several years before he had planned to, because he had met this amazing woman who drove him insane every time he got his hands on her. She was beautiful, determined, stubborn, smart, and had a heart as big as the sun.

"Who would have thought the sun wasn't big enough?" he asked himself.

He leaned in and picked up the painting. It was heavier than he remembered, but he lifted it out from the bunch with ease. He held it close as he squinted his eyes, but he couldn't see the flints of gold he remembered. Avery told him he was imagining things, but he swore that if he looked at the painting out of the side of his eye or with just a quick, stolen glance, he could see gold.

His mind was yelling at him now to put it back. Then he tried to reason with himself and say he was taking the painting to give to Avery, yet another gesture of goodwill. But he knew what his heart wanted, and he wanted to put it on the wall in his hallway. He thought, possibly, when he came and went from his apartment, maybe for a second he could pretend he was still there. There in that time when he had been happy and no matter what happened at work or with his crazy family, he had peace and love waiting for him when he got home.

"This is crazy," Carter said as he placed the painting back on the floor. He leaned it against a wooden chair and headed out. He could buy a new painting for his hallway. That was the right thing to do, to start over.

As he stepped outside the unit, Carter shut the door behind him and closed the lock. He took one step before glancing back at the painting one last time and froze.

He saw it! He saw the gold!

Turning to the gate, he reached in and tried to pull the lock open but realized he couldn't. He continued to pull at it and felt himself begin to panic because he couldn't open it.

"Damn you, Avery!" Carter yelled as he kicked the gate.

The first thing Leigh said when she burst into Max's D.C. office was, "Shut up."

Sitting at his desk with his cell in one hand and a thick document in the other, Max only got his mouth open before she started in.

"You wanted to know if I loved you?" she asked. "Well—"

"I already know," Max answered. "You do."

Leigh stood at the edge of his desk and placed her hands on her hips. "Excuse me?"

"You do love me." Max leaned back, resting the back of his head on his hands. "Did you fly all the way back to D.C. to see me?"

"You think because I flew here, I love you?" Leigh huffed. "How can you even fit your ego in this office?"

"I didn't say that you love me because you flew over here," Max said. "I know you love me because you said you did."

"When?"

Max pushed away from his desk, his chair sliding back. "When you threw your little tantrum at my parents' house."

"Tantrum?" Leigh asked angrily. "You thought that was a tantrum? That is nothing compared to what you're going to see if you stand here and tell me you agree with your parents."

"I told you in the car that I didn't," Max said. "You responded by demanding I take you to a hotel."

Leigh slammed her purse on his desk. "You didn't put up a protest."

"I don't cater to spoiled brats," he said. "Even if I love them."

"Well, I . . ." Leigh was both angry and confused. "I am not a brat, but I will not have my life dictated to me by your parents or mine."

"I never said you should," Max answered nonchalantly.

"Or you," Leigh added.

"Now, wait a second." Max stood up and walked around his desk to face her. "If I'm going to be your husband, I think I should have some say."

"You think this is all a joke, don't you?"

"On the contrary," Max said. "I take this very seriously, and if you do, too, you can't have a fit every time someone pokes their nose into our lives."

"For your information," Leigh said, "that is exactly what I came here to tell you."

"No kiss first?" Max leaned in.

Leigh pushed him away. "No. You have to know that I don't give a damn what your parents want me to be. I won't live my life according to any preset plan."

"Sounds good to me."

"Aside from your parents or mine, you need to know what you're dealing with. I'm not the mild-mannered, well-behaved woman you think I am."

"When did I think that?"

"Stop it." Leigh smacked him on the shoulder. "I'm being serious. I have passion for causes that are not so pretty and neat. They don't fit well within a political campaign. As a matter of fact, they are quite risky for anyone running for office. They're real and they are volatile. I'm going to spend my life speaking out for them, especially for those that involve women and children. I'm not going to temper them no matter who I'm with. I do love you, but I believe this is my calling, and I won't sacrifice it to be . . . appropriate."

Leigh waited a few seconds for a response, but Max only looked at her with a mildly amused look on his face.

"Well?" she asked.

"What could be more appropriate than a life of purpose?" he asked.

Leigh was confused. "How can I tell if you're being serious?"

Max's faint smile disappeared as a very serious expression took hold of his face. "You've eloquently told me what your passion is, and I respect that. But your passion isn't the only one that matters if this is going to work. Are you ready to hear about my passion?"

Leigh felt herself relax. "Yes."

Max leaned back and reached across the desk. He grabbed a copy of the *Washington Post* and held up the front page to her. The statement was clear. A very large picture of the White House was placed above the fold.

"Are you sure that it is what you really want and not what everyone wants for you?"

Max nodded. "I'm just like you, Leigh. We may not have the same specifics, but I have passion and I want to change the world just like you. The White House isn't the only way to do it, but it's the way I want to do it. You need to know that."

"But what if being with me hurts your chances?" Leigh asked. "Even if you end up with someone else, having been with me and tied to my family could hurt you."

"It could hurt me or help me." Max tossed the paper back on his desk and faced Leigh again. "But one thing is certain. I won't be there with anyone else. Leigh, I love you in a way that I never thought I could again. If I get into the White House, it will be because of the man you will make me by being with you, not because of your name."

"I can't imagine you'd be too much of a hindrance in my goals," Leigh said happily. "Not that I would be using you or anything."

"Now I'm disappointed." Max stepped closer and wrapped his arms around her waist. "Ever since you walked into my office, I've been hoping you could use me a little. Right on this desk if you have the time."

Leigh resisted the urge that the heat from his body caused. "This is going too well."

"What do you mean?"

"We're agreeing on everything." She held her hand against his chest to keep him from leaning in for a kiss.

"Dr. Chase," he said. "You have got to stop expecting everything to be so hard. Do you love me?"

"Yes," she said breathlessly. She certainly did.

"And I love you," he said. "Trust me, considering who we are, there will be plenty of time for the hard stuff. Let's enjoy the easy while we have it."

Leigh reached out and grabbed his tie, pulling him to her. She leaned forward and kissed him hard on the lips, savoring every bit of it.

"Lock the door," she said. "We don't want any pictures in the paper tomorrow."

SIX MONTHS LATER

Janet Chase couldn't imagine being happier, and as she sat in the front pew of a church that she had never been to before, she had to reflect on how lucky she was for this day to come.

Once Leigh told her that Max had proposed and that she had said yes, Janet was euphoric. Not because of what it could mean for the family, but because of the look on her daughter's face when she told her. Leigh was happier than Janet had seen her in years, and even though the media had gone full-court press once the engagement became public, Leigh and Max's relationship only got stronger. Their refusal to play it out for the press had in no way hurt his campaign. He was ahead by more than twenty points in an election only five months away.

Janet and Steven had done their part to make this as easy on Leigh as possible. They had a family "come to Jesus" meeting in which they asked all of their children to do the same thing they themselves promised to do: end the drama. At least in public. They knew that ending it altogether would be too difficult a task. Because of Leigh's decision to be with Max, the public eye would be unforgiving, and everything they did would reflect on the woman who had quickly become the most famous Chase.

To Janet's delight, the meeting had been somewhat unneces-

sary. Her children were already figuring out how to make sense
of their lives and limit the foolishness to a minimum, which for
them, was still more than most people. What mattered was that
there was a different aura and sense when it came to her family.
No, the dysfunction that took a lifetime to build wouldn't disappear in six months, but things had definitely turned the corner
for the Chase clan.

Well, at least for most of them.

Janet's gaze went to Haley, sitting to her left. Looking at her, it
struck Janet how beautiful and peaceful her baby looked. Of
course, $30 million richer, who wouldn't be happy? What was un-
explainable was that she had not yet divorced Peter and was not
dating anyone as far as Janet could tell. Janet refused to intrude
as to why. She had made a promise to Steven to let their children
live their lives. Although she wanted to believe that Haley had
calmed down and was considering what it might mean to be married and be an adult, she knew her daughter, and she assumed
Haley, being Haley, remained Mrs. Peter Hargrove because she
had her eyes on more than $30 million. One had to take their
blessings where they could with her youngest child, and while
Haley had moved out and gotten a place of her own, knowing
Haley was in L.A. to stay was good enough for Janet.

Sitting next to Haley, Daniel Chase looked incredibly handsome in his tiny suit and had done a perfect job as the co–ring
bearer with his brother. No playing around, they had walked
briskly and carefully as instructed, delivered the ring, and took
their seats in the pew. Evan, sitting next to Daniel, seemed much
more interested in turning his cummerbund in circles than the
wedding ceremony. He was healthy and happy and showed no
residual signs of his illness from the previous year.

This was the blessing that allowed Janet to reach within herself and accept what had come next. Michael and Kimberly's second wedding was something that Janet made peace with before
they had even announced it to the family. She had to in order to
prepare herself for the inevitable. Janet would never pretend it
was easy, but seeing Kimberly's pregnant belly softened the blow
considerably. Another Chase was on the way, and Kimberly would
be the one to give this gift to the family again. For that, Janet

would promise to try, and so far she had. As she looked at Kimberly sitting beautifully next to Evan, her hands on her belly, Janet could no longer convince herself that her hold on Michael was because of her exceptional beauty. As Michael had told her after announcing their decision to remarry, Kimberly was the love of his life, and there was nothing or no one who could ever change that. Janet intended to never try again.

Besides, their wedding, which took place three months ago, had only been the icing on the cake. After returning from the honeymoon, Michael had gone back to Chase Beauty and Steven appointed him as chief operating officer, one step closer to the crown and carrying on the legacy.

Then there was Leigh, and as Janet turned to look at her oldest daughter, looking as angelic as ever, she saw a different woman than before. She had always been the jewel of the family, the only really sane one among them. Janet had placed so much pressure on her to be the face of the Chase brand, because she was so beyond reproach. That pressure had led to good things and bad, and Janet blamed herself for Leigh's reluctance to accept who she was and how her last name meant more to the world than she might have wanted it to.

But now she saw a woman who knew who she was and who embraced herself completely. Only this time, it was on her own terms. She wasn't trying to be the good girl or please Mommy. She was pleasing Leigh and had taken complete control of her own destiny—which was to make history. Janet didn't doubt she would get into the White House, either as the First Lady or as the president. Either way, she was getting the happiness that she deserved, and to Janet's delight, she was putting up little resistance to her plans for the wedding of the year. They decided to wait until after the election, which gave Janet all the time she needed to make it perfect.

But for now she would enjoy today's wedding, and as she looked at Carter and Avery standing together exchanging vows, a sense of completeness came over Janet. It had seemed like a decade to reach this point, but they were here, and Janet couldn't help but believe that the union of these two was somehow a sign that the family was back in order.

Janet was amused at Carter's attempt to maintain his manhood regarding their reunion. He had told the family that they simply wanted to give it another try and warned them not to get too excited. On the other hand, Avery had told the truth. She told them all how she poured her heart out to Carter but expected him to reject her as he had been. But when he showed up at her doorstep telling some silly story about being locked out of a storage unit, unable to get a painting and suddenly realizing how much he still loved her and wanted to try again, excitement was an understatement.

From Carter, Janet had gotten the impression that they would take it slow, but everyone knew better. Seeing them together again was just too perfect and too right. Carter was happier than he had been . . . well, since he was engaged to Avery the last time. He continued to tell Avery he intended to be cautious and take it slow, but within weeks they were living together and within a month they decided to get married.

When Janet had asked Carter why the rush, he had simply told her it was out of his hands. Avery had owned his heart from the beginning and never gave it back. This had to be true, because Avery had accomplished what everyone believed was impossible. Carter had agreed to get married in a church. That was a miracle.

"This commitment symbolizes the intimate sharing of two lives and still enhances the individuality of each of you." The young preacher paused to clear his throat. "Carter, do you take this woman to be your wedded wife? Do you promise to love her, comfort her, honor and keep her in sickness and in health, remaining faithful to her as long as you both shall live?"

Carter looked into Avery's eyes, which were welling up with tears. She had never looked this beautiful to him, and he had never been this happy. He had run right from that storage unit to the Jackson home and bared his soul to her. He tried to hold on to his pride by making some demands, but Avery wasn't listening. She jumped into his arms and kissed him all over his face. After a while, he gave up and just kissed her back. They made love after that without any secrets or lies, without any husbands or girlfriends in the back of their minds. It was just each other.

This, Carter told her afterward, was worth it. It was worth everything.

"I do."

Avery felt the tension building up inside of her. With every second that passed, she was closer to her heart's desire. She was really marrying Carter, and they would be a family. Six months ago, when he'd shown up at her house, he was both cursing her and professing his love for her. It was somewhat confusing, but she got the gist of it. He loved her and wanted her back, and that was all Avery needed to hear. One second she had thought she would be alone forever, because no man could ever compare to Carter. The next second, she knew she would spend forever with the man of her dreams.

She knew she should have been scared and had doubts that she could actually get back what she had. With the history between them, she should have waited for something to mess it up, but she didn't. Each day, they connected more and the pain of the past washed away. They made new memories to replace the ones that hurt. They were once again parents, lovers, and friends. And now they were going to be married.

"Avery," the preacher continued, "do you take this man to be your wedded husband? Do you promise to love him, comfort him, honor and keep him in sickness and in health, remaining faithful to him as long as you both shall live?"

"You better," Carter whispered with a wink.

"I do!" Avery surprised herself at how loud she yelled the words, garnering more than a couple of laughs from the guests. She didn't care. "God, I do!"

Clapping had already started before the preacher could finish.

"Then by the power invested in me by the state of California, I now pronounce you husband and wife. You may kiss -"

Carter and Avery just couldn't wait.

GONE TOO FAR

ANGELA WINTERS

ABOUT THIS GUIDE

The questions and discussion topics that follow
are intended to enhance your group's
reading of this book.

DISCUSSION QUESTIONS

1. Do you think Avery deserved to be treated the way Carter treated her in the beginning of the novel?

2. Do you think Michael and Kimberly should have re-united?

3. Kimberly laid out some ground rules for Michael as a condition of their reuniting. Do you think Michael will stick to them?

4. Do you think Leigh genuinely came to love Max or was she just settling?

5. Do you think Avery and Carter should have gotten to-gether in the end? Was it all worth it?

6. Carter had moved out from under his father's thumb to an extent, but it was a longer journey for Michael. Do you think he's finally over seeking his father's approval?

7. Do you think it's a good idea for Michael to come back to Chase Beauty?

8. Do you think Avery knew Anthony could walk but just ig-nored it because, as she said, she didn't want to be alone?

9. What do you think of the effect Evan's illness had on Kimberly and Janet's relationship? Will the peace last?

10. Should Kimberly have told Michael about Keenan?

11. Do you think Steven really understood how his need to control his boys damaged his relationship with them?

12. Haley's marriage was a side story throughout, but what did you think of the way the family handled it?

Want more Angela Winters?
Turn the page for more scandalous exploits
from the Chase family. . . .
Available now wherever books are sold!

From *View Park*

1

That Chase mansion was something else. Nestled in View Park, the affluent mostly African-American suburb of Los Angeles, it is by far the largest house in the entire community. Glorious, elegant and intimidating begin to touch on it. Most people just call it big, not only because of its size, but because of its residents. A family couldn't be any bigger than Steven Chase and his clan, and no one was willing to admit how much they ached to know what went on behind the red brick and white columns.

The house, being only fifteen-thousand square feet, was not as big as it could be considering the money the family had. All of the homes they owned around the world focused more on elegance and class than size. Still, it was impressive with seven bedrooms and nine baths, not to mention the exercise room, game room, media room, and library plus more; the home had taken eighteen months to build. Steven had purchased it when it was 8,000 square feet, but as his millions grew, the house next door was purchased, torn down and his wife, Janet, had taken it from there. The stature that blended a sturdy East Coast feel with a flirt of southern gentility rejected any hint of West Coast flash. It resembled something more likely to be in Bel Air or Hollywood Hills with its tall gate, wide driveway filled with Mercedes, Jaguars and Lexus SUVs, large pool with cabanas, basketball court and a Caribbean colonial designed 2,000 square foot guest house. Contemporary frames, marble flooring, cathedral ceilings, granite countertops, five fireplaces and a double staircase that caused mouths to drop while making *Town & Country, California Homes,* and *L.A. Magazine* salivate delivered a lasting statement to those far beyond View Park.

The statement was class, sophistication and most importantly, power. It had to be. After all, the Chase family was one of the richest and most powerful African-American families in the country, the richest on the West Coast. No one could put a label to them, white or black, no matter how hard they tried, using every other rich family existing now and before them. The Chases never accepted any of those labels, seeing themselves as originals in every way. They were born leaders, attractive, well educated, philanthropic and seemingly unfazed by anything. They stayed away from the undesirable black wealth acquired by athletes, actors or entertainers. Only lawyers, doctors, businessmen, educators and politicians made up the world the Chase family ruled.

When it came to the various scandals, like any good rich family worth their salt, they had plenty. The general consensus among those who talk, and they all talked, was that the Chase family was special. Special in a way that any mistakes they made weren't as bad as their charitable acts were good. None of their misdeeds seem to trump their place as black royalty. It was a payoff that others were willing to accept. More like . . . willing to embrace.

No matter how intense the scandal was, there was never a feeling that the Chase family was out of control. Steven Chase, *the conqueror*, raised his children similar to the way he had built his business. The foundations were strong and well supported, not only meant to last long after he was gone, but to prosper and dominate far after that. He was the ultimate symbol of that power and his confidence left everyone in awe, especially his own children.

Only today, that confidence wasn't as visible as usual. In his home office, elaborately decorated in cherrywood and rich, dark leather, Steven, looking much younger than his fifty-three years, sat uncomfortably behind his desk. He was a distinguished man heavy on control and light on affection for anyone except his wife. Running his hands over his salt and pepper hair, he shook his head in disappointment, his chocolate skin darkened from spending the day before on the golf course, a rare retreat for him.

His eldest son, Carter, *the reluctant gentleman*, was thirty and better-looking than any man had a right to be. His conservative style and calm, quiet demeanor drove his intense father crazy. Everything about Carter drove him crazy. The boy seemed determined to defy him since the day he was born. He seemed to take delight in doing anything other than what Steven wanted him to and making a success of his defiance.

Steven didn't expect today to be any different as he looked at Carter sitting in the chair across the desk from him. Those incredible light eyes he'd inherited from his mother stared back saying he refused to let his father's anguish affect him.

"So," Steven said as he sighed, trying to focus on something other than why his firstborn son wanted to be his enemy. "When exactly am I ready to say we should panic?"

"You don't panic, Dad." Carter was unwilling to accept the blame this time. Whenever things didn't work out at Chase Beauty like they should, he somehow shared the responsibility even though he didn't work there.

"There's a first time for everything," Steven scoffed. "And I think this might be that time."

He looked back at Michael, *the favorite son*, who was standing behind him, leaning casually against the bookshelf. It wasn't Steven's choice to make Michael his favorite and he would never admit to anyone, not even his own wife, that he was. He'd wanted Carter, but it became clear early on that that wasn't ever going to happen. It was better this way. Michael was more like Steven: aggressive, hungry and willing to do whatever it took.

Twenty-nine-year-old Michael was tall and dark, looking like a young Sidney Poitier. Unlike the carefully concealed fire inside Carter, Michael's flame could be seen miles away. It drove him. It gave him immediate respect from men twice his age. It made him dangerous. It made him the mirror of his father.

Michael leaned forward with a confident smirk on his face. He was used to this game. His father made it seem like the world was falling apart to light a candle underneath him when he thought Michael was slacking, which he never was.

"We have seventeen of the twenty," Michael offered. "It's just taking a little longer than we expected."

Steven stared him down. "I'm disappointed in you, Michael. I thought I raised my sons to never make excuses."

Michael blinked, but never lost his composure. There was something about this man that ripped at him. His approval could make him feel like he was king of the world, and his disappointment made him feel like a five-year-old boy. This business deal was the chance he'd been waiting for. He would be the one to take the leading cosmetics company for women of color to the next level . . . a chain of high-end hair salons and that board of directors seat was his.

"You're still on the timeline," Carter said. "You wanted to take over twenty of the top black salons in L.A. by the first of the year. It's only September."

Steven turned to him, a sarcastic grin on his face. "I love how you use these phrases 'you' and 'your.'"

Carter rolled his eyes, knowing what was coming next. The almost daily reaming of accusations that Carter didn't love his father, his family and the family business because he'd decided to be his own man. It was a broken record and he didn't have the patience for it.

Steven leaned across his desk, staring pointedly at his son. "You may not work for me, a rejection I have learned to deal with, but you are still a Chase."

Carter felt his teeth grinding. Keep your cool, he told himself. He loves it when you let him get to you. "I know, Dad. I just meant . . ."

"So," Steven continued as if Carter hadn't spoken, "when referring to the success of Chase Beauty, 'we' is more appropriate."

Carter pressed his lips together, noticing the sly grin on Michael's face. His little brother got a lot of entertainment out of these scenes, and even though Carter loved him more than anyone on the planet, he wanted to sock him right now.

"Hate to say it," Michael admitted, "but Carter's right. And I wasn't making an excuse."

Steven wasn't getting through to them. They were young, but

they were Chases and that meant they had to act more than their ages. "Do you boys understand the point here? My vision was clear. We would buy these carefully selected salons and launch our own chain. The end of the year was the deadline to launch. Not buy the salons."

"Dad, we've offered them the world," Michael said. "Performance Salon and Essentials won't sell. It's time to get dirty."

"Like you haven't already?" Carter asked. "I've heard what you've been doing."

Michael smiled innocently. He kept very few secrets from Carter. Only sometimes, Carter's sensitivity to obeying the law made it necessary. "You haven't heard anything."

"How about Matt Leonard and those pictures you threatened to send to his wife?"

Michael laughed. "You thought that was dirty? I'm surprised at you, man. You ought to know dirty better than anyone. You're a lawyer."

"Michael is right," Steven said. "We have to—"

Carter raised his hand to stop his father. "Dad, I don't want to hear this."

"You're my lawyer," Steven stressed. "So it doesn't matter what you want to hear. Besides, I need your help with Essentials."

"I don't do your legwork." Carter watched as his father's eyes turned to slits.

"I'm your father," he answered back. "You'll do whatever I tell you to." Steven's gaze lingered a little longer on Carter to make his point before turning to Michael. "Michael, your hunger can go too far sometimes. Simple blackmail will . . ."

"I'm out of here." Carter stood up.

"Sit down, boy." Steven spoke in that tone that always got the desired result. No matter how big they got, he was bigger. He would never let them forget that, and as Carter sat back down in his chair, Steven knew they wouldn't.

"Blackmail won't do it, Dad," Michael advised. "We're gonna have to take it to a new level with them."

Steven didn't like it when things got this way, but this was business. He'd learned that the hard way when he started Chase

Beauty twenty years ago. He looked at Michael, his expression nothing less than deadly serious. "This needs to happen. So, do what you have to do. Carter will handle Essentials."

Michael's competitive spirit bit at him. He couldn't figure out why his father seemed to go out of his way to pull Carter in when he could handle this on his own.

Carter smiled, nodding. "Sure, why not? I've been looking for ways to lose my law license."

"I'm asking you," Steven said, "because we have to take the legal route with Essentials."

Michael smirked. "You get the easy stuff, Carter, since you're so soft."

Carter got up, starting for Michael, who quickly stepped around the desk, ready for him. With no patience for this, Steven stood up, the mere gesture having incredible power over his sons and they both immediately stopped, turning to look at him.

"Carter," Steven said. "Essentials has a shop in View Park and one in Baldwin Hills. They're both owned by Avery Jackson."

Carter shrugged. "Should that name mean something to me?"

Michael rolled his eyes. "She's the daughter of our chief of police, idiot."

"And she's not selling," Steven said.

"She's a bitch," Michael spat. "I've offered her twice what her piece of shit shops are worth."

"If they were a piece of shit, we wouldn't be going after them, idiot." Carter grinned while Michael gave him the finger.

Steven sat back down, focusing on the thick manila folder on his desk. "Revenue-wise, she's probably the weakest of the whole bunch. Location-wise, I've got to have those stores. I need a way to make her sell, but because of who she is, we can't use—"

"Me," Michael proudly offered.

Steven placed his hand on the folder and slid it toward Carter. Carter looked at it, but didn't pick it up, which he knew his father wanted him to do. "What exactly do you expect me to do?"

"You're the Harvard lawyer. You figure it out." Steven shared a stern look with both of his sons. "You need to understand the pressure we're under. Chase Beauty *is* our family's legacy."

Carter and Michael both sighed, having heard this speech too many times to count. Steven had built the business from scratch, ignoring the naysayers warning that an entire corporation focused only on black women could never rival the big players. Steven had showed them all, and he never let his sons forget it. He also never let them forget that a lot of people didn't like their success and were waiting in bushes like hungry lions for any chance to bring them down, and it was essential that they not get that chance.

"Nothing comes back to Chase Beauty," Steven ordered. "Do you both understand?"

"We understand," Carter and Michael answered in unison, as they had always to anything their father told them.

Janet Chase, *the socialite*, opened the office door without knocking, which was a sure sign she was angry. She didn't need to wonder if she had everyone's attention, because Janet always got everyone's attention. She was an exceptionally beautiful, elegant and classy woman who looked at least a decade younger than she was. That she was born into money was obvious to anyone with eyes and it took only a second's worth of time in her presence to see the best etiquette classes New York had to offer advertised in her every move and word. Including every look, like the dangerous one currently on her face as she eyed her husband and two sons.

"I knew you were in here." She placed delicately adorned hands on her trim, but curvy hips. She would not lose her temper. It wasn't her style, but she would be obeyed. "What are you doing?"

"Business, Janet." It amazed Steven that after over thirty years of marriage he still thought she was too good for him.

"Business is over." She had been Steven's mistress to his wife, Chase Beauty, for so long, but she wanted all the things its success gave her so she accepted it; only not today. "This is Leigh's day. She'll be here soon, and your guests are noticing your absence." She pointed her finger at her men, all of whom she loved with every inch of her. "I want you all out there in five minutes, and don't mess with me."

You just didn't mess with Janet Chase.

From *No More Good*

1

"What is this, Daddy?" Six-year-old Daniel Chase was standing over something in the hallway of his uncle's penthouse condo in downtown L.A.

"What is what?" Thirty-year-old Michael Chase waited for Evan, Daniel's twin brother, to get inside before closing the door behind him.

"It's a bra!" Evan rushed to his brother, picking up the lacy pink lingerie for his father to see, his little brown hand waving it in the air.

Michael sighed, realizing it might be a mistake to bring his boys over to his brother's place. He should have known something like this would happen. He'd been warned last month when he walked in on Carter and a Brazilian model having very loud sex hanging halfway off the dining room table.

"Put that down," Michael ordered. "Just drop it."

"These are panties!" Evan was reaching for the matching bottoms just a few feet away. They were lying on top of a silk cocktail dress.

"Don't touch that." Michael took his son's arm.

"Mommy has these." Evan struggled to get away from his father. "Is Mommy here?"

"All mommies have these, stupid." Daniel rolled his eyes.

"Uncle Carter needs to do laundry." Michael cautiously led his boys down the hallway, praying that he wouldn't have to explain the birds and bees to them today. That really wasn't on the schedule.

"Where is he?" Daniel asked impatiently as soon as they were at the steps to the living room of the three-thousand-square-foot, three-bedroom penthouse condo.

"He's probably working in his office," Michael answered. "Working hard."

He led his boys to the living room sofa and reached for the remote control. "You boys stay here, do you understand?"

Evan was already looking antsy, eager to get out of his church clothes. They were both used to being able to run wild whenever they were here.

Michael found a suitable television station on the large plasma screen on the wall. "Just watch this and don't move."

"Why not?" Evan asked.

"Look at me," Michael ordered, waiting until both of them did so. Keeping stern eye contact, he said, "Because I said so. Do you understand?"

Daniel nodded, but Evan just shrugged, always the difficult one.

As Michael made his way to the master bedroom, passing scattered pieces of clothing along the way, he wasn't looking forward to the reason he was sent over here by their mother. He had to remind Carter to show up tonight at Chase Mansion, their parents' fifteen-thousand-square-foot estate in View Park, to celebrate in his honor. Carter hadn't been answering his phone for three days now, so Janet sent Michael to track him down.

This wasn't the first time in the last six months Carter had "disappeared." Ever since his fiancée, Avery Jackson, left him, Carter would leave for long periods of time. Avery not only left Carter, but left L.A. and didn't want to be found. He'd gone ballistic when he realized she had no intention of coming back.

He had become a Jekyll and Hyde, moving between two states of being. One was an obsessed psycho desperate to find Avery, who he swore on the Bible was the only love of his life, using the considerable means at his disposal whether legal or not. The other was a reckless drunk who didn't care about Avery, swore he was better off without her, and wanted to prove it by nailing every woman he could get his hands on.

And the bra and panties in the hallway suggested Carter had been doing just that. This was the Carter that their parents were concerned about, the one who could get the family in real trouble.

And trouble for this family meant more than it did for others. The Chase family was American black royalty. They were not part of the entertainment or sports worlds, which high society looked down on. Those people didn't belong to, nor were they invited into, the world the Chase family ran in. No, the Chases were a cut above that. Filthy rich was where the Chase family stood—or stood out depending on how you looked at it.

The family was led by Steven Chase, a man from humble beginnings who built his cosmetics company, Chase Beauty, into a multibillion-dollar corporation. He had become an American titan and used the family's billions to influence business and politics all the way to Capitol Hill. His money was invested in several industries, including real estate in some of the most exclusive areas in the western United States.

Meanwhile, his wife, Janet, brought social standing to the family as the daughter of high-society East Coast lawyers with a strong heritage and several generations of wealth and community leadership. From their gated palace in the mostly black, affluent suburb of View Park, she single-handedly took over L.A.'s society scene, black and white, and created an empire envied by even the best East Coast families. Together, no one could rival what they had created.

And although it was Steven's money, influence, and power that put out the fires his children started, it was Janet who was the architect of the Chase family image and publicity. With the recent family scandals still lingering, she couldn't allow Carter to throw the family into another one. Especially not one of a sexual nature, which of course is what Carter was known for. He not only slept with lots of women, but he also treated them badly when he was through. Word was starting to get around, and that can be dangerous.

Michael stood in the doorway to Carter's bedroom and observed the mess in front of him. He could only smile because Carter was such a neat freak, almost to the point of obsessive, and here he was, living like a frat boy complete with a naked woman sprawled facedown on the bed.

Carter Chase's light brown eyes flew open as he heard a loud bang. Had something just happened or was it the awful pounding in his head again?

"Wake up!" Michael yelled, closing the door behind him. "It's afternoon, boy."

Carter struggled to sit up on his bed with his hand pressing against his forehead. He felt like shit. "What the fuck are you doing here, man?"

His younger brother, dressed in a sharp gray suit, sat down on the bed looking at him with a smirk on his face. At least Carter thought it was a smirk. Things were a little blurry.

"You know I brought my boys here," Michael said. "You got her thong in the hallway. They don't need to see that."

"Don't come by uninvited, then." Carter cleared his throat.

Michael nodded to the naked, chocolate body next to Carter. "She is?"

Carter turned his head slowly, because that was all he could do to keep it from exploding. Nice ass, was all he could think of. "I don't know."

"That's smart." Michael was envious of his brother's wanton freedom. With his having been married seven years himself, things were a bit more complicated. "This is what Mom is talking about."

"Can you not mention her right now?" Carter asked. He leaned back against the headboard. "What day is it?"

"She's afraid you're going to get some strange girl pregnant."

"Like you did?" Carter asked, reminding Michael of how he had introduced his current wife to the family seven years ago.

"Touché." Michael made a fist and socked Carter in the arm.

"Stop." Carter pointed to the half-empty condom box on the dresser. "I'm not stupid."

"But you don't know her name."

"Her name doesn't matter," Carter said. "She's getting out of here as soon as she wakes up."

The woman made a sound as if she'd heard Carter, but didn't move. It wouldn't matter to him if she sat up and started a scene. She was just some hot chick who had offered to buy him a drink at Level Three Nightclub. They moved on to one of the club's infamous beds with the curtains closed. Less than twenty minutes later, he took her home. In these matters, he preferred to go to the woman's place, so he could leave as soon as he was done, but this one had a kid and a mother at home and . . . well, a very nice ass.

"Mom sent you here?" Carter asked.

"No one has been able to reach you for days. I thought you'd gone off to chase after Avery again."

Carter felt his temperature boil at the mention of her name. "She's not in Tampa."

"Last month it was Atlanta."

"It was never Atlanta!" Carter swung around on the bed, feeling the room move around him. "I told you she was never in Atlanta. Her stupid sister used to go to school there, so I—"

"Hey!" Michael stood up. "Don't yell at me. I don't give a shit where Avery is. And last week you said you didn't either."

"I didn't," Carter lied. "I don't. She can be in hell for all I care."

"Who do you think you're talking to?" Michael asked. "I've seen you break down and all . . . this. Like it's not all about her."

"So you're my therapist now?"

Michael turned away from his brother, not willing to get caught up in this argument again. There was no talking to him when it came to his precious Avery. Instead he walked over to the full-length mirror and checked himself out, something he never tired of doing. He smiled at his fine, dark features. Everyone said he looked like Sidney Poitier at his most handsome, but Michael knew he looked much better than that.

"What about Sunday?" Michael asked.

Carter didn't feel like facing the family. He was tired of having to put on that perfect front that was such a lie. His life was a mess and he had embraced that. He didn't appreciate his mother making him act as if everything was okay.

After finding out Carter paid a woman to have sex with her fiancé, Alex, in order to win her away from him, Avery left him.

Despite everything he had done—the millions it had cost him to hide his mistake and all he promised never to do again—she handed him his engagement ring and walked away. Carter was devastated, but never considered giving up. He had come to love Avery, the middle-class girl next door, more than he knew he was capable of loving a woman. She was different from him, but she quickly became the only thing that mattered in his life. So there was no doubt in his mind he would win her back. It would take some time and a lot of work, but he would get her back. After all, he was Carter Chase and what woman could resist him?

Then Avery disappeared. Actually, she ran away with her family's help, and Carter hadn't been able to find her. It seemed impossible, considering he had the power of the Chase name and all its money and connections. If only her father hadn't been chief of police of View Park and her brother a detective, he would have been able to impose himself on them more. They were keeping an eye on everything he did in trying to find Avery, waiting for the chance to catch him breaking the law. He'd even gotten a call from the FBI after a bug was found in Nikki Jackson's car. They couldn't trace it to him, but they all knew he'd had it done. It was driving him crazy.

He'd begun trying to find her immediately, his only distractions being the law firm he ran and the commitment he'd made to his father to look after Chase Beauty while his parents were away for his mother's rehab treatment. He had everyone she knew traced and bugged. He put a flag on Avery's Social Security number and credit cards, but her family found out and he was blocked out after only one week. He tried to get the police involved, but Avery's father convinced them that she wasn't missing and of course they sided with him. They were getting in contact with Avery some way that satisfied Missing Persons enough. Even Carter's deep connections as one of the hottest up-and-coming lawyers in L.A. couldn't help him.

After a few months, he gave up and decided he didn't care. It was all a lie, but he knew it would drive him crazy if he didn't at least try to convince himself he didn't want her anymore. He called off all but one of the ten private investigators he had on retainer but still remained focused on the Jackson family. The

Jacksons knew he was following them and they were able to elude him at every step. Still, whenever they left L.A., Carter had someone on them, searching for Avery. The last trip had been to Tampa, Florida, followed by a rental car driven to St. Petersburg, which was where Avery's mother, Nikki, disappeared before showing up in Charlotte, where she caught a plane back home to L.A. Carter had sent his P.I. to Charlotte two days ago.

"You're coming to the celebration whether you want to or not. It's for you."

"My birthday was last month," Carter said.

"It's not for your birthday, asshole. You better come, you bastard!"

"Stop yelling." Carter covered his ears.

"Stop being such a—"

"She might be in Charlotte," Carter said.

Michael sighed, feeling pity for the brother he had always looked up to. Carter had never been this sick over a woman. "You don't have time for another trip."

"I'm not going until my P.I. comes back with proof."

"What about the board?" Michael asked.

Carter made a grumbling sound. "That's what the party is about, right?"

Michael couldn't believe this. "You're going to be made a member of the board of directors Wednesday, Carter. That's a big deal."

"I know," Carter said. "I'll be there."

"Do you have any idea how important this is to Dad?"

"Of course I do. It's important to me too."

The idea that he would be made a member of Chase Beauty's board was still odd to Carter, considering that when he made the choice to start his own law firm instead of going to work for Daddy, Steven had all but promised him he'd never be on the board. It had been a major bone of contention between him and his father and their relationship, which had always been on edge. It had been better some times than others, but never recovered from that decision to do his own thing years ago.

"Nothing is important to you anymore," Michael said, concealing his envy.

Michael was always a little on edge when Carter and their father started getting close again, even though he knew it never lasted. Still, this one-millionth make-up was lasting longer than usual and Michael felt left out. He was the favorite son and that position meant more than anything in the world to him. Chase Beauty was going to be his, and Carter's so-called invasion didn't make him happy. Michael had always been fine with Carter as the company's legal firm on retainer. He enjoyed working with him almost as much as he enjoyed working with his father. But this was more, much more. He loved his brother without question, but couldn't ignore that he felt uneasy about his formally joining the company.

"You better straighten up," Michael ordered. "Avery is gone. Stop being such a pussy and get over it."

Carter stood up from the bed and faced his brother head-on. Both a little over six feet, they met eye to eye. Even though his head was spinning, Carter stayed steady. "Back off."

Michael didn't blink. "You lost her, but you keep this up, you'll lose everything."

Carter smiled, because at that moment, he believed Michael, but he really didn't care.

From *A Price to Pay*

1

Thirty-one-year-old Carter Chase was standing impatiently in the foyer of his family's famous and often photographed home, the fifteen-thousand-square-foot Chase Mansion in View Park, a suburb of Los Angeles. He was impatient for a couple of reasons. First, his parents, Steven and Janet, were late. Church let out at eleven and it was twelve-thirty. They had promised to be home by noon at the latest. Second, he was always impatient to see his baby girl, Connor, especially considering he only had another eight hours with her before her mother would come pick her up from his house.

Connor Chase, the newest addition to America's wealthiest and most famous black family, was born six months ago and Carter's life was changed forever. Only a few months earlier, he'd been knocked in the face with the reality that her mother, Avery Jackson, the woman Carter loved and had wanted to marry, was married to another man, and pregnant.

He was only temporarily jealous of the other man, college professor Anthony Harper, because he had little right to be. Carter understood that he drove Avery away trying to control her and keep secrets from her. He was wrong and deserved to have his heart broken, which she did when she left L.A. to live in secrecy with relatives outside Miami. But he'd never stopped believing he would get her back. And as much as it hurt that she had been with another man, he wouldn't pass judgment on her. He'd been sleeping with any woman he could get his hands on in the six months after Avery left California, just to stop thinking about her for a few moments.

But the pregnancy was another thing. He was certain that Connor was his from the moment he saw Avery's belly, but Anthony had convinced Avery to lie and say the baby was his. He'd conspired with a local doctor who owed him a big favor to create medical records to support the lie. The idea that Avery, the woman he loved with all his heart, was having another man's baby had floored Carter.

Being a Chase, a member of America's black royal family, Carter had always gotten everything he wanted. He'd had a charmed life, always able to win any contest and influence or buy his way out of whatever he needed to. He was an heir to an empire, Ivy League educated and in charge of his own successful law firm; not to mention having that whole tall, dark, and handsome thing in his favor. He was six feet tall with chocolate brown skin and hazel eyes. His smile and style added to making him one of the most eligible bachelors on the market, with his pick of the best women. Which was why everyone was surprised when he hung it all up for a middle-class girl next door, Avery Jackson.

But they just didn't know. He hadn't expected to fall in love with her at all, but Avery quickly became everything in the world to him. She was perfect in every way that mattered. She grounded him, made him feel like a king regardless of his last name or his wealth. Carter felt a connection to Avery that he hadn't believed could exist between a man and a woman. But he'd made mistakes to get her away from her first fiancé, Alex, and even more mistakes to keep her. Unlike the other women he'd dated, Avery didn't care about the money, the glossy high-life or the power. She didn't care about all the things that came with being a Chase, so for the first time in his life a woman didn't put up with his crap, and she had left it all behind.

Like with any other obstacle, as soon as Avery returned, Carter was determined to win her back, regardless of her marital and parental status. And he'd almost done it. He'd gotten her to the point where she admitted she wanted him—loved him—but there was one problem. Avery actually believed in fidelity and the sanctity of marriage. She wouldn't cheat on Anthony and she wouldn't leave him even after the truth of Connor's paternity came out.

But he was a Chase, so there was always a plan B. It would take a lot of patience, but he would get Avery back. And although he had been angry with her when she finally told him that Connor was his, moments after giving birth, it only made him more determined to get her back. Now it was about more than the woman he loved; he had a family.

So while it hurt to see Avery with her husband, Carter knew it was only a matter of time before he'd have her back. Meanwhile, he took every moment he could to spend with his daughter, whom he loved to no end.

That was, he took every moment that he could get Connor away from her doting grandmother, Janet Chase.

"They're coming." Maya, the caretaker of Chase Mansion, stood at the archway between the foyer and the great room.

She looked tired, although Carter never really saw her do anything but cook. She always hired contractors to do heavy work, but he knew his mother loved Maya, who had been taking care of the Chase clan for almost fifteen years.

"I can hear the car, Maya. Thanks."

"Are you sure I can't get you somethin'?" Although she'd been in the country for more than twenty years, Maya's Caribbean accent was still very strong. "You know how she likes to stall when she has the baby."

"Not this time," Carter said. "I have to get going. I'm meeting Julia for lunch."

"How nice."

Carter noted that Maya rolled her eyes like she did whenever the name of Julia Hall, Carter's current girlfriend, was mentioned. Maya had loved Avery because Avery was kind and warm to her, while Julia maintained a clear class distinction in the very few times she even acknowledged Maya was there.

Carter smiled at the sound of his baby's voice. Before the front door even opened, he could hear her laughter and cooing.

Janet Chase, a woman of the best breeding, class, and social mastery, had always placed her family first. She was the image maker of the Chase name, and tough as nails when it came to her family. She was also a sucker for a grandchild, and her only granddaughter simply brought her to her knees. She hated giving her up, but as soon as she walked into the house, she could see from the look on her oldest son's face that she wasn't going to get away with her stall tactics today.

"Don't start," Janet said as she handed the baby bag to Maya. "We tried to leave, but they wouldn't let us. Ask your father."

"Who is they?" Carter asked, delighting at the squeal Connor gave as soon as she saw him and reached out for her daddy. She was so stinkin' cute.

"Everyone at church." Janet reluctantly handed Connor over. "I tell you, she looks more and more like Leigh every day. She looks ridiculously cute in her new dress."

Janet spent an obscene amount of money on dresses for Connor. There were two other Chase grandchildren, twins by second son, Michael, but Connor was a girl and that took Janet's indulgence to a whole other level.

"You're not letting people, strangers, hold her, Mom." Carter gave Connor a big, fat kiss on her lips.

"Of course not." Janet smoothed out her cobalt blue, Diane von Furstenberg cashmere wrap dress. She was a very beautiful woman, who still turned heads in her fifties because she looked at least ten years younger than she was, and she had an air of unattainability about her that men loved.

She turned to Maya. "Can you please serve lunch in the Florida room in about an hour?"

Maya nodded, handing the baby bag to Carter before leaving.

"Hello, son." Steven Chase closed the front door behind him, greeting his son briefly before reaching down for his vibrating smartphone.

Carter would have replied if he thought his father was paying any attention, but he knew he wasn't. Steven Chase was head of a billion-dollar empire, Chase Beauty, and that empire came first. There was no ignoring him once he walked into a room. From even his youngest days, Steven had a presence that sucked up all

the attention in the room. This included his own children, his
sons especially.

Carter and his father had been at odds as long as Carter could
remember, with brief periods of peace. Right now was a period
of peace where they got along, but that still didn't guarantee
he'd get any attention from his father.

"You're making me late for lunch with Julia," Carter said to his
mother.

"Why didn't you tell me you were having lunch with her?" Janet
asked. "I can keep Connor while you both . . ."

"No thanks," Carter said. "You'll see Connor again soon. We have
to . . ."

"You know," Janet interrupted, "this wouldn't be an inconvenience if you actually came to church."

Carter gave his mother an annoyed glance. "You know that's
not going to happen, Mom."

"You should open your eyes, son." Janet leaned forward to kiss
Connor on her tiny, brown nose. "That God you've decided not
to believe in gave you this blessing."

"Science and genetics gave me this blessing," Carter replied.
In choosing to govern his beliefs by logic and rationality, he had
made the decision while at Harvard as an undergrad to believe
in evolution over creationism, and his mother had given him a
hard time about it ever since. Avery gave him hell for it.

"Carter." Steven hung up his cell, getting his son's attention.
His salt-and-pepper temples added a distinguished look to his
dark, masculine figure. "Come in the office. I need to talk business with you."

"I can't," Carter said.

Chase Beauty was the largest client of Chase Law, the small
firm that Carter had decided to start instead of joining his father's
company. This, in addition to his sense of entitlement and assumption of power and control over everything, made Steven expect Carter to jump at the snap of his finger.

"I have to meet Julia for . . ."

"Now," Steven said definitively. He was already walking down
the hallway toward his office.

Janet joyously reached her arms out. "I'll hold her while . . ."

"Nice try," Carter said as he headed down the hallway with his baby in his arms.

"Close the door," Steven ordered without looking up from his desk.

"Dad, this has to be quick."

Steven looked up, ready to remind his stubborn son that a one-hundred-thousand-dollar-a-month retainer meant he could take as much time as he wanted, but thought better of it. They were getting along, as much as Steven and Carter could ever get along. These periods of relative peace between them never lasted long, so Steven let it go. "Did you read that Luxury Life report I sent you?"

"I read all the reports weeks . . ."

"No, this is a new one I had my marketing department put together. I sent it to your office Wednesday."

Carter shook his head. "I haven't gotten around to it."

"Dammit, Carter!" Steven leaned back in the detailed leather chair of his finely furnished home office, one of seventeen rooms in the house. "That's the only thing I asked you to do for me this week."

Carter pretended to bite Connor's tiny fingers as she put them over his mouth. She laughed as if it was the funniest thing ever. "You know I have that big antitrust case right now, and two new clients."

Steven sighed. "As your father, I'm glad your firm is growing. As your client, I don't give a damn. Read the report by Monday."

That was a lie, Carter thought. He wasn't glad as a father either. Although he had interned in the Chase Beauty legal department during Harvard Law, Carter's decision to go out on his own instead of join the company, as expected, had always been a sore point between him and his father. A sore point was putting it lightly.

"I'll get to it tonight, after I drop Connor at Avery's . . ."

"Carter, I know you're happy you have a baby and all that, but you can't let it interfere with your work."

"Maybe I can do like you did, Dad." Carter's voice was laced with extreme sarcasm. "Just ignore my kid altogether. I'm sure she'll understand like we all did."

Steven sneered, wondering if Carter thought he was too old to get knocked upside the head. No, he hadn't been the best father, but he was building an empire and they had Janet. He still loved them all more than his own life.

"You've never appreciated the sacrifices I've made for this family," Steven said, "but you seem fine with benefiting from them. Read it. I need to make a decision now."

Carter wanted to ask why his father wanted to expand Chase Beauty, which had already added real estate and a chain of beauty salons to its hair-and-makeup product line, to include publishing, but he wouldn't. He didn't have the time for the answer.

"Look, Dad, I was supposed to meet Julia at Beso five minutes ago. I'll read it later."

"She can wait if you tell her to," Steven said. "She'll do whatever you want."

Carter frowned. "What the hell does that mean?"

"You know what it means," Steven answered. "Julia wants to be Mrs. Carter Chase. She'll put up with anything if she thinks it will get her closer to that goal. I'll call her if you don't have the balls."

"You know that's not going to happen." Carter's tone reflected his confusion. "Why would you even say that? You know that . . ."

"I know six months ago you said that Julia was just a temporary amusement until you could get Avery back. She was part of your plan to make Avery believe you were over her so she wouldn't be so cautious around you."

"She still is," Carter said. "But it's not as if I don't like her. You don't expect me to be celibate until I get Avery back?"

"Julia is in love with you. She's told your mother several times."

Carter believed Julia was more in love with the idea of being with a Chase than anything genuine. "I can't do anything about that. I'm going to marry Avery. That's it."

"Tell that to your mother," Steven said. "She's already picking out invitations."

"Mom doesn't need to know anything about this," Carter said with a warning tone. "Dad, you promised not to tell her."

"I haven't said anything," Steven said. "Now just read the report."

Carter got pissed off when his father acted as if he didn't understand the master plan, which was two-fold. Part one was to make Avery believe that he had truly gotten over her, had no intention of interfering with her marriage, and only wanted to deal with her in terms of being good parents to Connor. It was working. Carter even believed that Avery was a little jealous of his relationship with Julia at times. Because of their chemistry, Avery had previously refused to be alone with him. That was changing. Once her guard was down, she wouldn't be so reluctant to spend time alone with him. That was all it would take.

Part two was much more complicated. Carter had to create a situation in which Avery would be willing to leave Anthony and not hate herself for cheating on him. This had begun by completely emasculating Anthony at every opportunity possible without it seeming obvious to anyone but Anthony. When placed against Carter, very few men could measure up.

Steven smirked. "You remember, kid, it was my idea for you to crowd her husband out slowly, before I knew she lied to you about Connor not being yours. I'd prefer you be done with her. Julia is more suited to our circles anyway."

"You're starting to sound like Mom," Carter said. He placed Connor in the other arm. She was getting heavy.

Twenty-six-year-old Julia Hall came from a prominent Dallas family of doctors. She had made a departure and had gone into corporate finance, but this positioned her perfectly for a financial analyst position at Chase Beauty. Janet had intended for her to distract Michael from his wife, Kimberly, but Julia had wanted Carter from the start. She was a bona fide, black blue blood like his mother: those who had money, power and social standing dating back to the 1800s.

No one else belonged in these circles. New money, acquired in only a generation, didn't count. What was worse was money from entertainment or sports. They always wanted in, and people like his mother and Julia always wanted to keep them out.

"That wasn't your background," Carter reminded his father.

"This isn't about me." Steven was well aware that his middle-class background would never have gotten him where he was now if he hadn't married a woman like Janet. "This is about you wanting a woman that has rejected you countless times and . . ."

"You're exaggerating," Carter said. "Avery admitted that she wants me, but all that Bible blah, blah and . . ."

"Marital fidelity isn't Bible blah, blah, Carter. It means something to a lot of people."

"Well, nothing means anything to me except Avery and Connor. So, fuck her marriage and that teacher."

"You better watch it," Steven warned him. "If your animosity shows, it will force Avery to side with her husband."

"Don't worry about me." Supporting Connor had been the perfect excuse to make Anthony look inadequate. "I've taken every opportunity, and his growing frustration has only worked in my favor. I've undermined him without Avery catching on. She seems more and more annoyed with him every day. I've got her keeping secrets from him, thinking she's doing what's best for his pride. But it's only making him more jealous and possessive and when those secrets come out, he'll explode."